SHIFTING AIR

A ROYALS QUEST

JESSICA KORALEWSKI

ARPress
45 Dan Road Suite 5
Canton MA 02021
Hotline: 1(888) 821-0229
Fax: 1(508) 545-7580

Ordering Information:
Quantity sales. Special discounts are available on quantity purchases by corporations, associations, and others. For details, contact the publisher at the address above.

Printed in the United States of America.

ISBN-13:   Softcover   979-8-89389-517-9
                    eBook   979-8-89389-518-6

Library of Congress Control Number: 2024920065

Table of Contents

Special thanks to my family, who encouraged me through this entire project. Thanks to my friends for being super supportive. And lastly, thanks to my dogs and tortoise for sitting with me as I wrote, edited, and illustrated.

CHAPTER 1

Time of Departure

In the heart of Onferwil, an oceanside city, stood the palace—its walls hewn from white stone and jade. It was four stories tall with three watch towers stretching far above.

The palace, constructed on top a steep rocky incline, commanded a clear view of the ocean. Its front gates framed the ocean's horizon. The pathway, from the gate to the shore, wound through meticulously cultivated gardens. The raised planter beds were nearly the size of the surrounding homes and staggered down the center of the path to the shore. An ornate fountain stood as the centerpiece of each garden.

All the beautiful architectural and graceful landscaping communicated peace to any ignorant person. The truth was these were dark days; no, dark years or even decades. Not many people living in this city could see it, they were protected upper-class; nonetheless, they could feel the tension in the air. It was suffocating.

Within the palace, on the third floor, Prince Laithrum Airslen occupied a room abandoned over time. He sat on a plain red-wood chair very close to a window. He felt like a blight on the décor. The room, designed for grand fetes, had walls adorned with fine art, colors, and freshly lit oil lamps. The casual and broken him didn't belong here.

The window he looked through was the center one of three. Of the trio, the center one bore a broad plate of gold, intricately detailed with regal sea dragons. One dragons' snout reached toward the ceiling. Its body crafted into a gliding motion. Its legs held to clasp the window with strong talons. This dragon symbolized strength and protection. Protecting was how Laithrum could relate. Strength was an unknown attribute.

Laithrum's gaze fixed to the space before him. He was searching, musing over so many things.

Surveying the mist-shrouded morning streets below, his amber eyes framed by unruly dark hair, he saw a threat. Somewhere out there in the dark was something colder than the icy air that grasped onto winter stubbornly. His gaze wandered, searching, hoping for answers. Still nothing cleared.

A labyrinth of thoughts held his weary eyes open. Ideas paths intersected only to cause more confusion. Perhaps, he was too tired.

Sleep eluded him for days—it was a mysterious desire rather than a life necessity. Some crucial responsibility was keeping him awake. How could he forget something so important that it would feel like this? He was supposed to go somewhere. Who would even whisper these now-forgotten words? And where was this obscure destination?

The questions lingered, stretching into eternity. He has suffered for two days now; they are haunting him? The phantom voice persisted, a one-sided conversation that deepened his daily troubles.

Yet the enigma of his destination surpassed even the mystery of its origin. Leaving the palace—an alien notion. Laithrum had never ventured beyond its walls, forbidden by illness and other, less tangible reasons. His older sister, Freyja, shared his suspicions. Why this confinement? The answers remained veiled. Some deep conspiracy maybe.

As Laithrum pondered, a man treaded heavily into the ballroom. He wanted to be noticed. It was Hondou Sentrose Unrey, captain of the royal guard and Thuthairryon's Crowned Knight. A military figure who became wrapped up in politics. Hondou had ascended to this position exactly one year prior.

Tonight's banquet celebrated the anniversary of his promotion and some victories in the war. It was an excuse to dress up, drink and strut superiorities. Hondou loved these events. He looked like the model Thuryon. He was tall with a broad, strong physique, light hair, and piercing blue eyes. His expression betrayed annoyance, muscles taut with anger.

Laithrum's cut through the tension by asking quickly, "What brings you to the southern wing, Hondou? You rarely tread these halls."

"I have come to speak with you," his deep voice sliced through the air, urgency propelling his words. Laithrum smirked, suppressing laughter that clawed at the silence.

"You can laugh at me later," Hondou spat, his tone sharp. "Now answer me! What evil approaches?" His abruptness hung in the room like a shadow.

"And how would I know the evil you sense?" Laithrum's calm retort could barely be heard. His gaze stretched beyond the window, into the distance, where those secrets were whispered in the wind.

Hondou's glare intensified. "Listen, child! You're no stranger to danger. Tell me—what plagues Thuthairryon? What darkness have you befriended WITHIN our walls?" His hand rested forcefully on the sword hilt, eyes darkening with suppressed anger.

"Stop!" Laithrum's chair scraped against the floor as he rose, eyes locking onto Hondou's startled gaze. "Unrey, no more! I may be an abomination of a prince, but you're merely a guard, albeit the highest ranked." His gaze dropped, shielding vulnerability. "Was that all? It'll comfort you that I have no friends within these walls! None, but my sister. Could she by the 'Darkness' you speak of?"

"Don't play dumb!" Hondou's voice trembled, unaccustomed to Laithrum's outburst. "How dire is the threat?" Fear edged his words.

"Unrey," Laithrum sighed, "I echo what you've heard. The threat ranks higher than you. Our capital city trembles in dread. When or whom, I cannot say. Only that it draws nearer by the day." His tone was soft but weighed down in worry.

Guilt flared inside Hondou's. "I feared this," he muttered, unaware that Laithrum's keen hearing caught every syllable.

With curiosity spiked, "Why my input? Have you consulted Seers? What sets me apart?"

Hondou turned, striding away. Laithrum's worry deepened. "Hondou Unrey, if your knowledge is helpful, share it."

"Nothing, Laithrum," Hondou's anger simmered as he stormed out. He didn't glance back, but Laithrum followed relentlessly.

Laithrum stepped in front of Hondou, actively blocking his path. "What is it?" he demanded, staring up into the knight's face. Hondou's gaze flickered, avoiding Laithrum's piercing yellow eyes.

Hondou gritted his teeth. "As I said, it's nothing. I no longer wish to speak with you." He circled Laithrum, swaggering away. Laithrum, defying his solitary nature, questioned again, "Why? Do you not trust me? I've never wronged you." His statement hung in the air.

Hondou didn't turn, alarmed by Laithrum's sudden persistence. "I don't completely distrust you I…," his words clipped. Laithrum observed that finishing those words would to unlikely. They'll stay unspoken.

Laithrum chose not to follow. He evaluated what had been said— and what had not. The answers they both sought wouldn't elude them for long. An event loomed. Something involving his father, the king. Its impending arrival shadowed the city increasing its potency. Laithrum would wait for the unveiling…right? It was less than he expected… hopefully.

His day had begun, the argument settled. He strolled through the palace, seeking signs. Along a long hallway, a decorative mirror reflected the sun's golden light. The warm rays evoked memories of his sister. For over a week, she'd battled illness, confined to her room. Laithrum's worry eclipsed his fear of contagion. He traversed the palace's labyrinthine corridors, arriving at the tall wooden door to Freyja's chambers. Would she be awake?

He turned his back to the dark door, sat down, and leaned against it. An hour passed, and then he knocked—each rap resonating rich and deep.

"Hello, Freyja. It's Laithrum," he said, each word standing alone. "May I come in?" Silence followed, but Laithrum waited patiently.

Sighing in defeat, he sat back down.

"The door is open," announced a clear, female voice from within. Laithrum straightened his legs and pushed open the door. Stepping into the spacious room he saw Freyja appearing perfectly healthy. Suspicious.

"Good morning, Freyja," he greeted kindly. "I came to see how you're doing." He remembered being turned away by her keeper many times. "Are you disinclined to leave your room?"

Freyja's fluent response held no hesitation. "My illness lingers. In some ways I'm worse than before. You've lacked kind conversation since my illness began, haven't you?" She, the only one who spoke openly with her mixed-blooded brother. She bore no superstitions, hatred, or fear of him. Her gaze met his, and she continued, "You've changed—more awake—bolder. Did you sleep well?"

Laithrum shook his head, his eyes heavy with fatigue. "I barely slept, but I'm more interested in you. Freyja, did you sleep well?"

Freyja's expression shifted from kind to bitter. "No, I didn't. I'm too upset to find peace in sleep. What Father has done recently is sickening. What he made happen...!" Her voice trembled with anger and grief. The recent war's devastation on Thuthairryon's people contrasted sharply with the nobles' banquet and celebration tonight; fairness was a distant dream.

Laithrum moved slowly to sit beside her. "This terror will only worsen. Freyja, if you don't recover soon, I fear I'll lose you to what's coming." His concern for his sister was evident.

Freyja looked down, her long, straw-blond hair falling over her face. She let it hang hiding her greenish-blue eyes, which resembled the ocean on a sunny day but were now clouded with sorrow. She knew a part of her was missing, and she knew where it was but not how to retrieve it. She realized Laithrum was right; she needed to lift her mind or risk losing herself. Closing her eyes, she forced a smile. She had chosen anger for too long; now, she would choose the opposite by embracing the day with positivity.

Abruptly, Laithrum stood and turned to her. "Sister, it's been too long since you been out. Come with me for breakfast. I haven't eaten yet; we both need to refresh ourselves."

Freyja stood beside him, her eyes hazy, and smiled. "And after we eat, then what, Laithrum? Do you have any plans?"

"I'll share my plans when the time is right, but you'll have to wait," Laithrum replied playfully yet maintaining his calm demeanor.

Accepting his answer, Freyja searched for a tie to bind her hair.

"Sister, won't you come as you are?" sighed Laithrum. "If you plan to brush your hair first, I'll leave, order our meal, and wait. It'll be cold by the time you finish."

Irritated, Freyja stood and accepted his statement. "Alright, little brother, I'll go as I am." She threw a long overcoat over her plain nightgown and followed Laithrum out of her barracks.

As Laithrum and Freyja walked, many turned to look twice. The joyous news of princess Freyja emerging from her room spread swiftly. The ears of King Niejill Airslen, their father, were reached.

He was a robust man with fair skin, light-brown hair, and narrow, dark blue-green eyes that gleamed like waves at night. King Airslen sat on a gold throne draped in silk. He cradling a flat object wrapped in dark cloth. The room held only him and the messenger. These days he commanded to be left alone.

"Where are they?" the king asked the royal messenger, Dairren, who bowed and replied respectfully, "Your majesty, they were heading to the dining hall for breakfast."

The king stood and commanded in a monotone, "Tell the chefs to prepare a grand dish for my daughter." He then turned to leave.

Dairren stared and waited, his blue eyes simmering with hidden anger, but no more commands came. Dairren bowed out of habit, not reverence, and swiftly went to the kitchen.

Outside the room, Niejill paced back and forth. Ripely annoyed at Freyja's roaming and irritated by her company; Laithrum. He grasped the covered object tightly, as if it were his own life in his hands.

. . .

After wandering through the white halls, admiring the golden trim, tapestries, paintings, and other decorations, Laithrum and Freyja finally reached their destination. They were surprised to find their breakfast already being prepared and the table set.

"Laithrum, was this your planning?" Freyja asked, but she noticed he was just as surprised. Before Laithrum could respond a housekeeper arrived and led them to their table. The two sat at the long table and waited until they were alone.

"Sister, why do you think they were waiting for us?" Laithrum asked, more to start a conversation than out of curiosity. Freyja played along and called over the messenger, Dairren. He came immediately and stood attentively by her side.

"How did you know we were coming?" Freyja asked kindly.

"The palace buzzed with the news that you were venturing outside your room. King Airslen ordered your breakfast when he heard," Dairren replied. Though glad she had emerged, he sensed trouble. "Is something wrong?"

"It is not meant for your ears, Dairren. I do not want this message sent to anyone, so I will not tell," Freyja answered, waving him away.

The Royal Messenger bowed and left, uneasy at the sight of Freyja's troubled expression.

Freyja's melancholy deepened. "Why didn't he come himself? Is he afraid to see me? He should be. Or is he just too lazy to come all this way? Like when I was sick! He didn't visit once. Maybe he sent this order to salvage his failing political image within the palace." She clenched her fist, her voice rising in anger. "His actions are clandestine and venomous." Laithrum watched her, his eyes sinking as he saw her anger and tears. He had never seen her so emotional; something was very wrong.

Staring at the dark wood table, Freyja whispered mournfully, "First, Father murders Lotus." She paused, as she always did when speaking his name. "Then he ignores my illness, not even one visit. Now, he sends Dairren to order our breakfast. His treatment of his subordinates and soldiers angers me too. He should have come himself."

Laithrum, confused, asked cautiously, "Freyja, what do you mean by 'murdered'? Lotus was sent to war, like many others. Isn't that so?" He regretted the question as soon as he asked it.

Freyja's face turned stern. She stared into his bright eyes. "Laithrum, how could you not know? Our brother was to be killed for crimes against the country, but he pleaded to fight to the death, for honor. After being granted his request, on that same day, Lotus was sent as the personal bodyguard for Adeyas." She paused, then continued, "Lotus was sent to protect someone destined to die. I call that murder!" She lowered her head into her hands, trying to calm herself.

When their meal arrived, they ate in silence, each lost in thought.

The warm light streamed through the window contrasted their gloomy moods. The brightness cast diamond-shaped shadows across the dining hall.

Freyja sat up, folding her hands on her lap, "Laithrum, I can continue. My mind has calmed, and I apologize for my tantrum," she said, life returning to her face.

Laithrum rose to his feet and gently pulled Freyja up with him.

"Come," he said, "Your fever has lifted. We must tell Mother. She has been depressed ever since you fell ill. You are her only remaining child now." Though he spoke mirthfully, his eyes were devoid of joy. He had love for… the queen, but realized he was the constant reminder of his father cheating.

"Mother can visit me or wait until I am finished with you."

Freyja understood his social rejection and the pain of his solitude. Even after eighteen years, no one warmed to him or respected him. Their mother had disowned him in her heart, insisting she never be called his mother.

"This country," she began, "has had unfortunate encounters with other races in the past… I'm sad that you are so unhappy here. People treat you poorly because of our fathers' choices and your racial difference."

"Freyja, I'm happy if you are. But I have had a troubling thought lately." He paused, and Freyja gestured eagerly for him to continue.

"Ever since the Saiyured joined the Trence fleet at the docks two days ago, something or someone has been on my mind. A thought demanding action has haunted me. Both fleets leave tomorrow morning. I hope these feelings will leave with the ships." His discomfort with waiting was evident.

"What is it, Laithrum? What's on your mind that you can't figure out? Discuss it with me, I need to know what you're thinking. I'm so very interested!" Freyja stated.

Laithrum realized he hadn't shared the subject of his thoughts. Freyja watched his eyes, waiting for an answer. She enjoyed being the same height, both nearly six feet tall, because she was never considered weak or small.

Face to face with his sister, Laithrum began to explain. "I need to do something, but I don't know exactly what it is yet and…" Freyja had never seen him so baffled before. He was usually able to foresee events.

"Brother, you used the word 'exactly.' You have a clearer understanding than you've shared. Right?"

He nodded.

She continued, "If you can put these strange thoughts into words, share them so I can be confused with you. Discussion might bring out the answer more quickly."

"Freyja, there's been a voice, not my own, speaking to me. It's telling me to leave, but I don't know where. The other thought comes from the first. It's telling me to do something. I have no idea where to do, what to do, or who is asking these things of me!"

She didn't answer quickly, struggling to find words. They stood in thought for a while, soon realizing the same thing. They should go to the ships. The fleet that seemed to bring the disturbance. Perhaps seeing them or being closer could provide an answer. Agreeing on their plan of action, they went to get ready.

After preparing to leave, Laithrum asked calmly, "Freyja, how am I to travel to the docks when I'm not even allowed to walk through the gardens on the roof? How will we get me out there?"

"Getting you out is simple for me. No one, unless foolish, will stand in my way. But before I let you go; I must know if you're willing to risk getting sick by going out."

The young prince smiled. "Being able to go outdoors will make up for any possible illness."

Laithrum and Freyja journeyed down stairways and through countless halls. Finally, they stepped through the front door. The fresh air was gratifying. It was late morning, the earlier clouds had dispersed, and the sun shone brightly. No one stopped them until they reached the palace gates.

CHAPTER 2

Into the Sea

The towering golden gates loomed overhead, guarded by two vigilant attendants. One of them, bold enough to halt their progress, stepped in the way and bowed. "Princess Freyja Airslen, I was informed of your illness and advised you should not be wandering. I apologize for not visiting you or writing you." He smiled formally.

"It is all right. I have only recently begun to feel better, Lattermere Seidei," she replied, anticipating his inquiry about Laithrum. Instead, he asked, "Princess Airslen, if you have just recovered, what brings you out here? And why is your brother accompanying you when he is not permitted to leave for any reason?"

"We both wished to be outside. I was unaware that walking around our domain was forbidden," she said, her annoyance growing at Lattermere's questioning. She continued before he could speak again. "Seidei, I am newly free from my room and only a hair away from anger. My short temper puts you in danger you continue to interrogate me. Be cautious, for I could pass an unfair judgment." Freyja warned as she and Laithrum moved forward.

Lattermere stared, frustrated, and genuinely concerned for both of them. He knew Laithrum was not permitted beyond the palace doors, let alone the gate. Reporting this would displease the royals, not reporting them would be breaching protocol. Either decision was a risk, but he trusted Freyja so the message would remain unspoken.

Freyja and Laithrum walked leisurely toward the endless sea. Normally, at this time of day, the water was a smooth, opaque pane stretching to the horizon. Today, however, the sea was dotted with ships, their sails furled, and their glossy wooden sides gleaming. The sight was beautiful yet foreboding.

The gentle breeze made the time outside pleasurable as it carried the sweet scent of flowers mixed with the sea. Again, it was beautiful yet foreboding. Was it the calm before a storm? They continued down the steep road.

When they reached the turquoise ocean, which sparkled with silvery reflections from the sun, they turned a sharp right toward the main docks. These docks, numerous and extending far into the water, were busy with people. Juxtaposed to the docks, up the shore, was a piling of supplies that continually grew from the city's prevision and decreased as they were loaded onto ships.

Observing the houses and people of Onferwil, Laithrum finally saw how clean the city was. It seemed untouched, which was contrary to what he had been told. Evenything was struggling because of all the conflict; right? His thoughts were repeatedly distracted by the raucous song of the gulls. Shore birds were everywhere. They were noisy and unafraid of people.

At last, Laithrum and his sister reached the port.

Soldiers and sailors were scattered across the beach. Their figures and belongings deceptively dark against the white sand reflecting the sun. Men moved to and from the ships, carrying supplies—weapons, food, and medical equipment. The sheer number of bodies made it difficult to discern the purpose of their activity. The two stood for a while, staring at the controlled chaos of teeming bodies.

Through the noisy crowd, and over the calling birds, Laithrum heard someone call his name. The voice came from an unclear direction. He looked around, but the area was too thick with people to identify a single, unknown person. Few were close enough to have whispered.

Laithrum glanced at Freyja. "Did you hear someone say my name?"

She responded with a light-hearted laugh. "Me, hear something you couldn't make out? Laithrum, don't be silly. You have much better hearing than I. Who knows you out here anyway?" After her retort, she pondered and asked, "What did it sound like? Was the voice familiar at all?"

Someone approached them from behind, interrupting their conversation. "Royalty shouldn't look so lost and be without assistance," a young red-haired soldier walked up beside them and bowed. The stranger continued, "Is there anything I can do to help you in your matter?"

Freyja responded, "First, I am not lost. I am, though, unsure of how I look, because the wind out here is tremendously strong," she teased.

"As for your offer, we'll accept your help. We are looking for someone or something, people or a person who may be able to speak in others' minds. An obnoxious company telling people what to do or where to go. We could also be in search of a visual item. Yes, something symbolizing leaving or something that stimulates engagement toward something," stated Freyja, trying to be so vague and confusing that the man would leave them alone.

She was eager to hear what kind of response this foreign man would give. His appearance suggested he was from Gourin, not Thuthairryon, an allied country. His red hair and vocal accent gave him away.

"Well... yes. I think I can help you," he stated.

"I know of two people who, it is rumored, could mind-speak. One is more frightening than the other, and I, personally, don't like speaking with either one. As for the item you're searching for, I know of nothing." The soldier said honestly, and quickly continued, "My name is Linus Lounleyossa, and I apologize for my informality toward royalty—princess Freyja and prince Laithrum." Linus bowed his head again when he spoke their names.

Freyja was slightly surprised that he recognized Laithrum and herself, as he was obviously from Gourin. She was grateful that he did not speak their names loudly. She was more surprised that he knew of people who could be speaking to Laithrum.

"Linus Lounleyossa, your last name sounds familiar. Do you know of a reason why I would know it?" Freyja asked, curiously.

A soft, rude chuckle echoed from another voice. "One of the captains is named Makoto Lounleyossa. He performed several remarkable acts for this country. Those achievements by Linus' daddy are the only reason someone like Linus could easily join the Thuthairryon forces."

Laithrum and Freyja turned to see the speaker. They saw a young woman, younger than themselves, looking up at them. Her shoulder-length hair was unnaturally pitch-black, too pure and dark to see the strands or folds, like a deep cave. The fluorescent, colorfully tinted, shine radiating from her hair proclaimed she wasn't human. Her cunning, pale blue eyes seemed to glow, untouched by shadow, and her skin was fair and bright. A very magical looking person. Beautiful like a gemstone.

Linus sighed, "Interesting, you're talking to people now, Raven?"

Annoyed by this person's presence, he continued, "This is one of the men I mentioned before, about your…" Laithrum and Freyja were both shocked to hear she was a man.

Raven waved his hand, silencing Linus. Pushing past Linus, Raven turned to Laithrum and Freyja and spoke shrewdly, "I have an idea who you want to find; however, before I continue, I need to tell you something. I've been listening to you for a while. I do not speak into others' minds. I only respond when spoken to. I know someone who can and would do so without any problem, but it's unlikely you'll meet him."

"Why is that, miss?" Laithrum's mix-up made Raven's eye twitch rapidly. Laithrum shook his head and corrected himself. "Why is that *sir*? He won't see us for what reason?" Laithrum knew Raven was baiting him to ask.

Raven teased, "Because he's going to help on the boat until we leave again. Not long now. Only the crew can board the boat, and ordering yourselves onboard would quickly reveal that you are out here." Raven maintained a consistent mocking yet mellow tone. Even though his tone was careless, and free of concern or regard, the expressions behind his eyes were serious. He was on guard. Looking for any seen or unseen threat.

"That would ruin your entire royal adventure, right?"

Laithrum couldn't quite understand Raven. Though dressed like a soldier of Thuthairryon, and radiating was magic, he bore unmistakable traits of the Seintroven—the enemy.

The people of Seitrova were known for their dark hair, light skin with a golden sheen, and a distinctive mark on their bodies from the bacteria in their land's soil. Raven's mark was visible: a red line, about a quarter-inch thick, extended horizontally from the top corner of his right eye to his hairline. Raven met Laithrum's stare, aware of the prince's unspoken questions.

Raven turned his gaze to Freyja as she began to speak. "Raven, would you kindly bring this man to us before we bother ordering ourselves on board?" she demanded, her voice dripping with venom at the disrespect shown to her and her brother.

Raven smiled maniacally. "He will not come if he doesn't want to. He is not under this realm's jurisdiction. I tell you the truth. Now listen, we're leaving early, so no soldier has time to heed your petty orders."

Just as Raven finished speaking, High General Vander Headorbron stood upon the rail of his ship, Warsped, the closest to the crowd on shore.

Responding to the general's raised hand, a soldier beside him sounded a horn. The soldiers immediately stopped and stood at attention, listening intently.

"Men," Vander shouted, "the new threat is close to the front lines! For this reason, we are leaving sooner than expected; move hurriedly. I command that every ship be prepared to depart by high noon." He then turned and headed back into the ships' housing.

The men loading supplies quickened their pace to a slow run. Other soldiers with sign-out lists ran off to inform their comrades, on temporary leave, of the new departure time.

Freyja and Laithrum looked at Linus and Raven, neither of whom moved. "Aren't you two leaving as well?" asked Laithrum. Linus glanced at him. "Not just yet, prince," he replied briefly.

Raven's silent laughter followed Linus' reply. Raven looked up at the two royals and explained, "We are stationed on the ship Derdrin, which is on the fourth and last line; consequently, we won't be able to leave for a couple of hours after noon."

Laithrum couldn't fathom Raven's calm demeanor; everyone else seemed anxious to leave. He couldn't care less. This passivity toward battle was strange and intriguing.

Laithrum felt a strange apprehension, as if he were leaving with them. Why? To him, being a warrior was akin to being a prisoner in a different guise. But would either of those be much different to his current life? His feelings dissipated some as he remembered his susceptibility to illness. He was trapped no matter where he was.

Staring intently at the ships he thought that he'd be fine if he went. Where were these thoughts coming from? He'd succumb to illness long before the battle. Wouldn't he?

Raven turned and began to walk away. He was uncomfortable in the group and bothered by their company. Linus, however, stayed with the royalty, finding their conversation refreshing despite the discomfort of their important status.

Freyja glanced at Laithrum. "What do you think went wrong at the front to create such urgency? And how did Raven know they would sail off early?"

Laithrum lowered his head but looked at her as he whispered, "I don't know. I could guess, but I have nothing to base any theories on." His mind drifting into thought again.

Linus also pondered the accelerated departure. "Prince, Princess, I can take you to our captain, Makoto Lounleyossa. He'll know. He must, right?"

Laithrum and Freyja smiled and agreed to go with Linus. The three navigated through the massive crowd of rushing men. As they stepped onto the beach, Laithrum noticed something in the distance. His eyes widened in surprise and fear. Though confused, he quickly commanded, "EVERYONE GET DOWN!"

He collapsed himself and Freyja to the ground. Linus followed, not knowing why. Raven, hearing from within the crowd, obeyed Laithrum's order. Many followed Raven out of respect, while others, unsure of what would happen if they didn't, also dropped.

At that moment, a powerful, howling, demonic wind roared over them. It was sudden and malevolent. So strong that even ships with their sails unfurled were thrown over. The closest ship turned completely over, up, and out of the water, landing on its deck. The sails and sides shattered under the ship's weight and momentum.

Debris covered the shore and grounded bodies. The wind stayed above ground, cutting upward. The men who didn't drop to the sand were carried up into the clear sky until they could no longer be seen. Strangely, none fell back down, and none were seen again by the men below. The winds had taken the roofs off beach houses, but only those closest to the docks were damaged.

Suddenly, the wind vanished, and the sea breeze resumed its harmless dance through the silent, frightened port. The men began pushing wreckage and sand from themselves. Raven jumped up and ran to Laithrum.

"How did you know that was coming?" he pleaded.

Laithrum stood and looked at him. "I saw it," he answered plainly.

This was the first time Raven noticed the brightness deep in Laithrum's yellow eyes. There was magic.

Raven grinned. "That gust was invisible until it struck. It didn't even move the water… yet you… so that's why…" He stopped, not wanting to provoke questions.

Linus hurried to his feet and offered his hand to Freyja to assist her up. Freyja stood up on her own, pushing away Linus's hand. She looked frantically around at the damage to the houses, ships, and people. Some ships lay on their sides, too damaged for use, but most remained untouched.

It was as if the wind dove toward them and thrown itself back into the clouds. Some soldiers were studying this fact as well. Somehow, Freyja knew the reason why but couldn't explain how she knew. Her stomach churned; anxiety gripped her.

Raven stood relaxed, staring at a cloaked figure in the distance. They exchanged looks as if having a silent conversation. Raven turned back and looked intently at Laithrum. Laithrum was too distracted to notice.

He watched a soldier with bound blond hair pull a piece of wooden debris, stained and dripping with blood, from another soldier's arm. Laithrum had never seen anything like this. It was awful, and he driven to respond but didn't know how.

Freyja regrouped herself and asked Raven, "Who is that?" gesturing to the cloaked figure. Raven didn't answer, ignoring her completely.

Linus grabbed Raven's arm. "She is one of your royals now, so show some respect… or be hanged. I'd like to see either," Linus spat as silently as possible.

Raven's expression turned into a glare. Linus backed away, chills running through his body. After this, Linus dared not speak, afraid of what might happen next. Whatever it was, it didn't make sense to him. In contrast, Freyja fearlessly glared back at the black-haired youth. "Raven, I'll know sooner or later who that man is, but you'd better hope it's sooner," she threatened.

Raven nodded in understanding, surprising her with his lack of intimidation. Freyja had never met anyone so hard, cold, and distant. She honestly liked the challenge he presented and would be sure to repay him if they met again.

"You wish for us to speak in private, don't you? If so, we should speak now," said Laithrum to Raven. Raven smiled, nodded, and started walking off.

Linus quickly but carefully grabbed Laithrum's shoulder. "Prince, I only started fighting for your country two weeks ago, yet I have been fighting for this country longer than him. Prince Laithrum, he was one of the enemies not too long ago. Please, don't trust him," he said in a hushed voice.

Laithrum met Linus's gaze. Linus tried to back away from Laithrum's amber eyes. Something didn't feel right. "Linus," he said, "if you're not going to trust him, trust me. I won't put myself in danger by speaking with Raven." Laithrum turned away and walked off to meet Raven, who was waiting up ahead.

Raven and Laithrum now stood on a clear road facing each other. "So, who was that man you saw? The one my sister asked about," Laithrum asked thoughtfully. Raven remained silent, prompting Laithrum to pry, "Raven?"

Raven rolled his eyes in annoyance. "I need to ask you to do something in someone else's place." Laithrum listened, hesitant yet eager to learn more. Raven continued, his voice deadpan. "You should already know what I'm going to say. It's been asked of you for two days now." He paused, waiting to see if Laithrum would speak. He didn't.

"Well, you have until noon to arrive at this spot to leave on the ships." Raven smiled cruelly. "You can talk with your sister about it if you want. She shouldn't dictate your decision; it's far too important and it's your commitment, not hers." He then turned and swiftly ran back to the port.

Freyja and Linus watched Laithrum come around the alley corner and went over to him. Laithrum's thoughts troubled him. He knew what to do but couldn't make sense of it. His thoughts froze when he heard his sister's voice. "Brother, what did you two talk about? What did he want?" Laithrum didn't answer immediately, so she continued demanding, "You will tell me everything that brat of a …thing said."

Laithrum nodded.

Linus observed and commented negatively. "Well, whatever was said, it must have been frustrating and confusing because he was speaking with Raven," He then looked up to consider the time. "I apologize, Princess and Prince Airslen, but I must get back to work. This is goodbye."

After wishing him farewell, they watched Linus run back to the port.

Laithrum glanced seriously at his sister. "Raven was being a messenger… someone wants me to go with them on the ships… toward battle."

Freyja looked at him with emotional eyes and then took his hand. Gripping it, she asked, "Do you need to go?"

Laithrum looked away in thought for a time. He glanced back at her. "I don't know, but it feels right," he said, trying to answer clearly but couldn't. He crouched down, fighting his instinct with his reasoning.

Freyja stooped beside him and gently whispered, "Go." He quickly looked into her bright ocean-blue eyes.

"Do you want me to die?" Laithrum asked, his voice breaking. Freyja smiled in amusement. "I don't want to be separated from you. I don't want any harm to happen to you. I'm trying to help you. Going might be what you must do. Please, I truly feel that you need to leave this place because here is worse." She paused, then added, "I don't trust *here* anymore. I plan to leave soon too. It's a gut feeling, I guess."

Laithrum remained silent, torn between two equally daunting choices. He glanced at Freyja, his confusion and unease evident.

"Come," Freyja urged.

"Where are we going?" Laithrum asked, following her as she quickly led him down the deserted streets.

They hurried back to the palace. At the gates, Lattermere tried to stop them, but they rushed past him. Freyja led Laithrum through the palace until they reached an abanded room. Anxiously, she unlocked the door, and they entered.

Laithrum recognized the room after inside; it had belonged to their eldest sister, who had died sixteen years ago. He felt a pang of sadness, remembering only her face. She had been Freyja's role model, though in recent years, Freyja had become her own person.

The room remained as Amethist Airslen had left it—spacious, colorful, adorned with items from many cultures. Freyja knelt by a large rock sculpture of a decorative fish, removed a loose stone from its base, and reached deep inside. She pulled out a long, thin package.

"This is something my sister wanted me to have if war came here. It's a long dagger that cannot dull with time or use. I will give it to you for your journey. See, I support you." Freyja handed him the package. Laithrum hesitated, then took the blade. The parting gift made his departure seem more real and frightening, but also less lonely.

"Go, Laithrum, and don't look back," she said with a sincere smile. Laithrum thanked her, embraced her, and said, "Goodbye, sister. Tell Ashtion the same when he arrives."

Parting was difficult, especially since Freyja had finally freed herself from her room. Yet, strangely, his leaving was what they both wanted, and they were glad to make the decision together.

Laithrum held the gift firmly as he packed a small sack of items from his room. He threw a light-gray cloak over his shoulders and ran quickly toward the harbor. With his sister's distractions, he managed to slip outside the gates again and swiftly returned to the rendezvous point.

"We were about to give up on you," Raven said from behind, clearly glad to see him. "What do you mean? I'm early," Laithrum retorted calmly.

Raven was surprised by Laithrum's response. "If you always spoke that way, you'd be looked upon with more respect," Raven said, adjusting the bag on his back. He walked toward the numerous ships that sat in the brilliant blue water, reflecting the afternoon sun.

Laithrum followed Raven onto the ship Derdrin. The person who had summoned him was aboard, but Laithrum did not stay inside to seek him out. Instead, he ran to the front deck to gaze at the city he was leaving behind. The ship began to back away from the white shores of Thuthairryon.

The wind filled the sails, and the rowers below deck started to turn Derdrin toward the open sea. Laithrum moved with the ship, running along the railing until he reached the stern. From there, he watched Thuthairryon fade into the distance. The young prince found himself in an unfamiliar place, the thought of making the best of it both hopeful and daunting.

"Goodbye, Freyja," he whispered into the cool sea breeze as the ship sailed into the vast expanse of blue and green.

CHAPTER 3

The New Home

Hours passed, and the land vanished beyond the horizon. The air was neither hot nor cold, yet the breeze clung to winter's chill. Laithrum stared at the water's edge where the city once stood. Not even he could see the city Thuthairryon.

Laithrum shifted his thoughts to his current surroundings. He had never felt he belonged in the palace, but now his home seemed like a haven. The vulnerability of being alone and in a unfamiliar place paralyzed him. He wished to remain hidden in his cloak.

The sea wind tossed back the hood of his thick, light-gray cloak. He lacked the energy to respond. The wind grew stronger, playing roughly with his shaggy dark hair. He didn't care enough to side brush his hair from his face. What lapse of sanity brought him here?

The air had changed since they left port; it was saltier, with a slight sweetness. Despite the pleasant smell of the sea, the sight of the endless greenish-blue ocean, and the freedom from his past lifestyle, anxiety grew him. He had never trained for combat, never physically trained at all, and only possessed a large dagger for a weapon. Laithrum felt hopeless for an answer. Solutions seemed elusive in this new, dangerous place.

Adding to his terror was the sense of impending doom he had felt in Thuthairryon. Hondou had sensed it too. Or maybe Hondou knew more about it than he himself did? The eerie feeling that something awful was about to happen was constant. Leaving his sister there alone, tangled guilt throughout his thoughts.

There was a reason he left; he knew it, and Freyja knew it, but what was that reason? And what was he supposed to do here? Who was this person who pressured him into this venture? Was he of good nature or evil intent? Laithrum feared the answer but knew it was the first he must obtain.

With eyes wide in apprehension, Laithrum looked down at the wake of the ship. He thought, "Where am I going to start? I know no one to ask…other than Raven. I want to avoid that trouble for now. Where is there to go in this small and crowded place."

After a while, Laithrum stopped asking himself questions; his mind grew overwhelmed by the inability to answer any of them. He dropped his head on the ship's rail, holding himself up with his elbows. His forearms crossed over his head. He tried hard to forget all that surrounded him—even if only for a second.

A cloaked figure stood back, watching Laithrum. His body was motionless until, suddenly and without sound, he ran up to Laithrum. The stranger now stood next to him, his composure straight and unwavering. He wore a dark-green cloak, its hood hanging low and shading his face.

The stranger looked ahead with an unseen but known smile. "I am glad you came," said the stranger kindly. Laithrum turned to the stranger. He speculated that this man had called him there.

"Who are you? And I'd like to know why you've called me here. Not that I need to be persuaded. I am here, and anxious about the reason why. This isn't surprising to you, is it?"

Waiting to respond, the stranger pulled back his hood. The man seemed amused. "Raven told me you were shy or timid in the way you spoke and moved. You are not shy nor without resolve, are you? You are ill and tired though."

Laithrum stared at the stranger in amazement. He shone with a light that wasn't from the sun. Though he looked young, his presence felt ancient, both strong and fragile. His long hair fell straight, with locks in front entwined with two golden clasps, woven like vines.

Laithrum's observations brought back memories of stories told by his siblings about elves. This man fit their descriptions. Laithrum focused his thoughts and asked, "Are you of the elfin race?"

Before the stranger could answer, the wind lifted his dazzling, light-gold hair, revealing long, thin, pointed ears styled in the manner of elves.

"Do not answer. I see you are. I am honored to meet one of the immortal people," Laithrum began. "Yet, why do you say that I am ill? I feel normal. If I seem tired, it's because I am. I haven't been able to sleep for the last few days because of you." Laithrum paused. "I'm not ill, not yet at least."

"You'll see and feel why I call you *ill* soon enough. As for what I did, you might thank me one day. Nevertheless, I am sorry for disturbing your sleep," said the elf.

Curiosity moved Laithrum to ask, "What will I feel and see? What kind of illness is it?" He waited, fearful of the answer.

The elf placed a light hand on Laithrum's shoulder, surprising the young prince. "Stand strong. The illness will soon disappear. It will not be painful or take long; the peak sickness will be short, even by man's standards. It will be completely gone after a day, mostly gone in a few hours. You'll be better off for it," the elf comforted, a slight smile forming on his face.

Laithrum looked closely at him, then turned his gaze upward, staring at the blue sky. "This all happened so fast," he sighed, eyes leaving the sky and returning to his elfin acquaintance. "I'm sorry for acting out of despair, confusion, hopelessness," Laithrum said solemnly but tried to smile. He knew he was complaining too much and was probably bothersome. "But will you answer one more question? What is your name?"

The elf, who watched Laithrum carefully, replied cautiously, "First, I'd like an answer from you. Why aren't you speaking openly with me?"

Laithrum's eyes widened in concern, fearing he had said something insulting. He intended to make a friend. "I am sorry if something I said makes you feel that I distrust you. I don't wish to be a bother, and I have no reason to dislike you.

But I'd like to know you before I trust you with my personal battles, or the thoughts and questions I'm concerned about."

"I understand your answer and am glad to hear you say it. Not everyone you meet on this adventure will be trustworthy," he said lightly. "Now, I'll tell you, my name. Trust me more. I am Onlortrens Reniviall Silvertree. If you want or need my help, but are too stubborn to ask, I'll try to help you," answered the elf, pleased that Laithrum seemed to be fighting his sickness already.

Laithrum's demeanor told Onlortrens that he had a decent chance to excel in the coming battle and endure the hardships that would follow. Onlortrens continued, "Feel free to explore, Prince Laithrum. I will not let anything happen to you until you are ready."

Laithrum stared at Onlortrens, bewildered. No one besides his sister had ever promised to watch out for him. But why? Onlortrens' promise to protect him was strange. Skeptical, he asked, "Why me? You don't even know me. I only saw you once before, at the port. Why would my life mean anything to you?"

Onlortrens' bright eyes narrowed slightly in worry over the young prince's lack of self-worth. "Laithrum, don't ask such things. Don't tell yourself or anyone else that you are not worth their help. It doesn't help anyone to be incredulous. The one who doubts will be without help, and the distrusted person will be hurt and discouraged from helping again in the future. So, let all who wish to help you do so in whatever way they can. Just trust them with their own resolve. Don't trust them with the work you have to do yourself."

"I'll remember that, but I still don't have an answer to my question. For what reason did you contacted me and continued to bother me until I came?" Laithrum replied, still pensive over Onlortrens' intentions.

Onlortrens smiled and softly laughed. "I want to assist you, but first, I need you to discover what I am talking about. Understanding comes in time." His voice then turned playful. "Laithrum, you're not going to make this harder than it already is by asking me to explain it all now, right?"

Amused, frustrated, and even more confused than before, Laithrum spoke quickly. "What are you talking about? I heard you in my thoughts before and I was excessively bewildered. But now that I've met you in person, the confusion from my, previously invasive, thoughts seem sensible. I already feel overwhelmed by so many things, both past and present. Conversation with you is both exhausting and surprisingly comfortable. Furthermore, I want to trust you. I only know three people in this fleet. Raven isn't trustworthy—obviously. That brings me to you and Linus."

"I will not tell you that I'm trustworthy because I don't want you to trust words out here. Don't be easily convinced because the enemy wants to deceive you. Often, we can't tell friend from foe. Treat others with positive regard, but let time and actions speak for integrity. Your absolute trust is what I seek, and I don't expect to receive it without earning it," said Onlortrens, hoping Laithrum understood.

Laithrum meditated on his words to find clear understanding. He stared toward the deep water, his eyes reflecting the ocean's surface but expressing deep thoughts. After his eyes reclaimed present apprehension, he relaxed to enjoy the view.

The sea was so clear that even the depth did not hide the bottom. The sight was beautiful, as if he were standing on the rim of a tall glass of spring water. This sight was also an intimidating, endless odyssey of water that he had never seen. Onlortrens looked down the side as well. He gaven Laithrum more time to relax. They both benefited from the moment of silence, and after a while, the elf commanded the next task.

"Laithrum, come with me. I have set aside suitable attire for this journey and for blending in," Onlortrens said, then added quietly, "Young Thuthairryon Prince, it is not safe for you. Your presence on board is best kept secret." He turned to lead the way.

They walked through the well-crafted halls of hard, dark wood. This was the war-boat Derdin, led by Captain Makoto Louleyossa. Built strong for war and crafted beautifully for nobility, it was a sight to behold. After navigating narrow halls, steep stairs, and open entryways, they reached the ship's storage house.

The room, lit by fire and glowing rocks, was filled with neatly stored and well-secured crates of supplies. Only a handful of seamen were present, each keenly aware of their surroundings and what they guarded.

One figure looked over—it was Raven. Easily identifiable on a Thuthairryon ship by his black hair and unhuman characteristics; furthermore, he resembled a female. Onlortrens approached Raven. In response, Raven quickly picked up a crate, placed it in front of Onlortrens, and mockingly bowed. "Onlortrens," Raven began, "He is now yours. I don't want anything else to do with him."

Onlortrens gazed curiously at Raven and stepped closer. "I understand that you don't like this. Please answer me, I'd like to know. Raven, what is on your mind? You seem abnormally distracted."

Raven reluctantly looked into the elf's rich blue eyes, shining clearly in the dimly lit room. His resolve failed and turned away from Onlortrens. Raven's sunken expression quickly turned darker and more defensive. "This doesn't involve you, high elf." Raven abruptly walked away, and Onlortrens let him go.

Laithrum looked at Raven thoughtfully. He noticed that Raven's attire had changed. The tough fabric, worn out from wear, he wore at port use now covered by thick leather, metal, and weaponry. He had two swords, one short and the other long, both tied to a thick brown belt on the left side of his waist. He also had four small knives, likely for throwing, two on his right upper arm and the others tied around the right side of his waist.

Laithrum looked back at Onlortrens. "Should I be expecting battle soon?" he asked thoughtfully.

"In times like these, your enemies are hidden all around you. I advise caution. Treat your weapons like a part of your body. Go nowhere without them. Again, I warn you, do not trust everyone in this fleet. The wind earlier was proof that someone is searching for you. They will find you again. There is no way to know what or who will be used," the elf answered grimly.

"The wind? You mean that force that struck us at the docks…" He stopped in disbelief. "It was meant for me. But why?"

"I can't tell the full story right now, because it wouldn't be fair to you, nor would it be safe. I will say this: you have something they do not want you to share."

After a long, thoughtful pause, Laithrum knew he wouldn't figure this riddle out—not yet. He chose to ask about another matter. "How much time until we meet up with the other ships?"

"It'll be five days if we maintain this pace." Onlortrens knelt by the wooden crate and opened it. "This will be your new wardrobe," he said, lifting dark clothes and lightweight armor resembling Raven's.

Onlortrens placed a set of clothes and armor in Laithrum's arms. He then handed Laithrum a sword and a field knife. The last item in the box was a quiver full of arrows and a bow. Along with the gift from Freyja, these items were the only belonging of prince Laithrum. He was poor.

"And Laithrum," the elf said, waving to capture the prince's attention, "I will start teaching you how to use these tonight." Confident that the prince would learn quickly, he continued, "Now we need to find you a place to change."

Finding no suitable place for Laithrum to change privately, Onlortrens looked inside the crate and teased, "Do you think you could fit and change in here?"

Laithrum nodded sarcastically declaring that he would fit, and genuinely trying to fix his own negative perspective.

"I tend to disagree. I don't believe you'd fit in there," Linus said cheerfully, walking up to them. When close enough, Linus inspected the box. Onlortrens glanced at Linus and said, "Perhaps if we tried."

Linus nodded in approval.

"I noticed you were listening to us; make yourself known sooner next time. Now for a practical solution: since you're here, you can help search for a private room and keep Laithrum's identity hidden," Onlortrens said to Linus. Linus seemed comfortable around them and accustomed to adjusting to diverse orders.

"Well, to start, he can stay in the same chamber as I," Linus began. "The room houses four, and I'm only staying with two others."

Onlortrens accepted his offer but then looked to Laithrum for his opinion. Laithrum smiled nervously. "And who are the other two men?" he asked.

"Well, you already know one." Linus looked disappointed. "It's Raven. So, there's no worry about one of the three keeping you awake at night; he's never there. The other man I haven't met yet. I believe his name is Dowen… and his last name is complicated." After Linus finished talking, Onlortrens started walking, gesturing for them to follow, and they did.

Onlortrens led them through a door with a hole for a window, covered by a small but thick blind. The door opened into a room with many beds. Sleeping quarters for commoners.

"Go, Laithrum, quickly change out of your princely clothes and wrap them in your cloak so no one will see them."

Laithrum did as Onlortrens said, though he felt uneasy since there was a doorway on the other side of the room. After a short while, he emerged dressed in dark-green cloth, leather, and light metal armor. He wore the sword on his left and a long golden-sheathed dagger on his right, the gift from his sister Freyja earlier that day. The field knife was attached to his shin, and he held the bow and full quiver in his arms along with his bundled clothes.

"Do you think anyone will recognize me?" Laithrum asked while positioning his hair over his face.

Linus doubted it.

Onlortrens grinned. "I think it will work. You look much different, not princely. I just hope you quickly get over how uncomfortable your hair must feel over your eyes."

"I hope so too, Laithrum," Linus stopped himself sharply, knowing not to call Laithrum by his title. Laithrum was content with their reactions but suddenly felt very tired and light-headed.

"Onlortrens," Laithrum began, almost too softly to hear, "I feel faint. Is this what you told me would happen?"

"Linus, lead us to your room. Laithrum must rest," Onlortrens said with concern. Linus quickly led the way to the forecastle area where he stayed, and Onlortrens assisted Laithrum in following.

The room wasn't far. They soon arrived and laid Laithrum down on one of the four flat beds, and he instantly fell asleep. "Let us leave him to rest," Onlortrens said gladly as he stood from his kneeling position and turned to leave the room.

Linus followed quickly, protesting, "But he's ill! We can't leave him alone while sick!"

Onlortrens replied, "We will bring him food and water when he awakens, but for now, he must sleep. Linus don't worry. This is the first step to Laithrum's recovery. In about two hours, he can be disturbed. You can go to him then." Onlortrens advised and then left.

Linus stood baffled for a while. He reminded himself that it wasn't wise to argue with a person thousands of years older. So, he surrendered his, seemingly, rational argument and exited the room.

After two hours passed, Linus went to eat and, in a small sack, smuggled food for Laithrum. When content with the nourishment and water he collected, Linus walked back.

Upon returning, he found Laithrum sitting up, holding his sister's blade, Freyja's parting gift. The hilt of the dagger was gold-plated steel. The handle was wrapped in golden-brown leather. The gold on the small guard was designed with flowing writing. The words read, "There Is Always Hope" on one side of the guard and, when flipped around, "When Fought For." Laithrum grinned broadly, remembering Freyja say that Amethyst often quoted this.

"You're up. That must mean you're feeling better," Linus hoped, handing over half a loaf of bread, a small cheese brick, and a piece of jerky. Then he set the water nearby.

Linus continued sympathetically, "Sorry, considering what you're used to eating, this is probably going to be terrible."

Laithrum, curious about the taste, ate some of the bread. It was surprisingly bad—dry with an irregular consistency, sour taste, and grainy texture. The meal deepened his forlorn emotions about where he was. Nothing about this place was normal to him, not even the food.

Then Linus asked, "Is there a reason you brought such a fancy dagger to this filth? It really isn't benefiting you in hiding."

"It was a gift from my sister," Laithrum answered. "She gave it to me when I decided to leave the palace for… this," he said, questioning the logic of his decision. Soon after, he wondered what his sister would face at the palace. What was that threat looming over the city? He hoped Hondou would employ proper controls to mitigate the impact. But Laithrum doubted Hondou's preparedness against the appending threat.

After seeing Laithrum's face display his broken and confused mind, Linus said nothing more. Nonetheless, he remained there, keeping Laithrum company until it was time to sleep, or the elf returned.

Much time had passed. Day turned to night, and most of the ship's men were heading in. Raven, hidden well in the dark, walked down the narrow hall to his assigned quarters. Before arriving at the room, Raven noticed a stranger heading in the same direction. Curious, he followed.

The only color in the darkness came from Raven's light blue eyes, which neither shadow nor darkness could hide. After a short while, Raven realized he was following Dowen, the third resident of room six.

"Be careful," Raven whispered from behind, a sarcastic expression on his face.

Dowen, startled by someone emerging from the shadows, demanded, "Who are you?" He actively searched for the stranger; his hand clamped tightly to the hilt of his sword.

Raven answered quickly before the man could draw his weapon. "I fight on the same side as you." He raised his hands to show they were empty, but it was too dark to see them. All Dowen saw were light blue orbs and a blurry silhouette.

"I just wanted to know if you were the other man for this room. And now I know you are," Raven explained.

"If that's the case, why did you tell me to be careful?" Dowen asked, staring downward at Raven's black hair and glowing eyes, both distinguishable in the dark. His hair was darker than the night, and his light blue eyes floated in the air.

"Fear, and questions are the easiest way to get someone's attention, and sudden confrontation is the quickest way to learn the innermost makings of a person. Now that that's clear, my name is Raven." After speaking, he pushed open the door and entered the room.

By the light of a glowing stone across the room, the two saw Laithrum and Linus. Raven sighed being disappointed at the familiar faces, but he didn't stop walking. Reaching the adjacent bunk bed from Laithrum's, he jumped to the top and tried to ignore the company.

Dowen counted his roommates and asked, "I was told this room had three people, not four?" He wondered about this group since none of them appeared Thuryon but didn't believe it was the wrong room.

"There was a miscount, so now we have four in our room," Linus informed, half-truthfully.

"Well, it makes sense. We do have four beds in this room," Dowen said with a friendly smile that faded when he observed Laithrum's pale appearance. Following his analysis, Dowen recognized Laithrum. He knew his face, but from where? Laithrum, too, seemed to recognize Dowen.

"Are you alright?" Dowen asked.

Linus looked over and said in a frustrated tone, "The elf says he's getting better from some illness he had, but he looked fine until this afternoon."

Dowen listened carefully, then laughed. "Trying to make sense of an elf is too hard. They speak from a completely different perspective. Since they never truly grow-old, even the ones they call 'young' are older than our considered old ancestors. Our cultures are just too different."

Linus nodded, having felt that alien perspective from Onlortrens multiple times before. Dowen paused and added with intrigue, "From what you said, I assume there is an elf on Derdin?"

"Yeah, there's an elf named Onlortrens Silvertree," Linus laughed.

"Since we are talking about him, I'd like to know where he is. So, if you know, please tell," Laithrum said, sitting straight and proper.

Linus shrugged, and Raven sat up, staring down from the top bunk. "He's probably outside singing and thinking. It's what elves usually do at night. They rarely need to sleep. Since he's stuck with an army of men, he needs a lot of alone time to get intelligent conversation…"

Raven looked away and sarcastically continued saying, "…poor guy. I feel his pain." He shrugged teasingly and continued under his breath, only for himself to hear, "There's no company here for an elf, nor is there company for me."

Laithrum pondered how Raven and Onlortrens knew each other and how many elves Raven knew. Was he truly experienced with their culture, or was he merely pretending?

Distracting Laithrum's thoughts, Dowen suggested, "I believe introductions are in order. My name is Dowen Kackveriage." He looked at Linus, gesturing for him to go next.

Linus gladly accepted. "I am Linus Lounleyossa, son of Makoto Lounleyossa."

"Captain Makoto Lounleyossa?!" Dowen exclaimed, astounded, as that was the man commanding the ship.

"Yeah, being the captain's son gets annoying at times. But anyway, this is Laithrum, and the 'guy' up there is Raven," Linus introduced.

They all jumped, startled, as the door suddenly opened. Onlortrens stepped in, his dark-green hood hanging over his face. Raven quickly sat up, and both Linus and Dowen reached for their weapons at the sudden arrival.

"Laithrum, come with me," Onlortrens said gently. Laithrum stood up to follow, though he relentlessly questioned himself about why he would go.

"Hey elf! I thought you said he was sick," Linus complained in frustration.

"Laithrum was sick, and now he is well enough to come with me," Onlortrens replied, turning around and leaving the small room.

Laithrum shrugged and followed, and Raven jumped down from the top bunk to join them. Linus followed bitterly, thinking out loud, "I wish I could heal that fast." Dowen, enthralled by what was transpiring, followed curiously.

CHAPTER 4

Where Nothing Is as it Seems

The five approached the front deck, enveloped in the blackness of night. They gazed out at the dark waters, which faintly reflected the moonlight and starlight. As their eyes adjusted, the darkness seemed to lift.

Onlortrens extended his hand, pointing to the distant water. "Now watch, but do not fear their coming," he said, his voice mesmerizing.

As Onlortrens fell silent, the water ahead ignited. A great fire soared over the sea, racing toward them. "Onlortrens?" Raven asked, her voice mingled with worry.

Linus glanced at the elf; his panic barely contained.

"We'll be just fine," the elf replied, tilting his head back to study the stars. Slowly, he opened his arms as if to embrace the approaching wall of fire.

The blaze drew nearer, its flames reaching fifty feet into the air, glowing red, yellow, and blue. The heat was intense, but not like fire— more like the hot summer sun. The flames sparkled like stars and smelled fresh and sweet.

As the wave of fire struck the ships, it sang with sweet voices. The ships appeared to be engulfed in colorful, glittering flames that consumed everything they touched.

Laithrum looked at his hand. It was burning. The flames licked through his flesh, yet he felt no pain—only warmth. It was comfortable. He observed the flames burning through every object and person in sight, but nothing was harmed. Upon closer inspection, the flames revealed themselves as tiny beings with round bee wings.

Laithrum turned to Onlortrens, whose light blond hair, blue eyes, and green attire were also ablaze. Cries of fear and surprise erupted from the other ships and the forecastle. People ran to the decks, spinning in confusion when they realized the fire wasn't burning anything.

I man of authority ran out. He gave orders and directions in the confusion. This was a play to distract his men until he could figure out what was going on. This man was Captain Makoto Lounleyossa. Once he spotted Onlortrens he hesitantly ran through the intimidating fire. "Onlortrens Silvertree, what is this?!"

"It's something that happens far too often these days," Onlortrens replied sadly. "Evil approaches, and the good turn and flee. But the Fire Fairies told me something. They said that if we are to arrive in time to help the other fleet, we must quicken our pace by twenty percent."

Captain Makoto, still in wonder and frustration, nodded and ran back to inform the other ships of the new information.

Linus stood in awe, paralyzed by the sheer amount of magic. Dowen sat on the deck, questioning what kind of evil could frighten so many powerful beings. There was something very wrong.

Laithrum felt that this menace was the seed of what threatened the capital. It was an exact feeling, but why couldn't he trace its origin? What was its source? He glanced at Onlortrens and asked, "Did you call me out to see this? And if so, why?"

"No, I didn't call you out here for them," the elf replied. "You must learn how to use the bow tonight."

Linus abruptly interjected, "He is not an elf; he needs sleep. Those fairies gave us quite a scare, and after what happened at port, we humans need an explanation and rest. I think he should sleep, and you could wake him before dawn instead," he protested in one anxious breath.

"And he will rest," Onlortrens said sympathetically, "but not until later. In fact, it's best if he doesn't sleep tonight at all. Please, go rest. By the events of the day, you've had a long one."

"Fine, fine, I'll trust your judgment…No, that was a lie…I don't trust your judgement, but I can't fight it. Just don't turn him into another Raven, making him sleep in the afternoon and roam at night," Linus pleaded, understanding no part of what Onlortrens planned.

As Linus walked back toward the barracks, he lifted a hand in farewell. Raven started to follow but stopped. "I'll be back after I make up the sleep from this afternoon—you've overworked me again, Elf," he said to Onlortrens, then sauntered off to bed.

Dowen began to follow, but Laithrum stopped him, "Dowen, I now remember where I've seen you before."

Dowen felt lost in this revelation but waited to hear more. Laithrum continued, "I saw you at port, helping another soldier with a shard of wood in his arm."

Dowen smiled grimly. "You remember right. The man I helped was one of my best friends. His injuries prevented him from coming. I'm grateful for what happened, really. His family had problems he needed to address. Staying behind gave him that opportunity. It may not have looked so, but he wasn't badly hurt."

Laithrum was pleased about Dowens outlook. He hoped that Dowens friend left the city promptly to go home. What remained sad was the fact that they, the men on the ships, were the ones who escaped terror. The city was not safe. Laithrum couldn't bring himself to speak. The guilt of leaving was too strong.

Dowen bowed his head in parting and returned to their quarters.

Captain Makoto approached Onlortrens again, "I ask for your help with a search. Explaining that wave of fire is unnecessary compared to this," Makoto asked, his voice firm but desperate.

"I don't have the time to commit, but if you tell me what you're looking for, I will keep both eyes open. I might already know about it."

Makoto glanced at Laithrum, then back at Onlortrens. "Will you send that youth away until we finish speaking? Or can he be trusted?" the captain asked doubtfully.

"He can be trusted as much as I can. Maybe even more," Onlortrens replied with playful truth.

Makoto hesitated before revealing the need. "When we were still in the city, something was stolen. Something the royal family considered very important; probably the most important. A sword, the Red-stone sword, properly named Ellowvast, which had been kept safely for five hundred years to give to the coming king of legend—the king spoken about for almost a millennium. According to historians, his time is near. The stolen weapon is expected to be on one of these vessels."

Onlortrens looked away in thought. "I will help you find it. That is indeed very important." the elf said, knowing where it most likely was.

"Are you not telling me something, Onlortrens? If you're not taking this seriously, I beg you to reconsider your resolve," the captain said angrily, though his words were muffled.

"Yes, I am hiding something from you, but I will not let that sword fall into the wrong hands, and to that, I promise. I have not taken this situation lightly, not even for a moment," Onlortrens replied, his musical voice strong.

"I don't like this. Will you at least tell me where you think it is?" Makoto pleaded respectfully.

Onlortrens shook his head. "Leave it all to me; it's safer that way. The individual or individuals who stole it must have the skill to do so. We need to be very discreet with this matter." He told Makoto to relax, then dismissed himself from the conversation and focused back on Laithrum's training.

Through the middle of the night, Onlortrens trained Laithrum in the use of the bow and arrow. As the elf expected, the training went well. Raven emerged from the sleeping quarters, reluctantly agreeing to help Onlortrens teach Laithrum the basics of swordplay. Morning arrived before they stopped training.

The late mornings of winter were ending, giving way to earlier and longer days of summer. The longer days seemed to fly by. Onlortrens, with Raven's help, had trained Laithrum intensively for three days. On the evening of the third day, Raven stood by the rails, gazing at the setting sun. Expression full of rage and determination.

"Wait just a little longer," he whispered into the breeze. "I'll be there soon, and I have something to help me this time."

Laithrum, Onlortrens, Linus, and Dowen, now forming a group, approached Raven from behind. "What were you thinking about?" Linus pried, trying to be annoying.

"Why would I tell an idiot? I'm too kind to give your small brain another subject to think about. A thought that might end in learning would be too much for you," Raven retorted sharply, glaring at the group.

Linus was ready to explode. After another long day, he had no tolerance for Raven's demeaning comments. This guy always irritated him. And he was so small compared to himself that the fight would end quickly.

"Raven," Onlortrens said sternly, then asked, "How many people are on each of these ships? I'd like to know for future reasons. So, do you know?"

"The future? That's vague even for you. The ships have around two hundred fifty to three hundred men each. There are fifty-five ships, but two are occupied by mostly animals, so don't count those. The first fleet originally had forty-three ships, but now there are an unknown number of ships ahead. They had the same number of people, but the current number is unknown," Raven answered, unaware of the question's importance.

Unexpectedly, a horn sounded. "There is a man overboard!" yelled a seaman from the watchtower. They noticed debris in the water. Some panicked as if they were too late to help the other ships, but most assumed it was from the first attack. A tall, thin man was pulled from the water. He wasn't badly hurt, but barely alive. Orders quickly went out to search for more men adrift.

After they carefully carried him inside, they laid the man on a cot. Quickly they placed his few remaining weapons—a short sword, a knife, an empty quiver, and a broken longbow—against a nearby wall. Without delay, they replaced his wet clothes. They dressed him in a dry robe and used a towel to dry his curly, chestnut brown hair, which was shoulder-length and unevenly cut.

Troi Onturner, the most experienced medic on the ship, chose to stay with him until he woke up. He was puzzled by how this person could still be alive after drifting in the salt water for so long. And based on his clothes he experienced major physical trauma but, somehow, no injuries.

More than an hour later, Troi looked at the young soldier again and, to his surprise, saw his eye twitch. Troi moved closer, placing his right hand on the soldier's shoulder, and gently shaking him. "Hello," Troi said kindly.

The young man cracked open his eyes, revealing their reddish color, and looked sharply at Troi. The medic spoke again, slowly, and clearly. "My name is Troi Onturner. You are now safely on the ship Derdin." The soldier seemed to understand but was too weak to respond physically, though he tried.

Troi stood up. "I must get someone. Can you stay awake until I get back?" he asked, relieved that the young man seemed to be coming around quickly. The soldier managed a weak nod, and Troi quickly gestured for another soldier to watch him as he left the room.

Troi found the captain and informed him that the young man was awake. With the captain, he returned to see the soldier. Laithrum and Onlortrens followed out of curiosity, having overheard the conversation.

Troi, Captain Makoto, Laithrum, and Onlortrens entered the room. Laithrum was surprised and filled with joy when he recognized the soldier. Just as he was about to speak, he heard the captain ask, "What is your name?" The soldier answered, but his voice was too soft to hear.

The captain, followed by Laithrum and Troi, sat down by the bed. "What is your name?" Makoto asked again. The soldier answered, "Lotus Florissurnna," his reply slow and in a mellow, soft tone. Makoto smiled at him, though he was truly disheartened by how malnourished Lotus was.

"Welcome to my ship, Florissurnna." He stood up. "Eat and drink if you can, and rest. We will speak tomorrow morning." Makoto, Laithrum, and Onlortrens left the room. Troi remained behind, trying to get Lotus to drink more, concerned about dehydration.

Laithrum hastily approached Makoto. "Tomorrow morning, may I be there when you speak with Lotus Florissurnna?" he requested.

The captain answered gratefully, "Yes, you may. I assume you know him; your presence might make him more comfortable." He paused. "Now go rest. You'll need it for the day to come. Our estimated reunion with the other ships is tomorrow." He paused again, then continued, "By the way, what is your name, soldier?"

"It is Laithrum," the prince answered.

With that, Captain Makoto Lounleyossa parted from Laithrum. After a few more breaths of the sea air, Laithrum turned in for the night, unsure about the morning. If Lotus revealed he was a prince, what would happen? He shouldn't have asked to be there; he wasn't thinking wisely.

The early night was mostly spent awake, the only sound being the breathing of the others sleeping. It was after midnight before he fell asleep.

In the morning, Linus shook him awake. "Get up, Laithrum," Linus said. "I want to ask y…" But before Linus could finish, Laithrum swung out of bed and ran to the deck, leaving Linus standing alone and perplexed.

Laithrum met the captain outside and followed him to where Lotus slept. As Troi exited, they entered and sat on two chairs provided by Troi. "Florissurnna," Makoto said calmly, checking if he was awake. Lotus opened his eyes, brighter than before, and turned his thin face toward them. He had regained some color, though he was naturally very fair.

"Unfortunately, I have little time. The only comforting words I can offer is it's a good morning. The weather is nice." Captain Makoto said, managing a weary smile.

Lotus grinned softly. "That is great to hear, sir."

The captain nodded and asked, "When was your fleet attacked?"

"A week plus three or four days more, I'd guess," Lotus replied, uncertain of his memory. It felt like just a moment to him. His head still felt engulfed in salt water, and his mind resisted the effort to remember, making him dizzy. "Are you alright, Lotus?" Laithrum asked, worried.

Lotus fought the surrounding pain, smiled, and answered, "We'll see." He paused. "Please, ask your next question, and I will try to answer as best I can."

"Tell me about the enemy—Their number, weapons, and strategy." The captain tried his best to stay focused on the nearing battle.

"Many, more than expected. Three of them to one of us, we estimated. They brought Sinjar, and large projectiles, and even explosives. I fought; it was my job." He paused. "I can guarantee you will hear… what I don't want to remember. You wouldn't want it from me, anyway. At least it's over… it's over, right?" Lotus's freshly formed smile quickly faded.

"More are on their way. That's why we are here," said the captain. "But we'll be fine, for the enemy is just expecting the fleet you were part of. They aren't expecting another one so soon, and even larger." As he spoke, he looked closely at Lotus once more. Lotus had a very youthful appearance, his face looking as if he were only in his teen years, though he was a fully-grown man. Makoto asked sympathetically but mostly out of curiosity, "Lotus Florissurnna, may I know your age?"

"Why?" Lotus pondered, unprepared for such a question.

Makoto answered lightly, "Your face is confusing me, honestly."

Lotus bowed his head, accepting the reason for the captain's question. "I am twenty-six years old, close to twenty-seven actually," he said as his routine response.

Laithrum then asked hesitantly, "Lotus Florissurnna, do you know where Prince Adeyas Airslen is, if he's still alive?"

Lotus looked down in sorrow, and although he tried to stay calm, his words were unstable. "He was taken by the enemy. A Seintroven Sinjar took him away. Possibility he is still alive, but if he is, he's not in comfort." He paused, his jaw shaking rapidly. "I'm so sorry. I was supposed to protect him, and I let him get taken. Please forgive me—I failed the king, Freyja, and you." Lotus, close to melting into his grief, weakly placing his thin arms over his face.

Laithrum knelt beside the bed and spoke softly, "I'd like to know the story of what happened to my brother. I'll come back later this morning; you will remain my friend no matter the outcome, no matter the story. Be assured of that." Laithrum encouraged.

Lotus nodded. Even though he agreed, Lotus knew that it couldn't be true.

Laithrum stood up and gestured for Makoto to follow him. The captain did, though he was annoyed and confused why this soldier acted as if he were the superior officer.

After leaving the room Laithrum quickly ran to find Onlortrens. Spotting him, he called out, "Onlortrens, I need a word with you." The elf turned, his expression questioning.

Laithrum searched for the right words. "I don't know how to deal with this. My friend, who was brought in yesterday, is deeply upset by something he couldn't prevent but witnessed. I don't know how to help him, or if I even can. Something feels very wrong."

Onlortrens gazed gently at Laithrum, understanding that he had never faced anything like this before. Deciding to assist, he first asked, "And in what way do you think I can help?"

"Onlortrens, you are wiser than I. You've experienced matters like this, haven't you? And you are caring. For these reasons, please help me support him in any way we can," Laithrum answered boldly.

"I'll help you if you need it. It seems you already know what to do. Just love him as a friend," the elf replied, hesitantly at first. After thinking deeply about what he briefly observed from Lotus. He grew very worried. This could be a problem that he overlooked.

"Thank you," said Laithrum gratefully, now understanding that the best action he could take was to be himself—someone willing to listen and not judge.

"Come, Laithrum, you haven't eaten yet this morning," Onlortrens said, leading Laithrum inside. After a long discussion over food and drink, they returned outdoors and were soon greeted by Linus.

"Laithrum," he started, "What was the big rush this morning?" Linus complained, then continued kiddingly, "Sad to say, sad for my own pride, your reaction earlier scared me. Is something terribly wrong?"

"I apologize," Laithrum laughed, remembering his actions.

"I have my doubts about that," replied Linus playfully.

The elf then stepped forward, saying, "Laithrum and I have someone to see."

Linus looked curiously at them and asked, "I'm confused again. Who are you going to see?"

"A friend," Laithrum answered, continuing the walk. As he walked, his body tensed. He remembered they were expected to meet up with the other fleet today. Linus, recalling who Laithrum was, followed them. He was transitioning into a bodyguard rather than a companion.

The three went to see Lotus. Inside, they found him sitting up on his cot, with Troi changing a bandage around his right foot.

"Lotus, it might be surprising and you're going to be unhappy to hear it, but I want you to try walking," Troi said, standing up straight. "You must build up your strength somehow. Your foot was not badly injured; the bandage will protect it from further harm. The things I most need you to do are move, keep eating, and drink." He looked toward the three who had just walked in.

"Laithrum, I hear you are a friend. Will you take him out and have him try walking around the ship? He's healing very fast." Troi didn't understand how this rate of healing was possible, but he was pleased to recruit their help, because he was too busy for such a task.

Laithrum nodded. "That won't be a problem." He stepped aside to let Troi exit the room. Laithrum and Onlortrens lifted Lotus out of bed and helped him into the bright outdoors. The sunlight enhanced the red in his eyes, giving them a bright auburn glow.

As they walked along the ship's rim, Lotus recounted most, but not all, of the unhappy story of Adeyas's capture. He explained how he tried but failed to help Adeyas in time, never revealing why he failed or what happened to him afterward. Silence followed the story, their minds troubled and stagnant in thought. Lotus's mind was still sore from the many events, and Onlortrens's worry for him grew exponentially.

For Lotus's sake, they walked slowly. When he couldn't walk on his own, they lifted him by the arms, keeping him moving as he hovered above the ground.

Lotus commented as they sat him down, "I wonder if this is what I'm going to be like when I'm old?"

They smiled but remained mostly silent until noon. The sun, covered by hazy clouds, did not scorch. The weather remained comfortable whereas the emotional tension grew all around them.

While they sat, Dowen found them and brought food. "What have you all been doing? Without me, I might add," he asked in a playful, bitter voice.

"Bringing our new pet for a walk," Linus exclaimed, pointing to Lotus. Lotus pretended to be offended but didn't care about the comment.

Onlortrens answered Dowen's question, "The truth is we were bringing Lotus on a walk. We were just engaged in discussion for a long while. Lotus had just informed us about what happened to Laithrum's oldest brother in the last battle." As Onlortrens spoke, they heard someone yell, "The fleet! You can see the other ships!"

Laithrum and Linus grabbed Lotus and jumped to their feet. Lotus stumbled between them, unable to keep up. Dowen noticed and easily threw the gangly youth over his shoulder. They ran to the crowded front deck.

Lotus clearly wanted to run. Leaving this situation was active in his mind. But he couldn't yet. This new company didn't understand—not yet anyway.

Many faces were amazed at the vast number of ships the two fleets created and at the damaged state of the first fleet. Some young soldiers looked pale and grim, knowing they would soon need to take up arms.

Laithrum could hear the men from the other ships. They were yelling and calling out in joy as they watched their hope sail in; allied ships had arrived.

CHAPTER 5

Left Behind

Later in Thuthairyon, on the day Laithrum sailed away, Freyja returned to her sister's old room. Standing on the balcony, she leaned back against the sturdy rail. Her long, weightless hair and open silk overcoat waved in the wind. Though aware of the movement she could feel nothing. Her mind burned with questions and worries.

She looked over her shoulder at the departing ships, watching them fade until they were mere specks on the horizon. She acknowledged the possibility that she might never see Laithrum again. She doubted it. The faith she had in their decision remained strong even though she felt so weak.

Freyja lowered her eyes and head, mouthing a final farewell to her brother. Standing straight again, boldly facing the clear ocean, she began to hum a fair, pleasant tune traditionally sung when a loved one departed on a long journey.

A woman softly approached Freyja from behind. She was aged but elegantly dressed and beautiful—the queen, Lilith Airslen, Freyja's mother. Queen Lilith wore a white silk and lace dress and a red sleeveless jacket that ended just below her light brown hair. Both her dress and jacket were loosely held around her waist by a wide, white belt. Such weightless, flowing clothes were uncommon for the queen to wear.

The woman stood next to Freyja. Freyja turned her eyes to Lilith and smiled. "It is wonderful to see you, Mother. I intended to visit you, but something distracted me. Although I'm late, I must ask, how are you feeling?" Freyja asked, smiling as the golden sun shone on her platinum-blond hair.

"Freyja," her mother began grimly. It was hard to look her daughter in the eye, but she forced herself.

"I want to acknowledge the truth about what's been happening lately. But I need you as a witness… and I aim to teach about some events that affect our lives presently."

Freyja paid keen attention to her mother. These words were set up so vaguely. Her mother didn't want to say what she came to talk about.

"But I must ask you something first," continued Lilith, glancing side to side nervously.

"Where is your brother, Laithrum?"

"He has left," Freyja replied, pointing to the departing ships. Lilith's eyes widened in surprise and wonder. "Gone…?"

"Yes, Mother, gone—he has finally left," Freyja smiled pleasantly.

"I am truly sorry." Queen Lilith lowered her crowned head in sorrow and amazement. Freyja gazed questioningly at her mother.

"What is it, Mother?" she asked with a bitter tone. "You have always hated and ignored Laithrum. What is this change of heart?"

Lilith answered reluctantly, "While I was fighting illness, I lay there drowning in deep thought, mostly about my family. I realized that, even if I wasn't physically his parent, I was the only mother Laithrum had. That was when I noticed how devilish I was being to your brother—it wasn't his fault that he was brought into this world by an indecent act of his father. And then given back to his father by his mother, who clearly didn't want him. Who, after giving him life…" she paused, then said with pity, "Freyja, there is another act against Laithrum I wish to tell you about. Your brother has been poisoned to keep him sick."

Freyja sprang up from leaning but waited angrily until her mother finished speaking.

"It was given to him by your father, and I am ashamed to say, I have been complicit by letting it happen. I now truly regret that action. So, if it is possible, will you forgive me for what I let happen to your youngest brother for so long?"

"Why was Father poisoning him? Why would he do this to his own son? Laithrum isn't dangerous. Is this just because of his mother?" Freyja demanded, her voice trembling with anger. Another question formed in her mind, but she held it back, waiting for answers.

"I do not know Niejill's reasoning," Lilith replied, her voice quivering under the intensity of her daughter's gaze. "All I've ever heard him say is, 'I'm not going to let him take away my home. I won't let him come to power.' But I do not understand it."

Freyja stood frozen, her mind racing with the revelations. Anger and disappointment churned within her. "What will happen now that Laithrum is no longer being poisoned?" she asked.

"I do not know for sure," Lilith admitted. "I expect he'll get better and not fall ill from the sudden change."

"Mother, I am confused. Why tell me all this now? Learning this has made me bitter toward you, and it will take a very long time to forgive," Freyja said, her honesty cutting like a blade.

Lilith averted her eyes from Freyja's harsh gaze. She didn't want to burden her daughter with the full truth. So, she decided to keep her suspicions to herself until she could prove them. She would soon realize that this decision was a grave mistake. "I didn't want you to live your life blind to this truth anymore," she stated instead.

Freyja sensed there was more, but she respected her mother too much to pry. "Mother," she began again, "when does tonight's celebration start?"

Lilith took a moment to switch topics. "It starts at four... that's what I've heard."

Freyja sighed, looking at her mother. "Today has been quite hectic. I wish to take a nap before the party. But if there's something else you think I should know, please tell me. Resting can wait."

Lilith shook her head reluctantly.

Freyja nodded, trying to maintain her composure. "Thank you for telling me what you did. I'm sorry Laithrum isn't here so you could tell him you care and that you are sorry. Perhaps it's better this way…"

Freyja and her mother retreated to their rooms to rest before the night's festivities. Freyja slept little, her mind racing with thoughts. She pondered the mysteries unfolding within the palace walls, questioning her mother's omissions and her father's intentions.

Questions swirled in her mind, relentless and unyielding, relaxing proved impossible.

When the time came, Freyja rose from her bed to prepare for the party. After washing up, she donned a thin robe and bath shoes, then approached her closet. She slid open the simple yet decorative door. Freyja was never particular about her attire; she calmly selected one of the many beautiful dresses hanging neatly.

She chose a predominantly white dress with lace sleeves that extended three-quarters down her arms. The bodice was also lace, and the two-layered skirt was light and unrestrained, gracefully skimming the floor and concealing her feet. Over this, she wore a green silk top with no sleeves, just a wing of fabric over her shoulders, ending with a thin gold band around her midriff. The fabric below the band flowed down the length of her arms, ending at her wrists. The back fabric cascaded gracefully, forming wings from the sides to the back.

Freyja left most of her hair down, pulling back just enough to reveal her face. A handmaiden presented her necklace collection, but Freyja refused. Her casual chain with a small silver pendant was what she wanted to keep. She placed a silver crown on her head. She adorned her right index finger with a thick banded ring and wore thick hoop earrings before exiting her room.

She headed straight to the ballroom where the celebration was underway. She was never early for these events because of procrastination and sheer distaste for them. On her way, she realized she had only one brother left; her other siblings had all vanished in various ways. Determined, she sought out her younger brother Ashtion, who was always traveling. He had returned home late in the afternoon while she was sleeping. He should be somewhere in the crowded room. He liked crowds and chaos.

When she found him, he was sitting alone at a small side table, looking bored and tired. Ashtion didn't seem to regard the celebration as important; his hair was messily tied back and unbrushed. His hair was shades darker than hers, and his eyes were a deep blue, brightening around the pupils. He wore a silver band with the family's symbol centered on his forehead, just like Freyja's.

Freyja sat down across from him. "Ashtion, of all the times I've seen you, I've never seen you look so bored."

He looked over at her, his eyes brightening at the sight of his sister. "It's the party," he began kindly. Freyja was puzzled; neither the music nor the people seemed dull or downbeat. Ashtion quickly continued, "This celebration is supposed to be for Hondou Unrey and all the soldiers fighting for the king and this country, right?"

Freyja nodded, still waiting to understand his point. "Father told the men greeting the guests to expect some soldiers tonight. The man gave Father a strange look, as if he knew who they were and their significance. I wouldn't recognize them even if I heard their names, so I didn't ask Father. But after hearing this, I checked the list to familiarize myself with the names. Surprisingly, I saw no unfamiliar names. I knew everyone on the list, and no one was a soldier. Now, I sit here, clueless about what's happening and where to start figuring it out. Hence, I waste away in boredom."

He sat straight growing intrigued. But his mind was in a slump, his eyes blank and unfocused.

"Ashtion, you are more in the dark than I was. Mother came to me this afternoon, and I learned some things about recent events," she paused. "Would you like me to tell you what's happening around here?" Freyja asked, trying to divert his mind from daunting questions that couldn't be answered.

Ashtion looked down in thought, then abruptly stood up. "I want to know what you've learned, but not here. I don't trust this crowd." Freyja smiled and stood to follow. She was ready to follow him wherever he wished to speak—anywhere was better than here.

Just as they started to leave, a familiar, arrogant voice called out to them. "People usually don't leave a party before it has truly begun." They turned to see Hondou Unrey.

"Well, good evening, Crowned-Knight Hondou Unrey. How is this celebration faring for you?" Ashtion asked cheerfully but quickly, hoping to keep the conversation brief.

"I am enjoying it; the company is grand, and the music is to my liking," Hondou replied. But then he wondered why that demon child wasn't there. He quickly inquired, "Princess Freyja, may I ask why you're not with your half-brother, Laithrum? It's unlike him to miss an event or be late."

Freyja looked at him sternly, detesting how Hondou treated her brother. She answered sourly, "You need not worry anymore, Hondou, for he is no longer with us." Hondou was taken aback by the possible meaning of her words.

"What!?" he asked, confused and concerned. He took a breath and continued in a calmer tone, "What do you mean, no longer with us?" His mind fluttered with thoughts and possible answers.

Freyja looked up at him with a cunning smile and responded, "He's gone; he has faded away like a speck on the ocean."

Hondou scrutinized Freyja's expressions, a knowing smile spreading across his face. "Why did you want him to go, Freyja? He's sicklied. You know he's going to die." She turned away, her voice steady. "It felt right, and he'll be better out there than he was here."

Hondou began to speak again but stopped when Ashtion raised his hand. "Unrey, I wish to be with my sister, and you are ruining my time with her. Please, leave us in peace." Hondou bowed and walked off, not wanting to further anger the young prince. Ashtion was now the one in line for inheriting the throne. To Hondou, this was a frightening thought because Ashtion was prone to run off on adventures to avoid responsibility.

Ashtion smiled at Freyja. "If you will follow me," he said, turning toward the exit. Freyja followed him.

They walked to the southern wing, the same room Laithrum had been in earlier that morning. Freyja broke the silence. "Before I tell you what I've learned, will you tell me what you've been doing for the past two years?"

"I'd be glad to give an overview. It took about two days for anything to happen, but once it did, it never seemed to stop. It was a tremendous, sad, and happy adventure. We quickly found ourselves in a large mess. The problems began with Ian, the troublemaker in our company, even more so than me. He was taken prisoner by an evil and powerful sorcerer wreaking havoc in a small Turwin village. After six months, I received something special. I'll tell you what it was after you tell me all you know. Deal?" Ashtion said, pleased with some of the memories, despite the overall misery.

"It's a deal, but what I have to say isn't pleasant. Mother came to me earlier this afternoon. She told me Father has been poisoning Laithrum because he feared Laithrum would take his throne."

"Strange," Ashtion muttered, then spoke up. "I can't see why. Adeyas is next in line for the throne. Unless he gave up his birthright, which I can't imagine, because he never feared responsibility. He enjoyed the weight on his shoulders. So why would Father think Laithrum is a threat?"

Freyja sighed. "Brother killed Trence Guritton."

"Guritton, one of the royal counselors?" Ashtion asked.

"Yes, he was. Why?" Freyja asked, baffled by his apparent happiness.

Ashtion laughed. "I'm glad someone finally put him in a grave." Freyja looked at him in surprise. "Finally!?" she cried.

"Yes, finally. I never liked him much, and if not for Adeyas, I would have done it sooner or later." Ashtion glanced around, then asked, "Where is Adeyas? I haven't seen him since I arrived."

"They were going to execute him for his blasphemous act against his own country. He pleaded to be sent to war for an honorable death rather than a criminal's. Father quickly agreed, likely because he didn't want his son to die a criminal's death. They sent Lotus as his bodyguard. Lotus didn't know why Adeyas was being sent out. I tried to tell him, but I couldn't reach him in time." Freyja looked down, sorrowful for both Lotus and Adeyas.

"You two had a relationship, didn't you? It's sad. Father must have disliked you being together. I know two reasons why. One, he's younger than you, though only by a year. Two, Father thought he had mixed blood, a Weresync. It's a pity. For the time I knew him, we were friends, and I saw nothing foreign about him." Ashtion sighed.

"I'm sorry, Freyja, but you should have expected it. What was Father thinking, sending someone as frail and gentle as Lotus? Everyone will figure out Father's motives; it's political suicide."

Freyja nodded, speaking softly, "I did expect it, but knowing doesn't always help."

"This whole situation is hard for you. I know you care a lot about…people. Is that all mother told you?" Ashtion inquired.

"That was about it." Freyja replied, noticing her brother's rapid questioning stopped suddenly, current silence. "Is there something else on your mind you want to ask me?" she said, standing firm on the marble floor. Knowing her brother well enough to read his expression easily. He was actively thinking about something.

"Freyja," he began, "I wish to know more about Father. He's been acting strangely. Did anything else happen?"

"He hasn't been around much. Strange isn't the only word I'd use. He's been dastardly," Freyja replied.

"Why not look into it?" Ashtion asked, thinking it an obvious solution.

"Are you mad?" she spat in surprise. "He may be our father, but he's also our king."

"So?" Ashtion questioned.

"We could be hanged for this," Freyja informed him, calming down as she thought about her father's actions against Lotus and her other brothers. After a moment, she spoke decisively. "If you go, I'll gladly go with you. They may not kill us both if caught."

Ashtion was pleased to hear her declaration.

The two agreed to visit their father's quarters, but as they left the southern wing, the royal messenger, Dairren, intercepted them. "Princess, Prince," he said with a bow, glancing down the hall. "There is something I must tell you before you go."

Freyja and Ashtion listened intently. "But first, I must ask for your forgiveness. I was eavesdropping on your conversation."

"I forgive you; it is your duty to snoop," Ashtion said understandingly. Freyja nodded in agreement.

"Thank you," Dairren bowed gratefully. "For the past four days, like Prince Laithrum, you too, Freyja, have been poisoned, but with a different toxin meant to end your life. I gave you the antidote yesterday in your breakfast. I waited for you, Prince Ashtion, to arrive so Princess Freyja wouldn't have to face this alone. Now it's safer to tell you."

Freyja, uneasy with this revelation, asked softly, "Dairren, how did you know? And how did you get the antidote?"

Dairren sighed. "I know almost everything that happens here because I listen. And I have associates who listen. As for getting the antidote, that's a long story. Can I save it for another day?" He saw their acceptance and continued.

"Dairren, was it Father who poisoned me? And do you know why he's behaving this way?" Freyja asked curiously.

"Yes, it was the king," Dairren replied in a weary voice. "But I don't know why he's acting this way. It might have something to do with an object he's obsessed with. That wrapped…thing he carries everywhere. I'm not sure when he obtained it, but the strange behaviors started after."

Freyja looked seriously at Dairren. "I have a bad feeling about tonight. Keep your eyes sharp and your ears open, but most of all, leave this place as quickly as you can." Dairren nodded, bowed, and departed.

"This is strange, Freyja. It's not right to be so frightened in our own home," Ashtion said, melancholy and confused. With new resolve, they headed to their father's room.

They stood before a set of tall, dark-red wooden doors. They were decorated with iron to be impenetrable. The light flickering behind them reflected a bright red from the stained wood. Ashtion briefly tried to open the door, but as expected, it was locked. He looked down in thought. Freyja knew another way. She grabbed his arm and led him to the adjacent room, Adeyas's old quarters, the king's most prized child.

Freyja ran through the unlit room to a clear window showing the black ocean outside. She opened the window and turned to her brother.

"Are you coming?" she asked teasingly.

Ashtion, surprised by his sister's adventurous spirit, quickly joined her, wishing he had taken her on his quests. With Freyja, he would never seek danger, aiming for a long life for his sister.

Freyja lifted the hem of her dress and slipped off her flat-bottomed shoes for better traction. Ashtion helped her out and followed quickly.

They held firmly to a small rail above their heads. The ground was far below. Inch by inch, they moved closer to their father's window.

A sudden, strong wind blew against them. They pressed their bodies against the palace's stone walls. Freyja felt the gravity of their decision; a fall would mean certain death. Ashtion, more accustomed to such risks, was less surprised by the sudden anxiety. The wind seemed to push at them for an eternity before it finally ceased. Ashtion encouraged Freyja to continue, and she soon heeded his prompting.

They reached the large window. "Hopefully, it's unlocked," Freyja muttered. Ashtion sighed, realizing he should have anticipated that. When his mind returned to the present, he saw Freyja already heading inside. He followed, jumping through the window.

Freyja immediately began rifling through papers and scrolls, searching under anything that seemed out of place. "We need to find anything that explains what's happening. I'm also looking for the poison he used on our half-brother."

Ashtion looked down, regretful. "I never got to know him well. I wish I had. Meeting a demon, or whatever people call him, sounds more interesting than not." Freyja turned sharply, glaring at him. "Laithrum is no demon. You'll have to call him something else," she protested. "It's not fair to label someone like that. People judge them as unkind, dangerous, and insensitive."

Ashtion raised his hands in surrender. "What you say is fine with me. Let's not argue, okay?" Freyja nodded. Ashtion resumed searching, smiling at her protective nature.

They scoured the room until there wasn't an inch left unchecked. They found nothing unusual. The room hardly looked lived in. Ashtion and Freyja stood up, exchanging glances. "There should be some kind of secret door here," Ashtion thought aloud. Freyja felt a nagging unease.

"We should leave. Something doesn't feel right," Freyja said. Ashtion, equally unnerved, quickly agreed.

They moved swiftly to the entrance and unlocked their father's door. Stepping into the empty hall, Ashtion glanced at the clock. "It's around six o'clock," he said. "When I returned this afternoon, Father mentioned something significant would happen at this time." He paused, concerned. "I wonder what he's planning." The thought of his father doing something so wrong was unbelievable and nauseating.

They stood outside the royal room, their thoughts interrupted by a shrill noise. Their hearts jumped and stopped. Time seemed to stop a well. It was the sound. A whistle, three tones blown nearby.

Ashtion recognized the sound and was struck with fear. He grabbed Freyja's arm and started running away from the whistle source. That sound was a call to attack, a Seintroven whistle.

"Hurry, Freyja, we must get out of the palace," Ashtion urged, panic in his voice. Just then, a yell echoed behind them. They turned to see an enemy soldier charging silently, sword drawn.

Ashtion and Freyja quickened their pace. Freyja grabbed a copper candle holder from the wall and hurled it at the pursuer. The soldier deflected it with his sword but stumbled from the force of her throw. Ashtion waved off the surprise of Freyja's strength and continued running.

They dashed down a stairway, heading to their mother's room. She hadn't felt well enough to attend the party and would need help escaping.

At their mother's door, Freyja tried the handle, but it was locked. Ashtion stepped back. "Freyja, move," he commanded. She jumped aside as he threw his body against the door, breaking it open.

Freyja rushed in. She froze at the sight of fresh blood pooled on the bed and her mother's torn, lifeless body on the floor. Freyja stumbled back, unable to breathe, too enraged to mourn. She fell to her knees, shaking. Ashtion, swallowing his pain, knelt beside her. "Come, we need to get out of here," he said softly. He helped Freyja to her feet, and they supported each other as they moved to the corner window. They knew a woody vine and trellis beneath it would allow them to climb down.

Freyja opened the window and began her descent. Ashtion waited until she had safe footing before letting go of her. As he turned to climb out, he saw an enemy archer at the doorway. Fear blackened his mind as an arrow sliced through the air, piercing his right leg. Ashtion caught himself using the windows flaming. Leaning against the blood-specked window he exclaimed, "Go!"

Freyja looked up in horror as her brother was pulled back inside by stained hands. Although knowing she could do nothing to help her grip released to reach for him. Gravity did not delay pulling her down. She tumbled down the vines and trellis, tearing her skin and clothes. She hit the ground roughly, took a few deep breaths, she should be dead. But she was fine. Why? She refocused and with a yell, sprang up and darted to the royal stables.

There, she found three horses saddled and ready. One was Aitroven, her white-coated horse. Another was Ashtion's, but the third was unfamiliar, not a royal steed. Freyja glanced around nervously. The walls seemed to move in on her. She reasoned through the dizzying reality—it was anxiety playing tricks.

"I'm glad you made it… where is your brother?" a voice asked from inside the stall where the unfamiliar horse stood.

"Who's there?" Freyja demanded in a hushed tone. A large figure emerged from behind the horse. It was Crowned Knight Hondou Unrey, head of the royal guard.

"Princess, I was hoping you'd make it out of the palace and would come here." He opened the gate for his horse and mounted it swiftly. "Now come. Once we're out of this wretched place, we'll speak freely, and I'll explain everything. But first, you must tell me where Prince Ashtion is. We have no time to waste; we must leave now."

In a rush, Freyja flung herself onto her horse's back. Hondou led the way to the back exit, and Freyja followed, though her heart ached at the thought of leaving Ashtion behind.

CHAPTER 6

On a Mission

After Ashtion was dragged away from Freyja, his hands and feet were bound, and the enemy soldier ripped the arrow from his leg. The arrow had pierced inches above his knee but missed the bone.

Blindfolded, Ashtion was carried downstairs and through halls until a door opened. He felt a cool breeze and smelled the ocean. He was outside. Why had they brought him out here? What did they want with him alive? Ashtion prayed for salvation before having to discover their plan.

The soldier threw him onto the rocky ground and began speaking to another enemy scout. Their conversation, laced with vulgar language, revealed their lack of honor. Despite the pain fogging his mind, Ashtion listened carefully.

"His majesty wants this whelp brought to him as soon as possible. But if he decides he doesn't want him, we get to do whatever we want with him," said the unkempt man.

"Oh, that sounds fun. This pretty boy needs a good listen. He's just so pretty," the other soldier laughed menacingly.

Ashtion heard only these two men, neither of whom seemed decent. He prayed again for rescue, refusing to give up hope. His spirit waned, and his body refused to move. Breathing felt like a nuisance, his lungs swollen with effort. Was that arrow laced was a drug. The injury wasn't severe enough to paralyze.

He heard another man approaching, leading a horse. The man and horse stopped, standing right behind him. Ashtion tried to shake off his blindfold to see who it was, but he couldn't. And I soon learned that he didn't need to see him.

The man spoke, "I am taking him to the base at the east side of the Ring Mountains. I will not need an escort."

Ashtion recognized the voice—it was the king, his father, the mastermind behind this treachery! Rage surged within him, but he harnessed it, waiting for the right moment to strike. Ashtion knew he could force himself to move now. He had too!

As the two soldiers were sent away, Ashtion felt himself lifted by his traitorous father, former King Niejill Airslen. He was tossed onto the back of a large black horse among other baggage.

"It is time for us to begin our journey. A quest of a father and his son," Niejill declared. He unwrapped a flat object, revealing a mirror. Niejill tore off Ashtion's blindfold, meeting his son's glaring, hateful expression.

"Don't be angry. Just look. Consult the mirror, and you will see the power we will have! LOOK!"

Ashtion shut his eyes and turned away. "I will not look into that horrid, black-magic monstrosity!" he snapped. Niejill grabbed his jaw, forcing his head toward the mirror. "Listen to your father!" he scolded.

"It seems I have lost him!" Ashtion retorted, his voice breaking. Niejill threw his head back down. "Soon enough, you will do as I say. Once you come to your senses, you will understand that I am doing what's best for this family!" the former king spat.

"What!" Ashtion cried in disgust. "What could you possibly be doing for this family? You sent Adeyas to die. You're trying to kill Laithrum and Freyja. You killed Mother, and who knows what you're planning for me! And what about the kingdom? Our people trusted you to lead them. NOT KILL THEM!" Niejill struck Ashtion across the face to silence him.

"Be quiet, boy!" he snapped. "They all chose their own fate! Now we can only hope you don't choose a similar one."

"What about the guests at the party? What did you do to them?" Ashtion growled, expecting the worst.

"What else?" Niejill replied coldly. "I poisoned the food and drink. By now, all the guests are dead, and if they tried to run, they were slain."

"What if I had eaten some of the food? Would you care if I died?" Ashtion cried out in rage.

"I'd be disappointed in your lack of wit. Yet I would be saddened at your fate, Ashtion," Niejill answered. He called for another horse and climbed onto its back.

Ashtion lay still, confused about whether his father cared for anyone. His father's actions disgusted and saddened him. He hated seeing what this man had become.

Bound to the back of the horse, Ashtion and Niejill rode hastily into the woods, heading to an enemy camp where nothing and no one would comfort Ashtion's broken spirit. Unbeknownst to them, two others joined their journey—beings against them both.

***

Freyja followed Hondou to a gathering of about fifty people. They had only a half-dozen horses among them. She was relieved to see familiar faces but surprised by the lack of warriors. A man with long blond hair approached Hondou and whispered something. Their expressions suggested bad news.

Freyja dismounted, grabbed the reins, and limped over to Hondou. "Unrey, can we speak now?" she asked, trying to mask her pain. "What did that man say?" she added, gesturing to the messenger.

Hondou examined her, noting her dull eyes and solemn face. The bloody cuts and scrapes on her arms and legs seemed to already be closed. Healing very quickly. Though he knew it was important to answer her, he felt pressed for time.

"Go speak with the man who brought the message," he said before jogging away.

Perturbed by Hondou's manner, Freyja decided to remain quiet. She stood lost in thought, her mind avoiding painful memories while her wounds stung lifted. She closed her eyes tightly, trying to escape her feelings. Soon she was jolted back to reality by an unsettling sensation.

The messenger noticed her bloodied arms and sprinted over. "Princess Freyja, are you alright?" he asked, while cleaning off the blood on her arms. He wondered why there were no cuts. Was the blood not hers.

"I'd like to believe so," Freyja replied, choking back tears.

The soldier took her horse's reins and bowed. "Come with me, Princess. I'll get you some care."

Freyja followed him gratefully. As her vision cleared, she recognized him—Lattermere Seidei, the front gate guard she had known for years.

Lattermere tied her horse to a small tree, next to a painted horse of white, orange, and brown. "Who's this?" Freyja asked, referring to the horse.

"He is Honfra, a gift from Haru Strowint. Haru is one of the leaders of this group," Lattermere explained.

Freyja pushed her damaged dress up against her knees and sat beside Lattermere. She watched him take medicines and bandages from a bag. He washed the remaining blood and treated her remaining wounds. His face showed his confusion about why her injuries were disappearing so quickly, but he felt no authority to ask.

"Haru Strowint," Freyja began. "I'd like to speak with him. I need to know what happened and our plans."

"Well, yes. But I think you should speak with Hondou Unrey about those plans. He knows more about it than Haru," Lattermere replied.

Freyja nodded and looked angrily down the road at Hondou. The man who had rescued her was one of the most questionable. He seemed involved in the events in Thuthairyon, he's in charge of the military forces, he hated her brother Laithrum—could he be trusted? Though she desired his downfall, she wasn't sure if it was a justified feeling.

"He's in trouble, isn't he?" Lattermere asked, his voice tinged with concern.

Freyja smiled faintly, appreciating his respect despite the dire situation. Lattermere leaned back, knowing he shouldn't be so casual with royalty, but he couldn't help it. After everything that had happened, he needed to talk freely, and Freyja was easy to talk to. Guilt gnawed at him, and he bowed his head low. "Please forgive me, Princess, for being so disrespectful."

"Sit up," she said calmly. "It might sound selfish or irresponsible, but I don't want the title or authority of being a royal—not right now." Her eyes turned to the ground as her mind replayed the horrors of the night. "The enemy has taken my brother and killed my mother. My judgment is clouded." She shook, overwhelmed with emotion. "Inside, I don't even feel like myself. There's something inside that doesn't belong."

Lattermere looked at her with compassion, unsure how to comfort her. He remained silent, fearing he might say something to make her feel worse.

Their conversation was interrupted by Hondou riding up to them. "Princess Freyja, we are heading out. One of our watchmen reported that the enemy is close behind. We have no time to linger."

Freyja jumped up, untied her horse, and mounted it. Lattermere cringed at her bare feet, bandages as the only protection. He gathered his bags and followed.

By morning, the company had moved only a short distance through the forest, slowed by the injured, the old, and the weak. They stopped at first light, the thick forest blocking much of the golden morning sun.

Lattermere approached Freyja, who still sat on her snow-white horse with jet-black stockings on all four legs. "Princess Freyja," he called boldly.

She looked down at him, breathing heavily. "What is it, Lattermere?"

He lifted his right hand, showing her a pair of leather boots. "They should be your size. Will you try them on?"

Freyja smiled at his gesture. "Thank you. You've always been very kind."

She slid off her horse and slipped on the brown leather boots. Lattermere also handed her a long, heavy dark-gray coat.

"Princess Freyja," Lattermere noted her heavy breathing, his concern evident. "How are you?"

"I'm recovering from an illness. I just hope I can keep up. I don't want to slow us down," she replied, knowing it was a believable story, though far from the truth. The truth was unclear to her, but the illness recovery was long over with. Whatever was happening was new.

Before Lattermere could respond, a messenger arrived. "Everyone not on guard duty must rest. After the break, we head into Forest-Drawl."

Freyja and Lattermere complied. After sleeping soundly for four hours all were roused to continue the journey into Forest-Drawl.

Three days passed. Freyja struggled on the first day, less so on the second, and by the third, she felt completely healed. Her wounds had completely vanished, leaving her puzzled. How was this happening?

Early in the morning, whispers spread that their journey through Forest-Drawl was nearly over. Everyone was instructed to remain silent and alert as they trudged through the dense forest.

Freyja felt worried. A growing anxiety choked her. She watched every movement closely, sensing an alien essence surging within her. She rode silently, her eyes sharp and alert.

The travelers pressed on, nearing the end. Ahead, a moss-covered rock bluff marked the transition to the fields of Nentranverce. But as they rounded the bluff, they were met not by green fields but by a unit of Seintroven warriors.

Arrows whistled through the air. "It's an ambush!" Hondou yelled, his voice filled with rage and confusion. Half the Seintroven men charged the scattering company. Freyja shed her thick gray coat and drew a sword from her horse's baggage. Instinct took over, and she charged forward, cutting a man from his horse with fierce power.

Seeing the enemy force on horseback, she knew their only chance was to take the enemy's horses. "Do not run! Fight and take their horses! It's the only way to escape fast enough to survive!" she shouted.

Lattermere heard her and drew one of his short swords. Without hesitation, he rode forward, shouting, "All who are true to Thuthairryon, stand strong and fight! Protect your princess and the women and children in grave danger!" He turned his sword to the enemy, and the soldiers and men of Thuthairryon joined the desperate fight.

Freyja charged, radiating an unnatural energy that caused the horses to buck their riders and flee. Soon, most of the soldiers were thrown from their mounts, continuing the fight on the uneven ground covered with tufts of prairie grass.

Even Freyja leaped from the back of her panicking horse. Her mind was too focused to question the beast's uncontrollable fear. Soon she was surrounded. Backed against a large tree, Freyja raised her sword defensively, fearless as a berserker. The enemy surrounded her. A man stepped into the circle of soldiers. Freyja examined his face, finding it familiar, and searched for weaknesses.

He spoke with an arrogant laugh. "Hello, Princess. Enjoying yourself?"

Freyja glared. "Who are you, and how did you know we were taking this road?" she snapped.

"Who I am is power," he replied maliciously. "I'm Houn Seidei, older brother of Lattermere Seidei. This puts a twist on things, doesn't it? And that should answer your other question. I led you here." Before he could say more, Freyja thrust her sword forward with outrageous force, the blade exploding through Houn's chest. She then threw his corpse backward; behind her.

A man, still shaking from what he saw, sprang at her from the side. Freyja stepped aside, kicked his foot up with her own, and directed his skull onto a rock behind her. She showed no more emotion as she fought.

The battle resumed. As another soldier attacked, she brought him down with a swift grab and twist of his arm. Freyja then took up her enemy's sword and fought the other charging men.

Her left leg was wounded above the knee, sending her to the ground, but she felt no pain. She looked up as another soldier lifted his sword high, ready to strike. At that moment, Hondou leaped over his own, falling, opponent and slashed Freyja's attacker. Hondou's sword cutting down slicing the enemy in two. Only one enemy remained close to them. He spun around quickly to cut him down. He looked side-to-side, clear for the moment.

Freyja stood and positioned herself back-to-back with Hondou. A far-off soldier near a tree drew an arrow and sent it hissing through the air. Freyja saw it too late. The arrow ripped through her right shoulder, spinning her to the ground.

Lattermere saw the arrow and the man who shot it. From a distance, he threw one of his short swords, piercing the man's bicep. The blade entered a tree, pinning the enemy.

Lattermere sprinted to Freyja, whom Hondou was defending against three attackers. But Hondou could no longer keep up and was struck over the head from behind.

An enemy, in a desperate attempt, ran full force into Lattermere, knocking him to the ground. Moments passed, and he didn't move an inch. He stayed flat on the ground. Dead?

Freyja watched her comrades fight and fall. Her eyes then caught sight of a man with grayish skin and black hair approaching from the hill. He wore the enemy's uniform, a Captain's cloth, and seemed untouched. His hair was neatly brushed back, his clothes still pristine.

Freyja glared at him. "What deal did your people make with my father? I'm guessing you'd know!"

The man smiled. "We agreed to win your land if he could rule it. Once we take over, we'll kill your royal family and place your father, King Niejill Airslen, on the throne. This victory will end the war. And he's sharing something even greater than peace: power. I'll let you go to your grave wondering how that could be. Oh, and your father wasn't the only one behind it. A Council member, Trence Guritton, assisted greatly. Sadly, things didn't work out for him. Since you didn't die from the poison, your father had to find another way to kill you. He thought this would work just fine."

He looked around with his blood-shot eyes, then turned to his men. "Who shot her down?"

"It was me, sir, Nourttaku Renvent," came a pained voice from a man pinned to a tree by his stabbed left arm. He claimed his accomplishment, hoping someone would rescue him.

The captain smiled eerily. "Well, 'hen, those who aren't well enough to come will be left behind." He waved his hand, and a soldier ran over to Nourttaku. The soldier grabbed the pinned arm and slid it down the blade until it was against the tree. Nourttaku winced in pain.

The soldier began tying him to the tree. "What are you doing?" Nourttaku cried out.

Without reply, they took his other hand, ran a knife through his wrist, and tied the knife to his thick leather belt. Nourttaku glared and cursed as they walked away.

"And why are you doing this?" Freyja asked in disgust.

"Now no one can say I wasn't the one who brought you down," the captain replied.

"If that's truly the reason, why not just kill h..?" Freyja thought. But before she could finish, the captain raised his sword, ready to end her life.

Freyja had enough. She grabbed a sword lying near her and, with unnatural speed, beheaded the twisted captain. She then swung her sword in a spiral, striking down two other men.

A tall, burly man charged at her. She stepped aside, using his own force to tip him off balance, then slew him as he fell. Freyja looked up and saw an arrow racing toward her. It tore through her chest and into her heart.

Freyja fell, disbelieving. She was still alive. Slowly, she took hold of the arrow, and as it lifted from her body, it disappeared in a burst of flames. Her hand and chest remained unhurt.

The man who shot her quivered violently in confusion and horror.

His mind blanked, and he could no longer see clearly. In panic, he yelled, "SHE'S A WITCH; SHE CAN'T DIE!"

Hearing this, the enemy soldiers who saw what happened fled. They yelled for their comrades to retreat. Freyja watched as they disappeared into the fields of blue-green grass. Was it over? It all happened so fast and now the memories were flooding her mind.

"Whatever happened—I'm thankful for it. At least…I think I am." Freyja rose to her feet, noticing she felt no pain. The memory of what had happened made her shake. She couldn't believe it. What happened made no sense, it wasn't possible. Fear of herself sent her staggering in circles aimlessly.

Lattermere, stunned and paralyzed for a moment, finally rose and approached her. He had seen her fight, saw her fall, and then stand again as if nothing happened. He was terrified.

"Princess Freyja," he said slowly, trying not to startle her. She turned to him, and he shuddered in intimidation.

"What just happened?" he asked. Freyja responded with a look of uncertainty. Tears welled in her eyes, and she couldn't respond in any other way but to cry.

Lattermere nodded, then turned his gaze to the enemy soldier left behind. "If you will excuse me, Princess," he said angrily, stomping toward the man who had shot her. Suddenly, Freyja called out, "Lattermere Seidei, do not harm that man."

He stopped. Freyja walked over to check on Hondou, who was still unconscious but alive. She smiled lightly and turned back to Lattermere. "Go and find people who can move...who can work. There are too few of us to travel safely."

At her command, he ran to execute her wishes swiftly.

Freyja approached Nourttaku. He remained silent as she wrapped his hands, bandaged his wounds, and bound his feet. She left enough rope for walking. After securing him, she tied the remaining rope to the tree he had been bound to. She commanded coldly, "You will help us reach our destination. Refusal will only bring you more pain."

He looked away, acknowledging her warning. After what had happened, he no longer felt loyal to the Seintroven people. For now, he would work for her.

Lattermere returned with disappointing news. He had found only three soldiers, a handful of uninjured, and Freyja's horse. He also reported on the living but injured. She still did not worry. Despite their small number, they had an abundance of supplies left by the enemy. She didn't care about the odds. She knew what they had to do.

Freyja told him they were going to rescue her brother, Ashtion. This was nonnegotiable. First, they needed to gather supplies for a long journey and rest. The injured will be treated and the unwounded, who weren't trained in combat, will care for them. After a short while, Hondou woke and assisted. Her commands were absolute.

The ground was tangled with old tree roots, making every step difficult. Supplies were gathered, and wounds treated. By afternoon, the newly formed company was ready to travel.

Freyja stood, arms resting at her sides, looking at a large, old tree. After a moment of thought, she carved into it a message and a warning: *Freyja is alive!* She slipped the chain over her head and laid it on a twisted, broken branch.

"This gift is for whoever or whatever stopped that arrow from killing me and healed me instead. You have my thanks." After speaking, she stood with her head bowed in silence. Then she took a breath, lifted her gaze, and with new determination, set her mind on finding her brother.

Traveling with Nourttaku as their guide was bitter for them all. No one wanted to trust him, and none had the energy to try. The pain from both healing and festering wounds slowed their progress, but the memory and realization of what had happened drove them forward. This was bigger than them, and revenge was on everyone's mind.

Freyja's quest had begun. Different from anything she had ever imagined, her mission to a strange destination began. The long, winding journey took her to the east side of the Ring Mountains—a place no sane person would dare to go.

CHAPTER 7

Together for Survival

The ships Derdin, Saiyured, and Trence, joined the battle-torn vessels waiting ahead. The leaders' ships sailed close, laying ramps to connect. Commanders gathered to discuss their plan of action.

Laithrum watched the proceedings carefully from afar. Everything felt different now, a cloud of fear and tension thickening the air. The young prince looked at his companions. "Now what?" he asked pensively.

Linus glanced at the prince. "We wait for orders. Once we get them, we work beyond haste," he explained. "Usually, soldiers don't go to the other ships. We wait for the captains to return with orders. My father will tell us what to do."

Lotus, set down by Dowen, spoke to Laithrum. "Since the ramps are lowered, we can board Kairer, the ship I was stationed on before. I'd like to see if my friend made it through the previous battle."

Laithrum considered. "I'd enjoy that, but shouldn't you rest or at least change clothes?" he said, referring to the off-white robe Lotus had worn since his rescue from the sea.

Dowen sighed. "It was his ship. You may be allowed on. But before you go, ask Lotus' doctor, Troi. See if he's allowed to leave or if he should stay on this ship."

"I would, but if I find and ask Troi, we might not have enough time to see the other ship's deck, let alone find Lotus' friend. My main concern is getting back before the battle," Laithrum said.

Dowen nodded, understanding the statement but curious what kind of life Laithrum led. He spoke as if he could do whatever he wanted. He must have been nobility or very wealthy. The intitled attitude might get him into trouble.

Onlortrens approached Laithrum. "Move quickly. You need to get Lotus back before the battle. He'll be safer here for more reasons than you'd expect." The elf advised, hoping Laithrum took his advice seriously. Many young humans he had worked with didn't fear battle and got killed for it. He had learned not to fully trust a young, inexperienced man with his own life.

Linus shared the same concern. He was convinced that Laithrum's battle readiness was even lower than Lotus, who was injured. They all had more battle experience than Laithrum.

Dowen looked at Laithrum and commanded, "You must be back in an hour. I'll tell Troi where Lotus is going because he's Troi's responsibility. When you return, you should find Linus and me in the storage department preparing for battle."

Laithrum and Lotus said farewell and set off toward the ramp, with Onlortrens following close behind.

When they reached the ramp, Onlortrens halted them and turned to Laithrum. "I will not be joining you this time. It is entirely up to you to bring Lotus back within the hour." Laithrum, puzzled by Onlortrens' sudden departure, opened his mouth to question him, but Onlortrens spoke first.

"I have an important matter to attend to, trust me. But first, one thing must be clarified." He smiled warmly, and quickly turned too Lotus, "Who is this person you wish to see?"

Lotus, his dark curls tousled by the wind, replied, "My friend is an IseamA who was about to share something important before we were attacked. Those are the two reasons I am traveling there: to see my friend and finish our conversation."

The elf's eyes twinkled. "An IseamA, from the Lands of Bluegrasses, or as we call it, Altorerinviss?"

"Yes. She was bringing news from inside the Ring Mountains. I was very curious about how much she knew."

Onlortrens' eyes widened with surprise and concern. "News from the dark land? It's unfortunate I have other matters to attend to. I would like to know what your friend knows." He stepped back, turning away. "Farewell and return swiftly."

Before Onlortrens could leave, Laithrum quickly asked, "May I inquire where you are going?"

"Laithrum, I am meeting someone about a matter of great importance to us both," Onlortrens replied vaguely. "Must I remind you, before I depart, that the enemy will be here soon? I would feel better if Lotus returned in half an hour instead of a whole one; hurry." Onlortrens glanced back at Lotus, suspicion clouding his eyes.

Lotus sensed the elf's unease and could guess its cause. He should avoid the elf.

Onlortrens, not wanting to pry further, asked, "You will remind Laithrum to get you back to the ship on time. He hasn't yet mastered reading the sun for time."

Lotus nodded, but dodged eye contact. He knew it was crucial to return to the Derdin promptly. If he found his friend quickly, they could leave in haste and talk later.

Onlortrens nodded in understanding and departed swiftly and silently.

Lotus, his expressive eyes filled with regret, looked at Laithrum and said sincerely, "I'll try hard not to be a burden." He then looked away with a hollow smile. Laithrum remained silent.

They began walking across the pivoting ship ramp. Laithrum was grateful for the walkway's sturdiness and his natural balance because any extra movement would make crossing nerve wrecking.

Ahead, two men stood at the ramp's end, ensuring soldiers did not retreat to the Derdin, keeping them on a vessel farther from the front. As Laithrum and Lotus approached, one man turned around.

"Where are you two headed?" demanded the left-standing guard. He stepped forward and positioned his spear to block their path. Laithrum looked up and answered respectfully, "To the front deck, sir."

"For what reason?" the guard demanded, his narrow eyes suspicious as he scrutinized Laithrum.

Lotus, summoning a cold, soldierly tone, replied, "I was thrown from this ship in the last battle. I need to know what happened after I fell."

The guard studied Lotus's face intently. "I believe you, Flurissurnna. We all thought you were dead. If you have time, I'd like to hear your story. I was moved to a distant ship before the battle. So, I can't help you answer any questions." He withdrew his spear. "You may pass."

Lotus smiled gratefully. "Thank you, sir. But weren't you told? I thought someone, who saw and survived, would have told you."

The guard lowered his head, his voice firm but hazy. "Yes and no, Lotus. I don't know what happened to you. Head to the other side but understand that no one will be pleased to see you."

Lotus's expression darkened with dread. He realized everyone on the ship knew what had happened. He wasn't safe, but that wasn't important right now. He lowered his head and turned to walk away.

They walked silently off the ramp and onto the wooden deck, which was brutally broken and splintered from the last battle. Lotus glanced around, haunted by phantom visions of the fight. He saw the warriors' struggles, the blood and life they tore from each other. In different circumstances, could they have been friends?

The painful memories made him feel miserable and nauseous. He feared the coming battle even more. Laithrum noticed another soldier on the deck recognize Lotus and quickly leave. The soldier ran with overwhelming fear. Lotus watched and accepted this reaction. Laithrum had no idea how to rationalize this. What could have happened?

Suddenly, Lotus stopped and spoke in a fast, ghostly tone, "Laithrum, I can no longer move." He tried to keep himself standing, but it was useless. His mind and body failed him, and he fell to the ground. Laithrum went down with him to cushion his fall.

"Lotus?" the young prince asked, worried. He examined his friend's cold appearance. Laithrum felt him shake and turn cold to the touch. Not knowing what else to do, he took off his hard leather jacket and placed it over Lotus's shoulders.

Hearing Laithrum's call, a strange woman ran around the corner and approached them. She wore a long jacket, a lightweight armored shirt, black pants, and shoes without toes.

Laithrum looked up at her. She had long black hair that ended two inches above her knees and soft, fur-like body hair. Her face was lovely and human-like, with bright blue eyes. She wore a massive, beautiful ruby necklace, and when she bent down to Lotus, Laithrum noticed her large, lynx-like ears.

"IseamA," his mind recalled the conversation with Onlortrens. "Lady, are you the friend of Lotus we came to find?" Laithrum asked as she sat beside him.

"I would guess so," she said, smiling as she watched Lotus's eyes open. "Hello, Florissurnna."

Laithrum and the woman helped Lotus to his feet, as he felt too dizzy to stand on his own. "I'm sorry," he murmured, trying to explain. "I saw the last fight and the moment Adeyas was taken. It was too much for my battered body to handle."

Laithrum, having never witnessed a battle, couldn't grasp what had just transpired. He hadn't been a skirmish nor even a heated argument. Relating, even a little, would take a lot of creativity. It was clear something significant had happened, something that filled people with fear and rage.

The foreign girl seemed to understand the problem. Unlike the others, who looked at Lotus with fear and disgust, she appeared indifferent to the past.

"Are you alright to stand now, Lotus?" Laithrum asked kindly. Lotus straightened up and replied, "Yes, I think so. Do you two know each other yet? I don't know how long I was out."

"You weren't gone for long," Laithrum answered.

"And I have never seen this man before in my life. I have yet to learn his name and he mine. I really want to have an introduction though." said the free-spirited female.

Lotus gestured to Laithrum. "This is Laithrum. He is the younger of Adeyas' two brothers." She looked at Laithrum in shock, never expecting to meet one of Prince Adeyas Airslens' siblings. She had heard so much about them. "So, you're his brother. What should I call you?" she asked.

"Simply call me Laithrum. I would prefer it if these people did not discover who I am," he replied.

She smiled and placed her hand on her chest in a gesture of respect. "It's a privilege to meet you, Laithrum." She bowed her head and continued, "You may call me Yiyumiss, but my full name is Yiyumiss Maifush Kongei. And if you don't know yet, I am an IseamA, a forest dweller commonly known as Beastmen. We have retractile claws in our strong, human-like hands and feet. The no-toe shoes protect them from our claws." Laithrum quickly noted her chatty and buoyant personality. "But contrary to popular belief we are civilized, and we don't bite."

After the introduction, they helped Lotus toward the ramp.

"Lotus," Yiyumiss asked, "how long were you in the water?"

Lotus looked down. "I was hoping you could tell me. I was only mentally present for a small amount of the time. Two days, I think."

She nibbed at her forefinger in thought, then answered, "I'm not too sure. You were gone for a good week; I think so anyway. In any case, I am glad to see you're alright. Well, *alright* in the sense that you're alive," she said gratefully.

Lotus knew he was fortunate to be alive, but he disliked the feeling. He knew his plans were flawed and could no longer live like this. He felt like a burden, a chore, a danger, and never brave enough to be honest. He had served this royal family for five years and now he was harming them. Had he let things go too far? He worried most for Freyja. He should never have allowed their relationship to become serious; she deserved better. He was guilty.

Laithrum had never seen the results of Lotus' work. Lotus worked in the gardens, but Laithrum wasn't permitted to go out, not even into the royal gardens. The gardens were even on the roof. It was safe, but he could only look through the glass. He had heard that Lotus had a fascination with mushrooms. The only reason they allowed him to grow them was because they were beautiful and non-poisonous. He'd have to ask about them some day.

As Laithrum and Lotus crossed to the other ship, leaders gathered in a tense conversation. Captain Makoto Lounleyossa, the last to arrive, entered the room where the commanders of the four surrounding ships and the fleet General were seated around an old wooden table.

Makoto approached them. "I apologize for my tardiness," he said, taking a seat. "Let us proceed without further delay." He was relieved to see that none of them seemed to mind.

General Vander Headorbron wasted no time. "The battle is imminent. This meeting is to ensure we all understand the situation. The enemy's objective is clear: to invade the royal city of Thuthairryon. Their tactics leave no other reasonable conclusion." The five men nodded in agreement.

One of the front-line commanders spoke up. "There is nothing new to report on their strategy. Expect anything in the upcoming battle. Last time, we failed to anticipate their bold, almost suicidal maneuvers. Moreover, none of their fighters were of the mortal race of men. The Seintroven were unlike anything we've faced. They weren't as *human* as before."

"Do you know if the enemy is bringing any beasts of flight?" Makoto inquired. "We prepared the ship Winwotheer, which carries our trained winged dragons. I'll want to inform the riders."

The commander, eyes widening in surprise, replied calmly, "As I said, be ready for anything. The enemy had winged monsters resembling wild dogs with bat wings, dragon-like tails, and human-like arms wielding swords. These creatures, called sinjar, appeared in the last wave of battle. I expect them to return, but nothing is certain."

Imagining the frightful creatures, Makoto looked up at the commander. "I have a question for you," he began. The commander listened attentively.

"You are Commander Hanner Tron of this ship, the Kairer, correct?" Hanner nodded. "A day ago, we found one of your men adrift in the water. His name is Lotus Florissurnna. He has dark curly hair and auburn eyes. Looks younger than his age. Do you know him?"

Hanner's eyes narrowed, and his face flushed. "He survived," he said, sounding utterly disappointed.

"Why are you angered by this?" Makoto asked, puzzled by the reaction to a soldier's return.

"The reason is understandable. You'll feel as I do once you hear it. There is a disturbing fact about the deceptively kind-hearted Lotus Florissurnna. It made me decide to leave him in the water after the battle. That soldier is…" Hanner paused, then continued calmly, "Lotus' blood is mixed, or he is a demon of sorts. He appears human but is something else entirely. Lotus is an unknown, unstable, and wildly violent creature. It is too risky to have him aboard any ship. That's why we let him drift. You picked him up without knowing better; now it is a terrible issue, a danger to our mission and our lives."

Makoto froze, overwhelmed by sadness and worry. He had never expected this from the youth. His mind hardened. "If this is true, I do not want someone so troublesome and dangerous on my ship, especially with my son Linus aboard. Lotus is ill and can hardly walk. I hear he is on your ship now. Please, keep him here. Your ship is closer to the front; he will have no place to escape. And all but one person on this ship knows what he is. He has no allies. The enemy will kill him swiftly." Makoto choked on the shame that followed his harsh words.

All the men agreed to the plan, though only Hanner and Makoto felt any remorse. They met him and liked the boy for that time. He seemed human and well natured. After the meeting, the four commanders, fleet general, and captain returned to their vessels. The ramps connecting them were quickly disconnected to ensure Lotus couldn't cross over.

Laithrum watched in dismay as the ramps were pulled up so early. He ran to the guard he had spoken to earlier. "What is going on?" he demanded.

"We are preparing for war. You must stay and fight on this ship. There is nothing else you can do," snapped the guard, though he knew the real reason and didn't approve.

"But what about Lotus? He is unable to fight in his condition," Laithrum argued calmly. Looking into the guard's darkening eyes he sensed the discomfort. The man didn't like the dishonorable situation, but wasn't about to help someone he didn't know. Laithrum read his emotions and chose not to fight him.

"Don't give me a hard time. Making me feel worse won't help you! If you want the ramps lowered, speak with the commander of this ship. If he agrees, he'll talk to the captain of your ship. If they both accept, the ships will reconnect, and you can cross. There's nothing I can do, so don't bother me further!" The grim warrior walked away, leaving Laithrum in troubled thought.

Feeling powerless, Laithrum returned to Yiyumiss and Lotus. "So, what did he say?" asked the IseamA, worried by Laithrum's expression.

"They're preparing for battle. There's nothing he can do. I'd have to speak with the commander of this ship, but I doubt he'll allow it. This feels wrong, not just because of the enemy's approach."

Lotus looked down, guessing the reason. "They want me to die. Leaving me in the water was just another way to get rid of me." He considered their attempt wise. Glancing at Laithrum, Lotus forced a smile. Thoughts raced, *if people fight around me and against me, what happened before will happen again.* Yiyumiss knew the reason too, but what troubled her more was that Lotus seemed to accept it. He agreed with their ethics. Laithrum could only guess, but he was used to that. He had never felt worse about not knowing what his companions knew. He had no clue why this was happening.

Yiyumiss stared into the distance, her hand shading her eyes to see clearer. The sight of the distant horizon was troubling. She saw the enemy ships approaching. In shock, Yiyumiss quickly turned and yelled to the lookout.

"The enemy is on the horizon!" Immediately, the man spun around and looked through his monocular in the direction she pointed. She was right. The news spread like wildfire. The enemy had arrived.

CHAPTER 8

With a Separate Undertaking

After Laithrum and Lotus parted ways, Onlortrens descended to the lowest segment of Derdin. The third level, a realm of smuggling and storage, was a stark contrast to the upper decks. The ceiling pressed low, and the narrow corridors were shrouded in near-total darkness. Everywhere was a tight fit; hard to move around. While a human would be rendered blind, Onlortrens' elfin eyes pierced the gloom effortlessly.

Crouched and cautious, he navigated the blackened halls, his magic illuminating the way. The biting cold was palpable, the thin air like ice against his throat. He conjured a spell to warm himself, but the chill lingered.

Ahead, a shadowy figure leaned against a large wooden crate. The man, clutching a long object wrapped in thick cloth, eyed the High Elf with disdain. "Why have you come? Why do you care?" he demanded, his voice slow and deliberate. He stepped away from the crate, standing straight despite his shorter stature, exuding confidence.

"Why did you take it?" Onlortrens' voice echoed, his elfin light casting eerie shadows. Raven shielded his eyes from the greenish glow, the sudden brightness stinging.

"And why should I tell?" Raven retorted bitterly. Feeling his resolve falter against the elf's presence. He owed Onlortrens but his debt wasn't as big as this.

Raven's hand moved to the sword at his waist. "Onlortrens, this isn't your problem," he said, his voice tinged with reluctant anger. He didn't want to fight his friend, but he would if necessary.

"You are mistaken. This is everyone's problem. When I asked Laithrum to leave his home, this became my primary concern. Now, Raven, you may have a reason for taking the sword, but it does not belong to you. If you need strength, ask for my help."

Raven stepped back, one hand on his sword, the other gripping the stolen blade, Ellowvast. In his mind, there was no one to help him, no chance for aid.

Onlortrens drew his silver blade. The surrounding walls barely missed. Even though Ravens small size gave him an advantage in the tightness, he remained confident. He knew Raven too well to lose.

"This is your decision. Leave the sword and take my assistance. If force is the only way, so be it. You can explain after you wake up and heal."

Raven knew Onlortrens would win. He needed a good plan. Desperate, he thought of a place above where he might escape. An open area with a ceiling hatch, just below the top deck.

He darted for the door, Onlortrens closed behind. Raven's knowledge of elves served him well. He knew not to listen for movement. Elves made no sound when they moved, their feet barely touching the ground.

They raced into the room Raven had aimed for. Onlortrens quickly noticed a ladder leading to an unlocked ceiling door, through which daylight streamed. He wondered why Raven had led him there but did not lose focus or take his eyes off Raven.

"This still plagues my thoughts, Raven. Why did you steal the Ellowvast? What are you going to do with it?" the elf asked calmly, hoping to talk him out of this rash decision.

Onlortrens' question made Raven's purpose clearer than before, strengthening his resolve. Yet, it also made him feel the mission was inherently self-defeating. Without rationality, Raven lunged forward, clashing swords with Onlortrens. After a high strike, he sank downwards, thrusting toward the elf's center. Onlortrens darted to the side, avoiding the blade. Raven turned his blade, side slashing, but Onlortrens blocked with his sword as a shield. Stepping back, recovering from Onlortrens' shoving away his attack, Raven knew his last move left him open. Onlortrens seized the opportunity, cutting Raven's side shallowly. He then used the flat of his sword to knock Raven's weapon from his hand.

Raven knew he had to act on his previous plan. With clenched fists, he bent his knees and widened his stance. Before he could move further, Onlortrens grabbed Raven's right arm and spun him down to the hardwood floor. Raven realized he had lost, but another opportunity would come soon. He'd have to be sly, but he'll make it happen.

"Will you answer me now, Raven? Why did you steal this sword? To be honest, I'm grateful you brought it, as it saves me the trouble of retrieving it myself. I am sure your reasons for wanting the Ellowvast are very different from mine." Onlortrens stood, patiently watching Raven, waiting for his answer.

Raven looked away, his eyes troubled, and did not answer the elf's question. Onlortrens' expression shifted from questioning to disappointment. He guessed at a few reasons that might be true. Knowing Raven for years, it made sense that he wouldn't answer. Why would he trust the person who had just struck him down? His past traumas would be triggered and applied to the present. Onlortrens pushed away his questions, understanding that Raven would speak when he calmed down. He always breaks down eventually.

Onlortrens glanced up at the ceiling entrance. As Raven stood, he eyed the sword that was slapped from his hand. It was too far to lunge for. But his thoughts shifted completely as he heard Onlortrens exclaim, "The battle has begun!"

The elf ran, bending without slowing to pick up Ellowvast. After gracefully grabbing the royal sword, he leaped to the top of the ladder. Raven followed, springing up with one hand on his cut side and the other gripping his retrieved sword. "Where do you think he is?" Raven asked the elf.

Onlortrens, surprised and almost amused at Raven's quick emotional recovery, replied, "I do not know, but he should be back on this ship—if your 'he' and my 'he' refers to the same person." Knowing they both meant Laithrum, they set off in search of him. Now, Raven and Onlortrens fought side by side as if nothing had happened between them.

***

On Kairer, after a short wait, Laithrum drew his sword as the ships came into view. Without turning his head, he spoke to Lotus and Yiyumiss, "Lady Yiyumiss, do you know anywhere on this ship where you and Lotus would be safest?"

Yiyumiss narrowed her eyes in annoyance and replied bitterly, "The Iseamin women fight alongside the men and do just as well. We are much like the elfin people in that gender does not dictate our ability to fight. There isn't a significant difference in strength as there is among humans. But to answer you…NO. This ship in its entirety isn't safe."

The young prince nodded, showing his understanding. He knew little about this outside world but respected it as best he could. He hoped that one day, others would do the same for him. Yiyumiss, saying it was completely unsafe, caused higher concern. She understood much more than he. Laithrum respected her assessment.

Laithrum turned to Lotus. "Do you know of any place in the fleet where you could hide?"

Lotus sighed and shook his head. There was no safe place on any of the ships. He would be a threat no matter where he was. At that moment, he saw sinjars soaring through the dreary sky. Their long tails swayed as they flew swiftly toward them. The long swords the sinjars carried gleamed brighter as they approached.

"Laithrum, there is no time to worry about me. The sinjars are starting this battle."

Horns and shouts erupted from both ships. The Seintroven ships slowed, forming a straight line. At the front of both the Thuthairryon and Seintroven ships stood lines of men with long-range bows, archers ready. The soldiers of Thuthairryon prepared to shoot the creatures with poison-tipped arrows. Some men held four-foot-long arrows in their quivers, worn like sheathed swords. These arrows had to deploy by a two-man team, one carrying a bow with tripod and other the man with the arrows. They waited with drawn arrows for the command to fire.

One of the second-row men saw the three and ran over. "What are you doing?" he yelled, grabbing Lotus and throwing him behind himself. Laithrum opened his mouth to speak, but the man interrupted, "If he is too weak to fight, throw him overboard!" He quickly added, "You must arm yourself to fight, or you will die without prestige and without assisting your comrades!"

Laithrum grabbed Lotus to drag him back up, but Yiyumiss quickly took Lotus from him. "I'll get him too somewhere safer." She quickly spoke the bowman, "Thank you for the idea." She easily hoisted Lotus onto her shoulder and jumped over the ship's handrail. "Laithrum, you better be alive when I return!" she commanded as they fell.

Leaving Laithrum alone on deck, Yiyumiss and Lotus splashed into the cool water. Yiyumiss helped Lotus surface. Lotus shook the seawater from his hair and glared at his friend. Without thinking, he lifted his arm to strike her.

Yiyumiss quickly moved aside, placing her hands on Lotus' shoulders and pushing him under the water. Following him under, she spoke loudly through the salty water. "Lotus, you know me! I am a friend, I am Yiyumiss! Just think!" she said passionately, hoping he wasn't too far gone to come back. His strong, hurtful grip lifted from her arm. With a lightened heart, she lifted him to the surface.

After coughing out the salt water, they locked their arms to float. Lotus looked at Yiyumiss with much redder eyes, showing his weariness and lack of control. "I'm so sorry, Yiyumiss," he whispered mournfully. "I never wanted to be like this… Just leave me, please."

Yiyumiss thrust him under the water again. After holding him down for a good while, she pulled him out and scolded, "You are never to say that again! Do you hear me? Never again! It's a waste of words because I'm not going to let anyone harm you. I'll try my hardest to protect you and everyone else from you. Try your hardest to survive this battle and whatever comes next. Do you agree?"

"Agreed… I agree."

They started swimming. She no longer needed to hold him above water, as his strength was growing due to the battle. Lotus watched with dizzy, fading eyes as the flying beasts of the Thutheirryon soared overhead. They were neintoe dragons, one of the two kinds of dragons that could be tamed and the only type with hair on their heads and necks.

Neintoe dragons had two sets of bat-shaped wings sprouting from spikes on each side of their backs. They were small put magical. The dragon's rider had to be specially trained to avoid aggravating the dragon, as its temper was short.

They had swum far in the deep, waving water, and were now behind the Derdin.

"Lotus, which ship are the dragons on?"

"I do not know. Why do you ask?" he pondered.

"Because that's where you'll be safest. If need be, you can ride one of them to a safer place. You'll be able to escape the battleground if things go wrong." As they spoke, someone listened from the back of the ship.

"I know where that ship is," said a voice.

Yiyumiss turned sharply toward the voice. "Who's there?" she snapped, drawing and raising her sword above the water's surface.

"A friend," said Dowen, springing over the edge. He held onto a rope to ensure he could get back onto the ship. "May I ask what you are doing with Lotus, lady?" Dowen was surprised to see a woman in this battle. Or was she someone like Raven?

"I am planning to take him to the ship of the neintoe dragons. Will you tell me which ship it is?" She continued, "He'll be safest there. You said you were a friend, and if you're wondering where I'll go after bringing him there, I will be returning to Kairer to support Prince Laithrum in the fight."

Dowen gently grabbed her arm, moving and speaking like a gentleman. "I'll take the boy there, for I know the way better." He then looked down at Lotus. "Is that alright with you?"

Lotus simply looked away, tiredly. Nothing was pleasant anymore. He had too much hostility in him to fight back anymore. His head ached from trying to keep them safe from himself. His current success in staying calm felt impossible to maintain. It was like two other people inside him both screamed something different. Sometimes he wasn't even in control of his body. This feeling never ended well.

Lotus was glad he was too tired to move. With more energy, he would harm these two instead of healing himself. Yiyumiss started swimming back to Laithrum, leaving it up to Dowen to take Lotus to the correct ship.

Linus, who had been fighting beside Dowen before he disappeared, cut down an enemy soldier and threw him over the side of the boat's rail. The Seintroven soldier fell directly in front of Dowen. Hearing Dowen's startled yell, Linus quickly looked down from the rail and saw him.

"Need some help, Dowen?!" Linus yelled, thinking Dowen had somehow fallen overboard.

"Yes, getting him onto the other ship might require another person. So, get down here!" Dowen demanded. Linus hesitated, initially thinking Dowen had gone mad. But with no time to waste, he jumped overboard, feeling awkward and somewhat foolish.

As Linus surfaced, he asked, "What are you doing down here?"

Dowen, not wanting to answer directly, replied playfully, "What are you doing down here?"

Linus gave up searching for the real reason and simply swam with Dowen until they reached the other ship. Dowen handed the fainted Lotus to Linus and started climbing up the ship's walls.

When Dowen reached the top, he ran to the front deck for rope. Turning a corner, he sprang back with his hands up as he saw an arrow drawn and aimed at him. "I'm one of yours!" he said, unnerved.

The soldier lowered the bow and stepped forward in surprise. "Kackveriage...? How did you get on this vessel, sir?"

"This is the safest place to be. You don't have to question my motives. I wish for a wounded soldier to receive sanctuary. He is in the water with another soldier, waiting for me to return." Dowen waited for the soldier's reply.

"We are in the start of a battle, and you decide to swim over here to give some petty, pathetic soldier a place to lie down and take it easy?"

Dowen glared at him. "Yes, but no. The person I bring is not petty. Pathetic, in a sense, yes, he is. But neither of those expressions matter. I order you to lead me to a place where he will be safer!" he commanded harshly.

The soldier backed away and responded respectfully, "I apologize, sir. Show me where he is, and I'll bring him somewhere safe."

"First, I'd like to know your name, so I can find you when I come back."

"Teirlandus Shyjule," the soldier replied, fearing Dowen's return.

After mentally marking the name, Dowen led the soldier quickly to Lotus. The soldier looked down at the two in the water and threw down a rope. Linus tied the rope around Lotus' waist, and Dowen effortlessly pulled Lotus up onto the ship. Dowen looked back at the soldier with a warning in his eyes. "Ensure nothing happens to this man, Lotus."

The bowman nodded. He caried out Dowens order the best he could in such a situation.

While Dowen and Linus swam quickly back to the Derdin, Lotus was brought to where the dragons were kept and placed in one of the empty stalls. The stall was in the corner of the room, next to a sleeping dragon whose strong breathing filled the space. Teirlandus, was convinced this was good enough. He continued his priory duties.

***

Laithrum and Yiyumiss were together again, fighting side by side. Sometimes they spun around each other, defending one another with instincts that were remarkably similar. The enemy ship ahead charged forward, crashing into Kairer. Boards splintered and flew from the decks. Some board shot straight up into the sky where most tumbled to the sides erratically.

The front-line ships became a chaotic mix of Seintroven and Thurtairryon. Clean swords quickly stained with blood. Beasts flew, battling each other, and dropping stones over their on-foot enemies.

Deep within the ship Kairer, an enemy soldier had ventured. He placed a weapon made of a special ground-stone and, with a deep breath, threw his torch into the rock-dust.

Outside, no one expected what happened next—not even the Seintroven soldier. Half the ship exploded into a fiery ball of flame. Its crew was either thrown into the sky, burnt to nothing, or blown into unrecognizable pieces. The entire ship soon disappeared beneath the blood-stained water or reappeared on top as unsightly debris.

Laithrum surfaced, trying to regain control after the violent thrash that had struck his body. He shook and jerked, unable to control his movements as he floated in the water. To his surprise, his mind remained clear. He knew where he was and what had happened.

In the past, his mind had felt as useless as his body did now, but now it was strong, seeing solutions instead of a hopeless blur. He concentrated fully on movement.

Yiyumiss swam slowly toward him. Despite being hit as hard as Laithrum, she wasn't badly shaken. Being an IseamA gave her greater impact tolerance than humans. She had expected him to be dead, but his eyes opened, and he said, "I'm so glad you survived this, Lady Yiyumiss. Now, will you help me onto Derdin?"

She smiled, barely able to contain her happiness that he hadn't died. "No, Laithrum, I will not help—I'll do!" Yiyumiss grabbed him and swam toward Derdin. She extended long, sharp claws from her fingers and toes, something Laithrum hadn't expected to see, though it explained the shape of her hands and feet.

The IseamA dug her claws into the hardwood plating on the outside of the ship and climbed to the top. Laithrum held onto her shoulders as she lifted him on her back.

Seeing an enemy soldier charging at her, Laithrum jumped off to fight him. The Seintroven soldier slashed downward, starting the fight. Laithrum blocked with his drawn sword, then swiftly drew Freyja's dagger with his left hand, cutting deeply across the soldier's face.

Laithrum grasped at the now lifeless man, freezing at the sight of what he had done. Another soldier, close behind the first, attacked him, but Yiyumiss defended Laithrum. She jumped onto the man, sending him down and knocking him out cold with a blow to the head.

Laithrum stood straight, focusing to regain control. He raised his sword to resume the battle beside Yiyumiss. The enemy remained strong, and victory was far from either side.

Though the battle wasn't over, Derdin was cleared of enemies. The Thuthairryon soldiers cried out in a single shout of joy for the victory. This was the second time Laithrum heard such shouts. He turned to Yiyumiss.

"Is it over?" he asked, doubting what he heard, as matters still looked bad and felt even worse.

Yiyumiss didn't like the way it felt either. "This is strange," she said. "There's no doubt we're fighting Seintroven soldiers, but it feels like the real threat is something else. Could there be more on the way?" Her instincts were sharp and usually right. So, she keenly searched the surroundings for indicators.

"If this is just a trick, I dislike the Seintroven leaders even more. What kind of leaders would sacrifice so many of their men for a surprise?" Laithrum paused, experiencing a moment of clairvoyance. "This feeling has nothing to do with the Seintroven," he proclaimed, waiting for whatever was coming to reveal itself.

Dowen and Linus returned to the ship. After climbing up on deck using the rope Dowen had prepared, they surveyed the area. All clear. Relief washed over them as they spotted Laithrum. They had thought he was lost in the explosion.

The two ran over. "Pr … Laithrum," Linus called out, "I thought you were on Kairer. I'm glad to see you got off in time."

"Do you know where Onlortrens is?" Dowen asked, shifting the focus.

"I don't know. I thought he'd be near me during the battle," Laithrum replied, worry evident in his voice.

At that moment, the elf ran to the same side of the ship, his eyes wide with shock and fear as he spotted an enemy vessel. The ship was cloaked by magic, invisible to all but him. Onlortrens quickly drew an arrow, strung it, and pulled back the string firmly. His elfin magic glowed in his hand. Quickly, transferring the magic to an arrow he strung and shot. It glowed with a green light and whistled sweetly through the air. It pierced and exposed the huge dark ship.

Now, everyone could see the ominous black vessel that appeared just beyond the other ships. The hopes of all the men were shattered as this new threat came into view. The huge black ship sent out an evil chill, causing both Thuthairryon and Seintroven soldiers to immediately stop fighting.

CHAPTER 9

Against the Hidden Enemy

As the faded, black vessel rolled inward, all trembled at its frightful size. Its shape was barely discernible, shrouded in a greenish fog. It glided swiftly toward them, its greenish-black sails resembling thorny wings.

Strangely, the ship made no ripples in the water. The most frightening aspect was that it did not disturb the water around it. The water it touched turned black and went still. The vessel maintained a fast pace.

Laithrum slipped as he tried to run from the edge of Derdin. He wondered why; he didn't usually fall. Yiyumiss moved toward him, but Dowen had already reached Laithrum, lifting him from the ground. The company ran quickly to the other side of the deck as the dark ship plowed through an entire ship, the remains of Kairer, and into Derdin. A sudden wave of force tipped the ship to its side.

The dark, massive ship stood three times taller than the Thuthairryon ships and was many meters longer. After crashing through Derdin, it plunged into the ship behind it, finally coming to a stop.

Laithrum surfaced, taking a deep breath of the salty air. Boards were still falling from the sky. His eyesight was too fuzzy to see anything clearly. Everything flashed into his sight and quickly disappeared. He tried searching with his eyes but failed. "Dowen, where are you?!" he called out.

Someone grabbed him from behind. "Laithrum, I was looking for you. Thank you for speaking; I cannot see well," said Dowen, greatly relieved to have found him safe. "Are you injured?"

"Besides my sight and feeling like I've been whiplashed and suffocated, I'm fine. This is my second time being thrown into the sea," Laithrum said lightheartedly. "How about you, Dowen? Are you injured?" he asked, rubbing the salt water from his eyes.

"I'll be fine. The shock from the fall was the worst of it. Luckily, I wasn't struck by a board or something. Our vision should return soon; mine already is. Laithrum?"

"Yes, I can see clearly now. My vision isn't sharp, but it's good enough," he said calmly, moving his legs and arms to check for injuries. Nothing seemed harmed enough to keep him from returning to battle. The eerie sound of battle soon cried from above.

The two started looking around for anyone else. Soon, a figure with long black hair came into view. They recognized her immediately, and she saw them as well. The three swam toward each other. Dowen spoke first, noticing something strange.

"You are an IseamA, right? I understand your people can take more physical impact than humans, but to come out of this without a scratch is almost unbelievable. What happened? It couldn't just be luck… Was it?" he asked suspiciously.

She answered reluctantly, "It was not because I am an IseamA, nor was it mere luck." She then lifted a chain from the water, revealing two-winged figures holding a large, glowing red stone.

"This is a blessed ruby. It has the power to protect me from dangers like what just happened." Yiyumiss paused, then shifted the topic. "Do you know where the others are? The redhead with the Gourin accent and the elf who fired the arrow are missing." Her mind drifted at the memory of Onlortrens; she longed to meet the elf. His colored magic, a shade of green, signified his noble status and great power.

"Yiyumiss?" Laithrum's voice brought her back. "Will you find Linus and Onlortrens, the elf you saw? Ensure they are safe and help them if needed. Dowen, are you well enough to return with me to the battle overhead?" The young prince's words refocused their thoughts on the immediate troubles.

Dowen nodded in response, his respect for Laithrum growing with each interaction. Yiyumiss pulled herself onto a large piece of wood leftover from Derdin. "You two, don't get yourselves killed, alright? I don't want to have to die just for the pleasure of scolding you in the afterlife." With concern for both, she turned and leaped powerfully from one piece of floating debris to another, soon disappearing.

Onlortrens and Raven ended up on the other half of the vessel. Onlortrens was safe, having shielded himself with magic as he fell. Raven, however, had been stabbed in the back by a broken piece of wood. The shard had fallen out, and the wound didn't seem too severe. They climbed onto a wooden platform of the broken ship, gazing at the vessel last crashed into by the dark ship.

"So, Onlortrens, what should we do now that Laithrum's gone?" teased Raven, showing no fear or grief. He winced from the pain but concealed his worry well.

"We will find him," Onlortrens replied, understanding Raven's true intent. He hoped Laithrum was still alive.

Switching to his native elfin language, which Raven had learned long ago, he said, "Laithrum would return to battle if he were alive and well. That is what I'll do. Your choice is your own. I wouldn't suggest coming with me since you're hurt." The elf waited for Raven's response, hoping his reasoning would reveal Raven's true motives. Even Onlortrens hadn't fully understood his purpose.

"About being hurt; I don't care! I've decided to help you, wherever you're going, until we reach land. There, I'll make my final decision. For now…" He looked up at Onlortrens, despite his efforts to hide his true feelings, Raven's eyes portraying nervousness and weakness. "You lead the way, Onlortrens. I will follow."

Onlortrens couldn't predict what choice Raven would make upon reaching land. He couldn't even guess why Raven had stolen the sword or what he was fleeing from when they first met. Maybe he was still running from it now. After a moment of reflection, Onlortrens decided there was little time for discussion but chose to ask, "Do you know why I am here?"

Raven shook his head, waiting to learn.

"Just know this. I am here because of something more important than you, more important than me, and yes, even Laithrum. As you follow me, understand that my commitment is absolute," Onlortrens declared firmly, his words carrying weight without bitterness. He simply withheld his kindness.

With weightless feet, Onlortrens leaped to another flat of boards. A short jump for him was a long one for Raven. Raven, experienced jumping great distances, managed to follow without trouble. Soon, they had no choice but to swim through the reeking, black water and climb onto the side of a Thuthairryon ship, adjacent to the ghostly vessel.

Yiyumiss continued her search for Linus and Onlortrens. Dripping with water, she looked around. Her bright-blue, sharp eyes, more like a cat's than a human's, scanned the area. Her hair, stretching to her knees, was tied at mid-back by a cloth strap, with shorter strands framing her face.

She finally spotted a figure with short red hair, standing with one leg bent as if hurt. Yiyumiss then looked at what he was staring at. What could be important enough for him to stand for?

She saw the person. He looked eerily familiar; someone she had met long ago. Remembering the disagreeable meeting, she leaped forward, urgently rushing to her disappointing reunion.

The figure was Linus, sword drawn, waiting for the stranger to make a move.

"Who are you?" Linus asked, trying to buy time, hoping someone would come to help.

The white-haired, dark-green-eyed human shaped being had clean, smooth skin. Easily recognized as male, he moved as daintily as a gentle lady, but some build masculine and had a deeper voice. He wore a gray and dark-red coat tied in the middle. Much too fancy for this setting.

When he spoke, his voice grew deeper and increased in malice. "Who I am doesn't matter, but you wouldn't know where the elf, Onlortrens, is. You're clearly a nobody. Therefore, you are of no use to me." With those words, he lifted his sword. Quickly jumping forward, he swung it down, missing Linus' head but hitting his arm, sending him down in pain.

Linus clutched his bloodied left arm, the shallow cut running from his shoulder to just above the elbow. Blood and seawater mingled, dripping from his stained hands. He noticed the enemy's frustrated expression and realized, with astonishment, that the slash had missed his head entirely by accident. His opponent was inexperienced with the sword, or just terrible at it.

The stranger's eyes flashed as he swung his sword again, but before it could reach Linus, Yiyumiss intervened. She blocked the attack with her short blade, pushing the assailant off balance. To avoid falling into the water, he leaped lightly to another cluster of floating boards.

"An IseamA!" he exclaimed. "What is a beastwoman doing in a human battle?" His playful tone belied the evil in his slender eyes.

Yiyumiss glared at him. "Leave or come and die!" she yelled. "Those are your only options." Without taking her eyes off the mocker, she helped Linus up from the swaying platform.

The enemy was not easily threatened. He leaped like an arrow over the water toward Yiyumiss, his body led by his sword. Yiyumiss pushed Linus down to fight freely. She raised her sword just in time to block, but the force of his leap sent them both into the sea. Linus watched the water, praying she was safe.

Under the bright surface, they continued their fight, both having lost their swords in the dive. They grappled with locked fists. Yiyumiss managed to lift her legs and place them on his chest, pushing him away with her claws. A fog of red filled the water from his wound, but as she swam to follow her attack she had to stop. Her eyes were met with a field of golden flowers. It took only a blink to dispel the illusion. He worked with illusions; it was his gift, his means of escape. As she broke the surface, he was already gone, likely fled to the dark-faced vessel.

"Are you alright?!" cried Linus, fearing she had been killed and that the enemy had simply forgotten him.

Yiyumiss swam over and pulled herself onto the platform. "Do you know where your elfin friend is, the one named Onlortrens?" she asked, her mind preoccupied with the recent events.

"I don't know. If he's alive, he's likely looking for Laithrum," answered Linus, then quickly added, "What was he? He seems to bother you quite a lot."

"His face resembled someone I met two years ago; it was unsettling. Though I can't say 'just like,' as they had different features. This boy looked manlier than the one I met back then. People change a lot in two years. The person I met before was just as mischievous. Who creates illusions of fields and flowers? As for your other question, he was a Julrainzak, a people who usually fight with their minds and magic, not swords. They have various magical abilities; some create wings, others strong illusions, but all cannot heal well. This one fights by playing tricks, trying to make his opponents walk off cliffs or similar traps to kill them."

"I don't know much about different races, like yours. If we have time later, I'd love to hear about your culture."

"I'd love to share."

Yiyumiss' expression darkened as she looked up at the dark ship with hatred. It had turned the water black, and the air was filled with a sulfur-like odor.

"We must get back up there. Can you use your leg?"

He began to stand. "Yes."

She turned her back to him, crouched, closed the gap, and lifted Linus onto her back. "Hold on," she commanded, leaping from one floating platform to another until she could claw into a Thuthairryon vessel. They climbed aboard the same vessel Laithrum and Dowen had ventured upon earlier.

The two then parted ways. Linus went in search of Troi Onturner, the main doctor on his ship. He had been moved for a special needs patient before the battle. Yiyumiss charged into battle, searching for Laithrum, Dowen, and mostly Onlortrens.

CHAPTER 10

They Come Together

Superficial injuries and muscular fatigue were slowing them down rapidly. Laithrum backed away behind Dowen to catch his breath between bouts. In doing so, he caught sight of Onlortrens and Raven climbing aboard far to his right. The pleasant reunion turned into a grim observation. On the dark ship, Laithrum noticed a band of enemies aiming a harpoon intentionally downward at Onlortrens.

In a swift, impetuous movement, Laithrum darted forward. Reaching the end of the Thuthairryon ship, he leaped toward the dark vessel, thrusting his long carving knife into its side. The ship, poorly constructed, offered many holds for his feet and hands when climbing. He scaled the ship's side until his foot reached a sturdy outcropping. Using the sturdy board he jumped for the handrail, he grabbed it and pulled himself onto the dark ship's deck. With two quick bounds, he was upon the enemies. Swinging his blade fiercely he mutilated the creature's weapon before it could fire.

Dowen quickly followed his acquaintance onto the dark ship's deck. Onlortrens and Raven watched the shy, inexperienced prince with pleased astonishment. Though amazed, they had expected such bravery.

Onlortrens, unlike Raven, did not laugh at Laithrum's predicament. His concern was too great for what would happen next. With much effort, Onlortrens gracefully leaped across the water, landing silently on the dark vessel's rough, thorny deck. The distance was too far for Raven to attempt jumping, leaving him to watch the battle from afar; or climb.

Laithrum ducked as a sword flew over his head. Losing his balance, he fell to his back and desperately swung his sword into the nearest man's foot.

The men on the ominous ship no longer resembled humans. Their faces were distorted, and they acted like wild animals, perhaps driven insane by disease. Their age was indiscernible; they all looked the same.

Laithrum was then attacked by the man who had aimed the harpoon. Before the enemy's sword could complete the strike, an arrow pierced his skull. He hurled to the ground, no longer a threat. Laithrum stared at the man who had nearly ended his life. The man head pillowed by a pool of blood, cold eyes staring blankly. The trade of his own life versed this man's life didn't feel fair.

Present awareness returned swiftly as Onlortrens pulled him up to his feet.

The young prince turned his head just before a sinjar dove at him. The sinjar's sword swung, causing Laithrum to lose balance again. The creature's sword ripped apart the deck where he had been standing.

Jumping back to his feet, Laithrum removed a hand from his sword and with his fingers and mouth blew a shrill whistle. The sound hurt the beast's ears, disorienting it and forcing it to land. Laithrum quickly clenched his sword and resumed the battle.

The beast charged angerly toward him but couldn't stand against both Laithrum and Onlortrens.

***

Inside the ominous ship, the atmosphere was dim, foggy, and uncomfortable in every way. The halls were uneven, and the wood was splintery and dry. The temperature changed from hot into cold in waves as if it breathed in cold and breathed out hot. In the deepest part of the ship, the captives were guarded by beings of greater intelligence than the mutant men fighting above. They were weresynics, like Laithrum, but evil and unnatural.

In one of the four cells was a man with gnarled, light-colored hair. The only light came from the greenish, glowing fog pouring over rims of large stone bowls attached to the walls. The figure looked down the hall, noting the guard's unusually long absence. As the guard came back into view, the thoughtful prisoner teased, "I was becoming worried. What kept you? Are you alright?"

The prisoner hung his arms over the crossbars of the cell's square holes. "Be quiet!" yelled the creature, its voice so rough it was barely intelligible. It glared at the man with livid, pale green and brown eyes devoid of whites. Its eyes surrounded by bright red skin that faded into a dark color; dull and sickly looking.

"If you wish to live another day, you'll stay quiet!" it warned, stringy white hair falling into its face.

"I must mock your threat," the prisoner replied. "I clearly remember your leader saying not to harm me. What will happen if I do not remain silent? Will you risk your life for a moment of pleasure? Harming me would be foolish."

The large, dark mixed-blooded creature laughed cruelly. "Foolish, you say? It's amusing, considering you did the same in your own country, Prince Adeyas. You're here because you let your anger get the best of you and killed someone you shouldn't have." His eyes glowed brighter with malevolent intent.

With one arm, he ripped off the wooden gate and, before Adeyas could react, lifted him against the ceiling.

"I will crush your bones one by one, and no one on this ship can save you." He laughed with a crooked smile, pressing Adeyas harder against the splintery boards.

Adeyas didn't wait long to act. He struck under the creature's pointy elbow, targeting a glowing red piece of flesh where the nerves were over sensitized.

The creature's grip loosened, and Adeyas seized the sword from its waist. The beast, regaining its senses, swung its arm to backhand Adeyas. Swiftly, Adeyas dropped to the ground and, with a leap, stabbed the blade through the creature's stomach, which was at the prince's shoulder level. Adeysas rested his raging thoughts momentarily. Did he defeat this huge creature? Was he free?

The white-haired weresynic's eyes glowed brighter as he spun and struck Adeyas, sending him flying down the hall. Adeyas' body hit the rough ground twenty feet away. The creature, pulling the sword from its middle and stomped toward Adeyas. It should have died from the wound. Adeyas' fear and astonishment froze him.

As the threat plodded closer, Adeyas stood up, mind racing. He couldn't win against such strength with his speed alone. Desperately, he glanced at a stone-bowl light. He grabbed it and threw it at the approaching monster, then darted down the hall.

The enraged creature hit the bowl out of its way, shattering it against the wall and filling the air with colored fog. Nothing could be seen. Expecting a surprise attack, it stood ready, but when the smoke cleared, it found itself alone in the hallway. Furious, it squealed, causing its dry skin to crack and bleed around its eyes.

He charged forward, only to find empty air and some of his own kind. In fury, he struck at his comrades, starting a fight. Adeyas found a torn blanket and threw it over his shoulders and head. Even a weak disguised was better than none. Moving more quickly than his body sustained, Adeyas climbed stairs and cleared halls. He had to avoid the vessel's leader, a young-looking, white-haired Julrainzak.

He crept down the last hall and bolted the last few stairs. Knowing he was close to the battle because of the sounds. After a couple steps more, he found a dead Thuthairryon soldier, clearly dragged from a distance. After lowering his head in respect and remorse, he took the soldier's sword and continued his search for safety.

Adeyas walked through faded wood doors into the dimmed brightness of the overcast weather. The deck was darkened further by the ominous cloud radiating from the vessel, its cause still unknown. He saw a Thuthairryon ship not far from the unwelcoming deck. Despite his bruises, his hunger, and his natural limitations he believed fully he could make the jump. He had too.

Just as he stepped forward, he was sprung upon from behind. A wild man with a small dagger brought Adeyas to the ground, knocking the sword from his hand while carelessly cutting his own. The attacker raised his unharmed hand, the dagger gleaming through the gloom.

As the enemy's arm descended, Adeyas shot up his unpinned arm to block the strike. Then he swiftly pushed the attacker off. Sitting up he followed the enemy's body. He eased his opponent forcibly with one arm and slammed his other elbow into the man's skull, knocking him out cold. Adeyas quickly retrieved his sword, sprang to his feet, and darted toward the other ship.

As he ran, a light caught his eye—something simple and pure he hadn't seen in a long time. He stopped, gazing at the source. It was Onlortrens' elfin light, fighting alongside another soldier who looked familiar. Without further delay, Adeyas refocused on his goal and sprinted at full speed.

Suddenly, he felt a presence behind him. Turning, he saw an enemy's blade plummeting down. A cold white light flashed before his eyes, but after the shock, he saw the man on the ground, an arrow piercing through him. Surprised but grateful, Adeyas hesitated. Another arrow flew in, hitting the ground near his foot, snapping him out of his daze.

Without further delay, he sprinted to the other ship, leaping across with all his might. As he crossed into the light, the brightness shocked his eyes and sent him falling to the ground. Onlortrens watched him fall, understanding why. The elf did not worry. Even if injured from the fall, Adeyas was safer now.

Overall, Onlortrens was surprised by Prince Adeyas Airslens' sudden appearance, but recalled Lotus' story of his capture. It made enough sense not to ponder.

"Laithrum!" called Onlortrens as he stepped closer. Now fighting closing side by side. He continued, "I need you to hold on to something. It makes firing my arrows too slow." With a purposeful swing of his sword, he struck the last nearby enemy soldier.

Onlortrens quickly tied the wrapped, clearly sheathed, sword over Laithrum's shoulder and around his waist.

Onlortrens backed away, and Laithrum glanced at him, then back at the battle. After a few more glances back and forth, he asked, "What is this?" referring to the item, partially upset by the extra weight.

"It's a test. I want to see if you can hold on to it," the elf replied in a slightly cheerful, teasing voice. Laithrum, flabbergasted by the idea of a test and the playful tone in such a dire situation, had to accept Onlortrens actions for now.

The battle raged on, men and mutant corpses staining the decks with blood. Dragons and sinjar lay scattered, dead on the decks and in the water. There were no signs of the battle ceasing.

The Thuthairryon ships fed each other men by lowering ramps. Lines of bowmen, both long and short range, positioned themselves in straight lines and, on command, began to fire. The rain of arrows, carefully aimed, sang through the air, and mowed down enemy soldiers on the dark ship and any enemy visible on the Thuthairryon decks.

***

There was a brief pause, giving Raven enough time to board the dark ship and run up to Onlortrens. Dowen also approached from the other side.

"Laithrum, I'm glad to see you standing," Dowen said.

"Dowen, you should be glad to see yourself still alive," Raven drawled, surprisingly with a hint of kindness amongst the rude sarcasm.

"Are you alright?" was all Dowen could think of asking. Raven looked dizzy and moved strangely.

Raven glared bitterly, then his expression softened. "I'm a lot better than you're going to be very soon," he said, honestly but cryptically.

Onlortrens clarified, "Raven isn't threatening you. He senses what I do. This battle isn't over. But it is about to change." He looked at Raven. "I need you to do something for me," he continued telepathically, sharing an important secret. Raven nodded and ran off.

Laithrum was about to ask where Raven was going when a loud, uneasy sound emanated from the ship's interior. The noise, with its many pitches, soon became unbearable. They covered their ears as the sound caused the beasts, sinjars, and neintoe dragons to grunt and thrash against the walls. The flying beasts landed hastily to regain their bearings.

Hearing the panicking sinjars from inside the dark vessel added to the growing apprehension. Dowen stepped back in fear. "How many sinjars could still be inside?"

Laithrum looked at Onlortrens, "Where did you send Raven?" He disliked that Raven had left, as it weakened their force.

Onlortrens didn't answer. His intense focus muted Laithrum's question; his eyes were closed, and his hands were folded high in front of him. His elfin glow brightened, transforming into an enchanting green light.

The gates of the evil ship burst open, sending wood and debris flying. Sinjar poured out. With a soft yell, Onlortrens sent the gate's roof crashing down with magic beyond Laithrum's imagination.

Behind them, a neintoe dragon landed, ridden by Raven. He jumped off quickly. "Dowen, you know how to fly one of these. So, I was told," he said, gesturing to the large beast.

Dowen ran over to the dragon and Raven. "How did you get him so quickly?" Dowen asked as Thuthairryons with shields formed an unwavering wall before them.

Raven looked away, then abruptly replied, "You might figure it out someday! The answer will most likely not come from me!" He hastily ran closer to the others to engage in battle. Dowen climbed onto the dragon, placing his legs between its two sets of wings, ensuring they wouldn't be snapped off or crushed during flight.

The beast took to the sky, and Dowen joined the aerial battle. The Thuthairryon men below depended on the dragon riders to control the sinjar, while the dragon riders relied on them to prevent harpoons, crossbows, and longbows from firing.

It had become clear to all the Thuthairryon and Seintroven; this enemy was against both sides. The two forces teamed and fought vigorously in this final, brutal wave of battle. The Thuthairryon bowmen did well to prevent the mutants from advancing too far into the other ships.

Laithrum, Onlortrens, and Raven were soon joined by Yiyumiss. She stood at the front as a shield, nervously hoping her red rock would continue to defend her even why abusing its power this way. It had refused to protect her in the past, but this time it seemed to grow stronger.

The enemy thinned, surprising them, as there could have been many more on such a colossal ship. People surveyed the area. They looked for signs of a surprise attack, enemy stragglers, and anything suspicious. Nothing was found. The battle painted the decks red, and the water was heavily scattered with bodies, but the signs of the new enemy were gone.

Shortly, after Yiyumiss arrived, the entire dark ship began to shake. The shaking caused the reaching to cease and the medical care to pause; fear and wonder replaced everyone's thoughts. What could move such a massive vessel?

Laithrum looked at the ship's sheltering top. A deep moan emanated from inside and beneath them, making the boards vibrate rapidly. Laithrum took two steps back and shouted, "Everyone retreat from this vessel, quickly!"

Without delay, Laithrum and the others darted to the Thuthairryon ship's deck. Spooked, the other men followed quickly. Right after the last Thuthairryon soldier made it off, the entire body of the dark ship exploded upward in many pieces. The ship, except the sails, was destroyed. The sails lifted, stretching into the air, and then, with great force, pushed down, sending a strong gust across the water. The ships turned and thrashed and nearly capsized. A huge black dragon rose from the blackened ocean; the ship's broken pieces raining down with the water.

The dragon looked at the ships in front of it, then turned its pointy snout and long, thin horns to the side. Yiyumiss, with her sharp vision, spotted a figure on top of its head—it was the Julrainzak she had fought earlier.

"He's getting away!" Yiyumiss growled as she watched the black dragon fly upward and past their ship to the next. It grabbed two Thuthairryon ships with its talons, lifting them only to hurl them back down onto other ships below.

Laithrum stood in shock at the losses around him. His mind was shaken as he realized the battle was over, they survived. If that dragon stayed, they wouldn't have won. But now what? Honestly, he never expected to survive this battle. Why was he so much stronger? Change like this is impossible; isn't it?

Laithrum looked up at the gray sky, a familiar question in his mind. Why did he leave home? Was this venture worth it? Although his body ached and his emotions fluttered, he felt better than ever.

As he looked around, his spirit sank at the sight of so much death and destruction. When he saw Onlortrens, he remembered the item the elf had tied to his back.

"Onlortrens," he called, "What is this item you placed on my back? Am I allowed to take it off?"

"I will tell you at a more settling time. For now, we should see if all our friends are still with us," Onlortrens replied.

Laithrum nodded in agreement. It was better to wait for a less hectic time. A time when his mind wouldn't jump to thoughts of his friends' and his home, mostly his sister. The two walked away and quickly found Yiyumiss, who knew where Linus and Lotus were. Though she could only guess about their survival. They knew Raven was alive but injured, as he had been with them when they jumped from the now-destroyed ship. Dowen followed them, riding the neintoe dragon Raven had fetched from the far ship's stable. Unbeknownst to them, Adeyas was already with Troi and Linus.

CHAPTER 11

Finding One's Place

Men quickly parted as the neintoe dragon, carrying Dowen, strolled through. The dragon's wings had sunken into its back, appearing as four long spikes spearing out from its body. Dowen's legs sat right behind the first set of spikes, his body bent over the animal's back.

"Laithrum, Onlortrens," Dowen called as he rode up behind the prince, elf, and IseamA. "I feel the need to bring Lotus back to this ship. So, if it's not a problem, will you two wait here for my return?" He paused as his eyes caught sight of Yiyumiss, who looked annoyed. "Oh, I'm sorry. Will you three wait here for your friend?"

"Yes," Laithrum answered, his chest heaving from lingering adrenaline, "but I can only speak for myself. I cannot answer for Onlortrens or Yiyumiss." He turned his golden eyes to them.

Dowen's eyes followed Laithrum's to Onlortrens, who gestured for Yiyumiss to speak first. She did. "I will stay here with Laithrum and wait for Lotus." She then turned to Onlortrens, guessing his response. "Since I am staying, elf, I'm guessing you will be going to find our other friends, right? Especially because you know they are injured." She waited for his remark; hoping her instincts were right.

Onlortrens lowered his chin and closed his eyes, finalizing his plan and the actions he needed to take. After strategizing, he lifted his head and reopened his eyes.

"Your guess is mostly correct. I have no need to explain things," the elf replied plainly. Onlortrens turned back to Laithrum. "I will meet you in the healing room, and there I will explain what I can about the questions you might have." He watched Laithrum carefully.

After a long, thoughtful pause, Laithrum nodded, though he had much to say. The Thuthairryon prince sensed something strange was afoot. Was it something he saw or heard, or was it something he would soon be part of? Laithrum glimpsed the path ahead, but it made too little sense to comprehend.

"Good," interrupted Dowen. "I would like to hear all this conversation. So as not to delay it longer, I will go now and not take long." He spoke from his elevated perch, three to four feet higher than if he sat upon a horse.

Dowen lay further down against the dragon's back, slipping his hands under the two horns that swayed out to the side of the dragon's head. He gripped the coarse hairs attached to the most sensitive skin, making it the only place to steer the powerful beast during battle. Dowen turned around, carefully maneuvering so that the long tail avoided hitting anyone nearby.

Laithrum watched the Neintoe Dragon sprout wings and lift off from the deck. He briefly wondered what riding a dragon would be like, but no single thought held for long. Laithrum and Yiyumiss leaned over the ship's railing. They talked off and on about pointless things that came to mind, but even with nonsense topics, they remained mostly silent.

Dowen, had almost reached his destination before he noticed his senses. The weather was mostly sunny, neither hot nor cold, with a soft breeze. This beautiful weather did not belong to such a day. While soaring, he surveyed the damage. At least some ships didn't look broken.

As the small dragon glided closer to the destination, Dowen focused on the ship's landing deck. He smiled when he saw it wasn't damaged. He rode straight down to the deck and landed by some other riders standing by their tamed creatures. The dragon's wings retracted instantly after landing.

Dowen jumped off its back. "Fellow riders," he called to the men, trying to distract their troubled minds. "Do either of you know Shyjule?"

One of the men looked puzzled, but the other ran up to him. "Teirlandus Shyjule?" the soldier confirmed.

"Yes, Teirlandus Shyjule. Do you know him?" Dowen questioned. After a moment, the soldier recognized him. "Commander Dowen Kackveriage?" he said in surprise and quickly answered, "The man you're looking for is down in the stables, sir."

Dowen thanked the soldier and headed in that direction. Upon arriving at the Neintoe Dragon stables, Dowen found Teirlandus quickly.

"Shyjule," Dowen spoke sternly from behind him. Chills ran down the soldier's spine when he heard Dowen's voice, yet he calmly turned to face him. "Commander, you came back quickly."

"Surprised, Teirlandus?" Dowen said teasingly. He watched the soldier look down, filled with anxiety.

"Well, sir," Shyjule started, standing straight and as confidently as he could, "I am guessing that you came to get that man you brought in."

Shyjule started down the sloping ramp. Dowen followed, asking, "Did he wake up while here?"

"No, he did not. I was looking forward to meeting the man who could make two men swim that distance during a battle. I do have a question about him. If you will tell me, I would like to know his full name. All I know is his first name, Lotus," he said, nervous of the answer.

Dowen, noticing his fearful expression, commanded, "What do you think his name is, and what or whom do you fear?"

Shyjule stepped off the ramp and answered, "If his last name is Florissurnna, I heard something from some other soldiers. They said that some of the ship commanders were looking for him. It wasn't for anything positive; even I could tell." He paused, then asked, "Do you know the reason why?"

Dowen jumped off the ramp and answered, "No, but we did find Lotus half-dead in the water from the last battle. They might have just been looking for their man. How long ago was the search?"

"Just heard of it, sir. I do not know when it started. The tune behind the messenger did not portray caring concern." The soldier answered truthfully. But they both understood the situation the same. Shyjule continued leading the way to where he had put Lotus. Lotus was still asleep when they arrived. Dowen didn't hesitate to carry him out to the Neintoe Dragon that waited on deck.

"May the winds be kind, Commander, though it is unfitting that today is so beautiful," said Shyjule as the dragon's two sets of wings shot out from the four spikes. Dowen grinned broadly at the comment, thinking the exact same thing earlier.

Neither spoke again before the dragon took off into the sky.

Lotus lay under Dowen's chest, draped over the dragon's neck like a scarf. The clouds began to dissipate, letting the brightness wash over the ships and water.

The light touched Lotus's eyes, waking him. He leaned to his right side and started looking around. Was he still dreaming. He was flying. Calming down, Lotus realized that he managed to survive the battle.

They landed back on the ship where Laithrum and Yiyumiss were waiting. Dowen lifted his hand to call them over. They ran quickly to him. With folded wings, the Neintoe Dragon walked closer. Dowen lowered Lotus to Laithrum, who was waiting with his hands outstretched. After transferring Lotus, Dowen jumped to the ground.

"Go on back to the ship you belong to, girl," Dowen said to the dragon before following the others. Soon, he reclaimed his place as the brace for Lotus. Though he soon found that Lotus barely needed help anymore.

The current ship was much different than the one first stationed on. The design was simpler, the boards plainly cut and of a different, lesser quality wood.

The company found directions to the healing room. The first person they saw was Troi Onturner. Troi quickly ran over when he saw Dowen bracing Lotus.

"Was he injured in the battle?" the doctor asked, worried, while looking at the young man's strengthening body.

Dowen answered directly, "No, he has been asleep throughout the battle, so I have been told. I am glad to see you survived, Troi."

Troi sighed at Dowen's words, turning his mind back to his work but keeping a positive tone. He replied with a separate topic, "Sleep was good for recovery. At least we know he was able to rest and be safe." Troi then gestured for Dowen to lead him into a more hidden room. The entrance was too small for carrying injured. What could room be for?

Troi then said to Laithrum, "The elf Onlortrens Silvertree is waiting for you inside. He told me that you would all be coming."

"Thank you, Troi," Laithrum said tiredly, yet he maintained the pristine manners he had been taught. Troi slid open the narrow door for the group to enter the separate, almost mysterious room. As Laithrum stepped through the door, Onlortrens greeted him.

"Laithrum, you should be looked at by a doctor. I would suggest Troi. Though this skirmish you're collected many injuries, and you will notice them before the day is over; your mind will replay all that happened."

Laithrum looked down, sickened by some of the memories. But, yes, he was still numb from shock. The images played tricks on his sight, appearing and disappearing, and events from earlier were distorted. He was unaware of the shaking throughout his body. His hands, knees, and eyes rattled visibly. But for now, his body was sensationless; not even could he smell. This did not make sense to him, but only a few things did in this place.

Onlortrens continued speaking to Laithrum, "The Ellowvast," Laithrum eyes widen sharply, startled at the foreign yet familiar word. He had heard it before, but its origin remained unknown. The elf continued to explain, "The item I placed on your back. Ellowvast is what it is called."

"Ellowvast," Laithrum repeated. His eyes caught the motion of Dowen walking up to them. Dowen inquired, "Did I already miss most of your conversation? I was talking with Lotus, who seems to be just fine."

"No, we just started, I…" the elf was then interrupted by another familiar voice.

"I'm over here hurt, not over here dead," Linus said cheerily yet tiredly. He calmly stood up from his bed, his left arm bandaged and held bent by a thick cloth band.

"Linus," Dowen said, returning Linus' cheerfulness in his own voice. "You're looking great." He laughed at his companion's interruption and the state of Linus' normally straight red hair. Linus' hair flared out, stretching and bending in every direction, like wind striking a flame.

Dowen turned back to Onlortrens. "It seems like you bear all of us as a burden, again," Dowen mocked as the elf's face fell, expressing disappointment. He truly needed a break, or burnout with going to defeat him.

Onlortrens focused on all of them. He wondered how this company had formed over such a short time; so diverse and yet with the potential to become functional.

Linus soon interrupted Onlortrens' thoughts, "And, as you know, Onlortrens, there's now one more person you need to include here." Linus then glanced at the bed beside his former one. At that moment, Adeyas turned his body over and opened his deep blue eyes. His gaze passed over them and stopped at Laithrum's golden gaze.

"Yes, Laithrum, your brother," Linus started. A lock of red hair fell back over his brow before he continued, "He escaped from the dark vessel…that was actually a full-sized dragon." Although spoken to, Laithrum never lifted his sight from Adeyas. He was too surprised to do anything else.

Dowen had taken a step back from Laithrum, gasping in shock, "Brother?" Pausing, he then asked to clarify what he had just heard, "Laithrum, the youngest son of King Niejill Airslen?" Laithrum nodded and shut his eyes tightly. He did not know what to do about

Dowen knowing as well. Laithrum pleaded, in a desperate voice and spirit racing around the unknown, "Please Dowen, do not tell anyone. I do not wish to be treated like a prince here. I was not treated like a prince at home, and don't want any more trouble out here. Not now."

Dowen looked intently at Laithrum, his voice tinged with sadness. "I would like to ask you so many things. I will wait, not to ask, but to be told. I can't act against my values. I will listen to and report to you, but I will keep your identity a secret."

He then turned to the group. "How many of you already knew who Laithrum was?"

Adeyas was the first to raise his hand. "I had been suspicious for a long time. I am glad to know I was correct in my assumption," he said sarcastically about his half-brother. Adeyas quickly continued in a more serious tone, "Laithrum, unfortunate for him, has been found out. But if we continue speaking like this, more people will know. Let us forget it was brought up and move on—now it is time to hear what Onlortrens was going to say about the sword on Laithrum's back. I very eager to know."

Laithrum agreed, eager to learn more about the mysterious item. After this, a silence fell over the room—not from negative feelings or surprise, but because no one chose to speak after Adeyas. The only person permitted to speak now was Onlortrens.

Dowen stared at each of them with his slate eyes, waiting for someone to speak. As expected, Linus spoke first, addressing Laithrum and Onlortrens. "If it is not too much of a problem, can we all be included in your discussion? Onlortrens, are you going to pick up where you left off?"

Laithrum turned to face Onlortrens, waiting for the elf's answer. Laithrum wanted clarity. His questions have sat for a long while and didn't know you should or should not know. Onlortrens knew the answers and had promised this discussion.

Onlortrens did not answer immediately, though the longer he paused the more intensely people stared. Laithrum and the elf exchanged glances. Onlortrens, telepathically, told Laithrum that it was his choice: to speak broadly as a group or to delve deeply into the issue.

The prince's golden eyes lowered for a moment. His mind raced through thoughts and questions. What should he do first? Should he speak seriously with Onlortrens or engage in group conversation to learn what happened to his brother?

"We shall all speak. My own questions can wait until we are not already gathered." This firm decision surprised Adeyas. He had not forgotten his brother—he was tired and weak and didn't often make decisions.

Dowen spoke next, taking a deep breath. "Well, we should get the others, and then introduce ourselves to Prince Adeyas."

Linus nodded, though he disliked the idea of seeing Raven again. Adeyas sat up in his bed, slightly surprised. "You mean there are more in this group? Not just the four of you and Yiyumiss?" He looked over at Laithrum. "I am confused. Who are you, really? To guess that you are in a company of more than two is unbelievable. But still, is it true?" His face remained upright, though his eyes reflected much distress.

"Yes, there are others," Laithrum started slowly, "if you want their count, it three."

After Prince Adeyas was answered, he commanded hastily, "Well, do not just stand there, go. Go off and bring back your friends so I can meet this odd fellowship in its entirety."

As he spoke, Linus and Dowen stood at attention. When the prince finished, both bowed and ran to complete their orders; Yiyumiss casually followed as well.

Laithrum smiled as he watched. His sister had been treated this way, and the memories of her were comforting and painful. He thought deeply about their home. Maybe he could glimpse what happened. The images were all so blurry but that fact that something terrible happened was clear.

"Laithrum," Adeyas said, his tone and expression changed. Once he had Laithrum's attention, he continued, his voice hard and his glare cold. "Before I start, sit down on Louleyossa's former bed before you fall to the floor."

Laithrum hadn't noticed his knees bending from exhaustion. He did as his older brother instructed and sat on the thin bed. Onlortrens stepped closer to clearly hear what Adeyas had to say.

"Laithrum, what are you doing here?! Were you sent away? And if so, for what reason? Why did you leave Freyja alone in that place where chaos was growing so quickly?" He paused, trying to settle his growing, passionate anger. "AND WHAT IS ANOTHER 'DEMON…!'" The words burst forth without being fully directed at Laithrum. Adeyas clenched his teeth to stop himself. He then continued, more controlled, "What are you doing here in Thuthairryon's armies?!"

Laithrum was stunned, fear and confusion from the outburst left him speechless. Adeyas continued, but now his body language and words were melancholy.

"Why did you have to leave home? You're sickly, you always have been. Being out here will just kill you. I—I…" Adeyas stopped, his gaze heading downward. He saw and thought nothing, but he shook from an unexplainable feeling; much of it was worry, but the rest he could not identify. Maybe it was rage.

Laithrum sat frozen, his eyes round and filled with more emotions than he had ever felt before. Soon his eyes fell like his brother's, but he was in deliberate thought, not confusion. "Brother, I am no longer ill. Something happened. I can breathe and be in the outside air without worry of illness."

Prince Adeyas Airslen picked up his head, light blond hair covering half his face. He stared at Laithrum for a time, then asked, "How could that be?"

"I am not entirely sure, but I believe Onlortrens knows," he said, looking over at the elf who had been carefully watching and ready to defend if needed. "He said he would answer my questions. All the ones he knows the answers to, in any case."

Turning to the elf for verification, Onlortrens reassured, "Yes, I will answer the questions I can, and also some of the questions that you might have, Prince Adeyas Airslen." He felt a need to offer after seeing some of the tension tied up inside him. Watching this reminded Onlortrens of another…

"I thank you," Adeyas answered, looking down, reluctant to even think of an apology to give Laithrum for his outburst. That display of tension was only a small percentage of what was bundled inside.

A short time later, Dowen re-entered the room where Laithrum, Onlortrens, and Adeyas were waiting. After walking in, he could feel the situation. There was still a thickness in the air from Adeyas' outburst and the tension that followed.

Lotus, fully awake and moving well, came in with Linus. Lotus looked over at Adeyas with a smile on his face and brightness in his eyes. Although soon after seeing Adeyas, a sharp pain hit him; the sharp pain was caused by memory. Remembering the events that happened back on that ship quickly soured any joy felt.

Yiyumiss silently walked in behind Linus and Lotus; Raven followed after Yiyumiss. Raven was surprisingly easy to find. Stranger still, he agreed to go with them without fuss.

"What happened here?" asked Dowen about the tenseness in the air, or whatever it was.

Onlortrens looked over at Dowen. "Something between brothers. It has been resolved for now, so do not pry."

Dowen looked surprised. "Already? Siblings are amazing that way," he sighed. "My brothers and I hold on to the most trivial things for ages. In the end, though, we are always there for each other."

Linus laughed. "I never had too much trouble with my siblings." Dowen and Onlortrens both gave him strange looks. They struggled to believe him. "So serious," Linus continued, "maybe there really is *strength in numbers*."

"Well, how many do you have? I have three brothers," Dowen argued.

Linus, not liking where this might be headed, answered reluctantly, "I have thirteen siblings."

Dowen stepped back, astonished. "I never would have guessed you came from such a big family."

Linus was about to reply when Raven stepped out from behind them, moving to Linus's side. "Is this why you called me here? To discuss family size?" he grumbled, looking up at Linus, who towered over him by at least nine inches. It wasn't unusual for Raven to be the smallest in the room, but it made him uneasy that even Yiyumiss was taller.

"No," Linus replied curtly. Unable to be near Raven any longer, Linus grabbed Lotus roughly and dragged him away to Laithrum. Raven smiled smugly at this action and walked farther into the room; Yiyumiss followed him.

Laithrum looked to Adeyas, who was already learning the new faces. "They are all here," he said, then turned to Onlortrens. "There is something you wish to say to all of us, correct? We are gathered and ready to hear it."

Onlortrens looked curiously at Laithrum. "I did wish to speak to the group, or at least most of them. Did you know or were you guessing?"

Laithrum hadn't guessed. He saw the desire and believed it to be reality, so he acted on it. "He just asked!" Raven yelled, growing impatient, which wasn't normal for him. "Can we just hear what you have to say? Further engagement in meaningless conversation about siblings or quality in problem-solving will truly drive me insane. So please, can we get started?"

Linus angrily looked over at Raven and hissed, "Will you ever stop thinking only of yourself?" These words seemed to hit Raven deeper than Linus expected. They caused him to remain silent, smoldering in a constant repetition of what he felt from what he had just heard. It choked him up; he shouldn't have let the statement matter—but it did.

Watching this, Onlortrens quickly ran over and stood between Linus and Raven. "Stop this!" he commanded. Raven was glad to back down. Linus believed he had won the dispute, but the victory soon felt bitter. If only it could have been a physical fight; a verbal felt despicable. Hurting feeling was dishonorable.

"It seems I made some bad air," Adeyas said quietly to Laithrum as they watched the flaring tempers subside.

Laithrum quickly spoke, "We should not go on speaking without them; it might restart the fire." This was the end of the first conversation Laithrum had alone with his brother, Adeyas.

Adeyas stood up and grabbed Laithrum's shoulders, forcing him forward and folding his body over his legs. Taking away the sword, the older brother said, "We shall speak of this, but first I wish to know your names. Each person will speak for themselves."

Linus started, "I am Linus Vorenter Louleyossa."

"Commander Dowen Trence Kackveriage," Dowen said with a bow.

Lotus glanced at Adeyas, questioning if he should say his name. The prince's eyes narrowed defensively as he nodded. Lotus bowed his head and said, "Lotus Florissurnna."

"Onlortrens Silvertree," the elf answered, finding this quite strange.

Yiyumiss spoke reluctantly, "Yiyumiss Kongei. As you know quite well, Prince Adeyas."

Raven had no wish to say his name, but he did so, nevertheless. "Raven," he said as plainly as he could.

Adeyas waited, then asked, "Do you not have a last or first name? Or is your name Ra and your family name Ven?" He doubted it.

"No, I do not have a 'family name,' and no to that ridiculous Ra-Ven idea!" Raven spat. He glared with his glowing eyes, unusually irritated, and disliking his own temper. Everything was annoying him, and it wouldn't stop.

Onlortrens was also quite surprised. The reaction showed something was very wrong, but what? Troubled, the elf would have to wait for the answer.

Adeyas regretted saying anything but continued, "I apologize, Raven, for bringing it up. I would like no more interruptions, so do try to use some self-control."

In all honestly, nothing that happened bothered Adeyas. He was too hardened to care. This numbness toward Raven's obvious distress was unthinkable to Laithrum, who cared about all these people. He disliked that Linus and Raven did not get along and that Lotus was distant and untrusting.

Laithrum looked into each person's eyes. All of them contrasted with each other, all were empty yet crowded. Some focused on something, while others seemed to avoid a thought. The young prince retook the sword that Adeyas had taken from his back. It was still hidden in heavy cloth.

Raven walked over to Laithrum, who sat on a bed, and sat on the floor at its foot. He did not lean on the bed, because of the wound on his back. He had no intention of having it cared for, but he prayed for it to heal. The trouble it could bring was frightful to say the least. He got this when that ship exploded—it was this or death. Did he make the right choice?

Yiyumiss then spoke up, redirecting Raven's thoughts. "I'm sorry, I have been quiet. There was a person in the last battle that I would have liked to speak with. Well…speak will after knocking him down, but he got away. The event has put me in a bad mood." She paused before saying, "What are all your problems? They can't be all that bad, and if they are, you should get some help." She scolded, unable to take the bitterness, hidden fears, and anger these people carried anymore.

Onlortrens laughed while most of the others were still quiet, surprised and offended by her accusations. She was right and they didn't want to admit it.

The elf then asked, "Yiyumiss, I was told you came with news from the lands of the Ring Mountains."

"Yes, but first you must tell us the significance of that sword, if it has any. That is the kind of trickery I would expect from an elf," the long-haired IseamA said accusingly.

"Trickery?" Onlortrens repeated questioningly, as he never saw elfin games as trickery. Trickery was such a harsh word. He thought back to her question. "Dismissing what else you said, the sword is named the Ellowvast, or as most know it, the Red Stone Sword. Yes, the one treasure that was being saved for when 'the king' was to come."

All were at a loss for words after hearing that. Adeyas seemed the most taken aback. His family were the keepers of that sword. "How did it get here?" he asked, confusion radiating from his face.

Laithrum looked over at Onlortrens. "Yes," the young prince said as he remembered. "Captain Makoto Louleyossa was looking for this, right? You two spoke a few nights back about it. I recall this now." After Laithrum spoke, he looked down at the sword. "Why would you test me with this, whatever kind of test it was…with something like this… if he, or whoever else he trusted with the knowledge, saw me with it, I would have been killed." Laithrum questioned what Onlortrens wanted out of this, or what he wanted to see from it.

Onlortrens could not tell him the full reason just yet, but sharing a lesser truth seemed wise. "The sword liked you, Laithrum. You came into this room with a weak, shaking body. Your brother had to tell you to sit down. The sword has now healed the worst of your wounds. You will just be tired; you'll have no marks from battle. Nonetheless, even though you are healed, do not strain your body further."

No one was expecting that reasoning. To see if the sword would heal Laithrum or not would never have crossed their minds. This was strange, and most didn't know if abusing its power or not. Laithrum could have been killed without it and because of having it; nevertheless, no one doubted that that was the elf's reason. No one in the room could say what the right way to use the sword was. No one knew what abusing its power would look like. Was this a misuse of the blessed sword? Since no one there disliked Laithrum, they were satisfied with the action.

Dowen said, with a controlled but noticeable panic in his voice, "We must get that sword back to the capital of Thuthairryon, Onferwel. If we do not, who knows what will happen."

The room fell silent as individuals reasoned with the matter. Laithrum's mind strayed away from the sword and traveled to what he was going to do. Questions raced through his mind: what would happen to him once he got back home? What exactly happened to his home after he left? Ashtion was supposed to come back the day he, himself, left. What happened to him and Freyja?

Laithrum thought clearly: Am I ready to return? To go back home. Whatever I am going to do, or wherever I am going to go, I need the answer before we reach land. He experienced similar pressure like when

Onlortrens was speaking to him in the palace. But a feeling or voice hit him. It said to give up and go home. This wasn't an ally.

He knew giving up wasn't an option; it was an irrational thought sent by an enemy. Laithrum searched the room, not knowing what he was looking for. What he just felt, what he heard, was from someone close. Maybe someone in the room.

There was a struggle or a task that they had to do…Laithrum caught a glimpse—there was more than one person there with a heavy affliction. Were they in the same situation or both different? How many of them were against each other? So many ambitions that felt as fleeting as dreams, yet it was also their one hope. The future looked overwhelming; almost impossible.

Breaking Laithrum's vision, a soldier hastily walked into the room. "Linus Louleyossa," the Thuthairryon soldier called.

"Yes. What is it?" Linus answered, surprised at this man's entrance.

The soldier looked to both sides at all the people and watched as Raven went out the back door. "Can we speak outside?" he said, seeming distracted by something.

Linus, exasperated, followed, and waved farewell back to his company. When outside, he asked the soldier, "What do you want? I was in a meeting. If this is not very important, I'm not going to bother with it."

"Well, I came to tell you something very important, yet first I would like to know what that Seintroven is doing on this Thuthairryon vessel? Why is he not with his people?"

"Don't mind him. He has been with Thuthairryon for a long time now and fought in the battle with us," Linus said bitterly. "Now, what did you come here to tell me?"

The soldier pulled out a letter. "Your father is alive, and he told me to give you this." Linus' eyes widened and quickly focused on the letter. He snatched the folded paper from the man's hand. Linus did not open it right away. He wouldn't until the man took his leave.

The soldier quickly stepped back and turned around, parting from Linus who was staring at the letter. The sun was now setting quickly, its red and golden rays swallowing everything in sight. The white sails turned more brilliant with every passing moment. Linus finally opened the letter and read:

Linus, my son,

I was glad to hear that you were still alive, overjoyed really, and I wish that the moment was more peaceful so that I could write as just a father; but there are still jobs. One that I would have you do if opportunity arises.

Lotus Florissurnna survived the battle. Linus, you must listen; since he did survive, you must avoid him and not protect him. His death would be best for the safety of everyone...

The letter continued, but Linus read no further. The confusion in what he had already read stiffened his lungs and moved him to fold the letter back up. His father couldn't write that. Never would he wish death on an innocent...innocent? Was Lotus innocent?

Laithrum soon walked out. "Linus, what did that man..." The prince stopped when he met Linus' eyes. "What's wrong?" The answer was something Linus could only think, for aloud, no words could break his darkening thoughts.

Linus forced away his expression of fear, disgust, and confusion, though confusion seemed to dominate and linger. Linus wanted to respond to Laithrum but remained shocked. Perhaps, *doubtful* would be another way to describe his thoughts. Who sent the letter? It couldn't have been his father, he reasoned, for why would he say that? He didn't want to finish reading out of fear of what the rest said.

"Laithrum, to mostly answer your question, I got a letter from my father."

Laithrum was only more confused. "Then what was the questioning expression about? Did the letter say something that could surprise you so much?"

Linus looked away. "It just said something very strange, that's all." He picked up his head to look at Laithrum again. "May I ask why you came out?"

"Troi came in and told us to continue some other time. He wants you, Adeyas, and all the rest of us to rest or get to work. If I understand correctly, he had a lot of work to do, and we were in the way."

Linus nodded as he walked back in. His eyes turned far away from where Lotus sat. Lotus noticed and wondered what was wrong. What could Linus have heard to make him look away like that? Probably the truth.

Dowen walked over to Lotus. "I spoke to Troi, and he said that Linus would be spending the night here. The special treatment is from being a captain's son. So, would spending the night with us be alright with you? There are four beds in our new room, just like when on the other ship."

Lotus smiled. "Yes, that would be great. Thank you for asking."

Dowen went to help him up, but he rose easily by himself and walked out of the room quickly. As they left, Adeyas' eyes followed, glaring at Lotus. Linus saw this and thought that perhaps Adeyas knew what his father knew. Adeyas might know why his father wanted Lotus dead and seemingly wanted it in haste.

When everyone left, Linus knelt at Adeyas' bed. "Will you tell me all you know about Lotus? Please, for my father wrote something very strange in this letter. Please, I ask you; will you try to explain it to me?"

Adeyas pushed back his hair that had fallen in front of his face. He examined the man asking this loaded question. After a short pause, he told Linus everything important he knew about Lotus. The information was not much, but it told Linus the reason why his father wrote what he did.

Before heading to bed, Laithrum met up with Onlortrens, who was watching the sunset as it weakened from its prime. The mission was draining. He wished to have not been the only volunteer.

"Onlortrens," Laithrum started weakly, but continued more certainly, "I have a few questions that I really…desire answers to…" He was going to go on, but Onlortrens interrupted.

"Laithrum, I will not answer the question of where you go now. You should be able to answer that question on your own. Many of your other questions, I am running out of answers for. Don't expect too much from me." The elf looked back at the sky. "I now have far too many questions myself."

Laithrum peered down, not focusing on any material item. The red glow from the setting sun reflected off him like a fire's glow, but his mind felt like the raging fire emitting pure chaos. He was willing to go and fight or return home and rest. He was ready to move on, but to where? And to do what?

He looked back up at Onlortrens. "While I was in there, I felt something, but could not pinpoint it. It was more like I heard a feeling. It happened right before that man walked in and called out Linus."

Onlortrens gazed across at Laithrum and said, "It could have been many things. Will you tell me what the feeling was?"

"To let go of something, to give up. It almost felt like a command or warning. But it also seemed like they did not have a choice in the matter. Then it split into two, as if hearing from two individuals." He paused. "This thought couldn't have come from me. I do not know why I would feel like that."

Onlortrens looked intently into Laithrum's eyes. "You have been gifted as a seer. Could you go back to that moment and see if you can clarify who it came from?"

"I do not know. I have only seen things through my own mind before. This was from someone else's thoughts. I will try."

Laithrum then picked the sword from his back and handed it to Onlortrens, but Onlortrens did not take it. "Keep it, Laithrum. I cannot use that sword in any way. It will reject me," he said firmly.

Laithrum protested quickly, "I cannot! It is not mine. I have no right to keep it, and if just to guard it…why me? I am not as strong or as experienced as any of the others!"

Onlortrens then said to end the conversation, "You must start choosing your own way. Although you are confused about many things, I think it would be good if you start learning from yourself and other men, not just me. I will be here and stand with you, but I will no longer lead you around as if you cannot see. Be led by what you believe and know to be right. This advice cannot be said to any other person than you. Most people's minds are fickle and messy. Many of our companions are led by their emotions, feelings will send or throw them anywhere. So, don't tell people to do the same." With that, he bowed and, while walking off, said, "Tomorrow we will speak again. I am sure you have more to ask." Onlortrens left without another word, knowing that Laithrum needed his sleep.

Laithrum accepting this turned in for the day. The three others in the room were already asleep. Many dreamt but the dreams were nightmares. The rest was not very pleasant. Recovery was important but sleep refused to help after such a day.

Early, before sunrise, Lotus got out of his bed and slowly walked out of the room. He looked down the hall and through the door that led outside.

"We are moving," he told himself. When he walked outside, he remembered what woke him. It was something Laithrum said when he came in earlier that night: *To choose my own way… and do what I know is right?"*

Lotus studied the ships, and indeed they were moving, quickly too. The breeze was strong but not so hard that it made it difficult to steer the ships. Both Thuthairryon and Seitroven ships maneuvered easily through the deep water.

Lotus smiled at the sight of the sun finally touching the sky and painting it mauve. The wind, blowing firmly, played with his soft curls that turned out in every direction. He was a mess. Both physically and mentally damaged and dysfunctional, but the weather was orderly and beautiful, at least for the moment.

His large red eyes sank with the thought that his body was already healed. Overwhelmed but still determined, he told himself, "I need to try harder to get better, the natural way, before the next battle, before… that happens…again."

Linus woke and walked out as well, but when turning the corner, he saw Lotus and stopped. Linus watched for a while. He had come out to wait for the sun, to read the rest of the letter. But now, how could he focus? He wanted to know what the rest said. It would not have mattered what the letter said two weeks ago or maybe even just one. He used to do everything his father told him to, no matter what. "Father, things have changed. I do not know what I should do."

Land was the destination. They traveled in hast because they could feel a bad storm coming. They knew of a protected cove nearby.

The Seintroven and Thuthairryon people sailed peacefully together. What helped this was mutual understanding and confusion about what had happened. That dark ship: that odd, heinous ship that came in so quickly and left so strangely. The two fleets still didn't trust each other. They both kept prisoners for leverage. The current plan was to hand over prisoners when land was reached.

CHAPTER 12

In a Forest of Danger

The ground had straightened since passing out of Forest Drawl; consequently, they traveled in longer increments. After a three-hour bout of hiking, they entered an older, more open woods. Freyja considered these woods very beautiful. Her companions cared nothing for nature's beauty.

The sun fell through the treetops, warming the air. The light rays moved gracefully through rustling leaves. The light made the greens brighter. New leaves glow on the forest floor. The large leaves were surrounded by little pink flowers and carpets of moss. The forest's small flowers were radiant and sweet-smelling. The scent and sight Freyja found almost too glorious to accompany a journey of this nature.

She felt alone. The forest might groan if it knew she was the only one enjoying its display. The others with her had all their senses focused sharply on internal matters. She considered their rigid and overly dramatized opinions as weakness. They were so stressed and on edge.

The three people Lattermere found for this mission were as follows: First, there was Kound, an adult man with mostly white hair. Kound was proud and arrogant with no known right or reason to be.

He often argued to kill Nourttaku, the poisoner, and the volunteer guide. Kound claimed he would be a better guide. But clearly, he had no idea where they were going.

The second soldier was young, around Freyja's age, and called Yohain. Yohain was diffident and didn't say a word for the entire trip. Freyja was impartial to Yohain because he, at least, was well-behaved. Kound was unbearable to be around; his self-seen greatness and promotion of his greatness proved stomach-churning.

And lastly, Haru, a very large, strong man with a short beard and keen eyes that always surveyed the surrounding forest for hazards and enemies. No one seemed able to lessen the relentless stress he put himself through.

Haru, Hondou, and Kound never allowed themselves to break for sightseeing or enjoyment. Freyja was surprised they weren't all experiencing burnout. They believed they were always working toward their distant goal and mission. In truth, all they were doing was trying to outwalk, outtalk, and outthink one another. The conspiracy theories knew no end.

Nourttaku and Lattermere did not join in this competition often. They couldn't care less about what those men thought of them. This was all they had in common. Lattermere's thoughts and emotions were directed toward the fallen capital city and how they would fix the mess; he thought much about Freyja. Since she was his royal, he aimed to impress her. But ever since he saw her in battle, he had a difficult time speaking to her. Toward her, he felt much fear and confusion.

Nourttaku, certainly, had no desire to impress the princess. He didn't care about their capital city. Future payment or prestige did not interest him out here. His plans, wishes, and ambitions all had to do with getting home and receiving medical treatment for his festering wounds. Beyond that he didn't care.

Princess Freyja played in her thoughts about these men. She tried to guess their thoughts and actions. Since they were so flamboyant she often got the answers to her guessing game. Sadly, they were predictable, and she was usually right.

This team needed some adhesive. A break from competition to conversation was needed. A plan, at least, would lend itself to focusing these individuals into a similar frame and state of mind. She soon called for a break and a meeting.

The six traveling with her sat down for discussion. Focus' were where they were headed and the plan of implementation once there. Nonetheless, an awkwardly long while passed before matters were addressed. Freyja systematically glared at each of these stubborn individuals waiting for the conversation, no, argument to start.

"To start this important discussion, let's define where we are headed. Certainly, we cannot bring the woman on the complete hike to the mountains. Her ankles will fatten and make finding someone to marry her even more difficult. She's already frightfully too tall." Said Kound, before lifting a canteen to his mouth and consuming the last drops of water in it. Freyja held in her anger; if she allowed any out, she might murder him for his echoing sexist comments.

"We are going to Jien. It's a small town close to here. We will stop for the supplies we need and rest," Freyja answered sternly and continued. "Our destination is not far now. Prince Ashtion Airslen has been taken to a base outside the Ring Mountains. We have Nourttaku to lead us there, and hopefully, along with us, we will receive assistance from this town. This town has been very loyal to Thuthairryon and is filled with brave men. Kound, I will not be leaving the company. When we get to the town, I will let all of you decide if you will or will not come with us. Two of you do not have a choice." She turned her eyes, gesturing to Hondou and Nourttaku.

Hondou responded, "Why do we need the Seintroven? Certainly, we can get a map at the town."

"Yes, we can get a map, and he can show us where to go, but will it tell us enough? This is a well-guarded base next to a dangerous environment. The territory is poorly mapped because it's so dangerous. Security will always be keen, because the threats are constant. Nourttaku knows the rotation and entrances."

All were uneasy with putting their lives in the hands of that "thing." She acted as if Nourttaku was trustworthy. He didn't help them out from loyal duty. He was just doing enough to stay alive and would betray them at the first chance.

Nourttaku tired of this treatment, but it was expected from enemies. Since he was betrayed by the Seintroven earlier. Did it mean he had no allies anywhere? He shut his eyes tightly, remembering he was different, and that difference should have made him expect to be betrayed and rejected. He was hated and ostracized by his unit for the same reason he was envied and respected in his village.

Kound looked toward Nourttaku and suddenly said, "So, what are you anyway? You're mixed in blood, aren't you?" The others were startled by this claim. "Your eyes aren't right. They are brighter, and the darkness of shadows doesn't touch them. So, what are you?"

Nourttaku glared, knowing the risk of answering equaled that of silence. Honesty might keep him alive, so he chose his words carefully. "I am a man of Turwin village near Seintrova. Part Julrainzak due to outside magic—though not much." He kept it brief, rolling his eyes at Kound's lack of understanding. He wasn't multiple races, species, peoples, or whatever this judgmental man choice to label him as.

Hondou and Haru rushed over, tying a rope around his back like a net. Kound advised Freyja, "You better use caution, princess. That race has powers that influence the opposite sex. Another reason not to bring women on quests."

Freyja rounded her eyes and hoped to be rid of this man soon. She didn't want to admit it, but she started wishing him dead. Executions were never a promotion of hers, but an exception may have presented itself.

"You're an idiot!" Nourttaku scolded. "I wouldn't use that power even if I could. It's only explicable to a real Julrainrak. And don't single out her, the lure could be used on men as well." He protested, turning to Hondou and Haru. "And what's with this binding? The ability to sprout wings is rare, common only among full-blooded Julrainzak!"

Nourttaku was maybe in a worse spot but at least he was still alive. These people trusted him even less. The truth, as vague as it was, kept him alive, but it made him less trustworthy; ironic.

Frejya and the others, except Yohain, had been trained to hide emotions. They maintained a coldness toward the prisoner. Once Nourttaku was secured, they resumed their business. "The town isn't far. If we leave now, we might reach it by late morning tomorrow, with breaks and sleep of course." Said Hondou.

Most knotted at the statement. It sounded like a fair plan.

Yohain felt bad for Nourttaku but dared not speak. He was raised to respect all races, even those he disapproved of. Out here kindness was seen as weakness. Considering the injuries and mental strain, he finally spoke. "We should rest a little longer." He paused, peering through his strawberry blond bangs.

"We don't have the time," Hondou said bluntly.

"Yes, but some of you have serious wounds that need attention. I have bandages, ointment, and pain medicine." Freyja looked at him, surprised and amused. The only one with serious wounds was Nourttaku. His play was obvious, and she commanded him for it.

"Why didn't you tell us? Didn't you think we'd need it sooner?" Kound complained, disappointed his wounds were stinging all this time.

Kound continued snorting. "Acting slowly gets people killed. Your age and foolish nature show."

"Shut up," Lattermere snapped, leaving the conversation to speak with Yohain. "Thank you for speaking up. I'm sorry for forgetting. What is your name?"

"Yohain Onel," he replied, amused that he had forgotten. Lattermere nodded, committing it to memory.

Freyja distracted Kound from complaining about his shallow cuts and random bruises with more steps in their plan.

They decided to spend the day resting and tending to their own injuries. Freyja formally entrusted Yohain and Lattermere with holding their medical supplies. Those two could be trusted not to waste them.

Sleep was elusive for some, plagued by physical pain and worry. Freyja was one who couldn't sleep. Sometimes she felt like she didn't even need it. It became a want, at least in sleep her mind might get a break. She kept telling herself, "Rest is beneficial."

As the sun began to brighten their campsite, they packed up and pressed forward.

The morning was calm, devoid of wind, but alive with the busy songs of birds. Their melodies, whether for mating, territory, or warning, filled the forest. The ground, now flatter, made hiking a joy compared to the rugged terrain of Drawl Forest. New, brilliant green growth still covered the ground—shrubs, vines, and ferns unfurling from the earth, alongside a myriad of other plants of various shapes, shades, and sizes. Though the ground was flat, rocks scattered here and there, some covered with moss and surrounded by small, fragrant white flowers.

The view was as beautiful as before, but Freyja's mind was too preoccupied to appreciate it. She felt the need to apologize to nature for her human worry. She became more and more distracted the closer to the mountains they got. The mission odds were terrible. They all realized that this venture could end in death or capture. This was the likely outcome, nevertheless, victory against the enemy or getting Ashtion back was worth the risk for her. Ashtion was her brother, and she had to try.

It was obvious that this endeavor required strategic, seamless planning and excellent communication and teamwork. Yet, their current social state was far from ideal. They were closer to being enemies than allies. Teamwork was a joke. This group working together for each other was the most unlikely thing she could think of.

Before they realized it, their path turned rocky. Short, sparse trees scattered the landscape, and fewer plant and animal life marked the change. Freyja glanced back, still able to see the green lands. The sudden shift brought anxiety to the group.

Soon, more trouble arose. Their hike was abruptly halted by the sound of thunder from swiftly approaching greenish-grey clouds. Hondou immediately scanned the surrounding rocks.

"We should find shelter among these rocks to avoid the rain," he instructed Haru, who had keen eyes and outdoor experience. "Quickly, find somewhere suitable."

The difficult terrain took its toll on the company. Nourttaku, under Lattermere's watch, felt near fainting. He longed to complain about his numb hand and throbbing, swollen arm. Lattermere, too, wanted to voice his hunger, the burning in his stomach, and the hot saliva that seemed to dissolve his teeth. Yohain's legs shook, and tunnel vision began to set in, but he remained capable.

Freyja, on the other hand, was perfectly fine. Her endurance, strength, rapid healing, and heightened senses frightened her more each day. She no longer recognized herself.

The horse carrying supplies sensed the growing danger and became restless. The wind picked up suddenly, followed by sheets of rain. Haru lost sight of the group on his return. Too far to shout, he pressed forward through the hammering rain until he could see them again.

Hondou spotted him first and shouted through the rain, "Haru, did you find any place to go?!"

"Yes, it's small, but our group will fit!" Haru answered loudly, glancing quickly behind him. "Follow me!" He waited for everyone to understand before moving.

Navigating the slippery rocks proved hazardous, and Freyja felt that berserk energy building inside her again. It was the same feeling as she had in that battle.

The horse, sensing the growing threat, refused to follow. Lattermere, Yohain, and Freyja grabbed the gear and supplies to protect them from the rain and prevent them from being lost with the frightened horse. Freyja hoped her horse would find them after the storm passed. But she soon realized that she was the …thing… her horse feared.

Yohain helped Nourttaku through the rocks, while Hondou and Lattermere assisted Freyja. Kound, refusing to help anyone, frantically searched for the shelter Haru was leading them to. It seemed to take twice as long to reach it as it had for Haru to find it.

Once inside, they were relieved and quickly opened their bags for dry blankets and clothing. They stripped off their cold, wet clothes in haste to avoid hypothermia and dressed in dry ones. Even Nourttaku was given a dry undershirt and new pants.

"Are you men crazy? You gave the prisoner the survival items we clearly need! So, which of you will go without if soaked again?!" Kound complained, standing in the driest clothes. His original innermost clothes were dry from the water-resistant cloak he had worn before.

"You're the one leaving people out! You have the most suitable clothes for this weather!" Lattermere argued.

Kound quickly spat back, "I only want the worthy to dress in what is dry! Don't give such monsters things you need! In that attack, two of my closest friends were killed. Why should we give him comfort? If it wasn't for that stupid, tall woman, we wouldn't have to care for that trash!"

"ENOUGH!" Hondou yelled, slamming Kound against the rock side. The cave wasn't tall enough for them to stand, but Hondou crouched to avoid hitting his head.

"I don't care what you've gone through! I've put up with your comments long enough! If you talk obscenely about her again, I will kill you, SLOWLY, with my bare hands! DO YOU UNDERSTAND?!" Hondou's eyes and the force of his arms pierced through Kound's confident calmness, causing him to feel nothing but fear. Kound shook too hard and panicked too greatly to respond.

Frustrated, Hondou tossed him down, again showing the difference in their strength, and walked to Yohain to receive his new dry shirt. Yohain sat with the shirt presented in his outstretched arms, fighting the urge to laugh and applaud what Hondou did.

It took a while for Hondou's large, muscular frame to stop pulsing with heightened adrenaline. For the first time, Freyja was frightened by this man. Yes, she finally found him intimidating.

CHAPTER 13

Dark Comes

The rain continued outside throughout their sleep. The puddles grew into a lake that hid the path and most of the rocks outside the cave. The thunder kept their sleep fragmented but was eventually ignored after a few hours.

Unable to be ignored, a loud noise shattered the night, waking everyone. Instantly alert, they were met with the musky smell of rain and a nauseating sense of dread. Something was very wrong.

Hondou and Lattermere rushed to the entrance, trying to identify the source of the noise. Nourttaku, half-awake when it sounded, struggled to place it. "I know that sound from somewhere," he thought. "But where? If only I could hear it again." The realization hit him like an attack, his face turning white, eyes dilating in shock.

Lattermere glanced at Hondou. "What do you think it was?"

"Not something," Nourttaku interjected, "someone. Get away from the opening. Someone's out there."

Understanding that Nourttaku knew more about the area, they obeyed. His eyes, wild with fear, told them enough.

"And why should we listen to you?" Kound challenged.

Nourttaku shot him a threatening look, eyes glowing in the darkness. "Quiet!" he hissed through clenched teeth. Hondou approached him calmly. "What's out there?"

"That sound, it is made by one or more Dark Elves. They know we are here and are looking for us. This is both bad and good—it woke us up, got us thinking and preparing, but our talking will make it easier for them to find us."

Hondou began distributing armor and weapons. "We have to prepare for the worst."

Kound, panicking, approached him. "The worst? Do you even know how to fight them? Have you ever done it before?" Hondou ignored him, continuing his preparations.

Yohain turned to Freyja. "Dark Elves are born violent, using power to burn you from the inside out. They aren't always descendants of Elves; that's just their origin."

Freyja didn't want to acknowledge the threat. It explained her own anxiety, but she feared losing control again, as she had in the last battle. Dark Elves were widely spoken of, though little was truly known about them. Folk tales really, most people didn't believe they existed.

Lattermere, knowing nothing about the enemy, approached Nourttaku. "What is a Dark Elf anyway? I hear Elves are kind, beings of light. Are Dark Elves the opposite? Are they Elves or not?" Nourttaku, startled, pondered the question.

"I don't really know. Some are born Dark Elves, some turn. Not only do Elves turn into Dark Elves, but most are from Elves. I'm not sure about anything else, sorry. Was say it's a parasite, some say a virus, others still say a curse." He stood to prepare for what might come.

Lattermere, paralyzed by fear, felt that moving would lead to their discovery and death. His fear of dark magic seemed unshakable. Remembering what he saw Freyja do, he knew his strength and skill would fall short against this foe. Biting his lip, he told himself he could do more. He could make a difference.

The water crashed against the rocks, so loud and relentless that they couldn't hear themselves think. They waited, tense and ready for whatever approached the entrance.

Outside, two Dark Elves tracked the company hidden in the cave. Even through the rain they could maneuver and search quickly. One, with golden eyes glowing through his light lemon-colored hair, asked his companion. "How many do you think? And should we really bother with them?"

Water fell over their faces, but neither blinked. Their steady expressions painted in malaise.

The other Dark Elf, with dark brown hair, shot a glare that made his companion shudder. The golden-eyed elf knew his companion was the stronger of the two. The dark-haired elf's expression, filled with a thirst for blood, silenced any argument. This was their mission. They prepared for their next move.

Freyja felt uneasy, her eyes glued to the entrance, imagining figures staring back at her. Surely, they would have attacked by now, right? The others would have seen them, right? She turned away, trying to re-gather herself. She struggled to stop picturing the last massacre that she had …embraced. When did she become a monster?

She glanced at Nourttaku, wondering if he knew his mission was an ambush, a massacre of fleeing civilians. How did he feel about it? Was he more of an enemy than she believed? Could he have approved of the slaughter, or was he unaware? Nourttaku felt her stare and followed it to her, surprised. When did I make her angry?

Hondou evaluated Yohain and Nourttaku, knowing they were their biggest handicaps. Yohain finished securing his armor. As he looked back at the cave's mouth, he saw one of them—a tall Dark Elf radiating black fire, centered at the entrance. The physical appearance of the enemy was not foreboding, but the spirit was. The Dark Elf brought with him feelings of fear, loneliness, rejection, helplessness, and anger. A tragic miasma flooded in from his presence.

In that moment, Hondou motivated himself to attack. He struck at the Dark Elf, despite the rush of emotions. Hondou fought with his sword against the blond elf wielding a short glaive. The Dark Elf was both pushed back and jumped backward by choice. Once outside, he was joined by the other Dark Elf.

Haru turned to Lattermere. "What are we going to do? We can't stay here; we don't have the room to fight. Out there, with them, isn't any better."

Lattermere answered quickly, "We are at a disadvantage. So, must go where they lead us—but we stick together. Come on!" He ran to join Hondou, and Haru followed bravely.

Nourttaku stood and informed them as they left, "It is most likely only the two." He sat down, continuing to himself, "The highest number of Dark Elves traveling together ever recorded is eight. Before that, it was four." He paused, worried about his next question. "Did Thouthairryon get in trouble with the Ring Mountains?"

Freyja shook her head, indicating she knew nothing of the matter. She stepped out to join the battle.

The Dark Elves listened to the company still in the cave. The darker one sneered, "They don't even know what they did." Growing impatient, he threw a spell inside the cave. The magic burst into gas, purging the cave of the company.

Hondou managed to rejoin Freyja. Haru stuck with Yohain, soon joined by Kound, Nourttaku, and Lattermere. Haru was relieved to see them but knew he was the strongest and felt the need to defend the weak and wounded. Kound, however, was only concerned with defending himself.

The dark-haired enemy stepped in front of them. Nourttaku knew that if the situation worsened, Kound would abandon them. He glanced at the binds around his back, knowing they were breakable, but unsure of the damage it might cause. He had only one shot and had to stay with the company, no matter the cost.

The Dark Elf charged. Haru blocked his blade, using both arms to buffer the attack. The Dark Elf's strike aimed high, and in a flash, the pressure lifted from behind the sword. Haru swung his leg, kicking his opponent, but the enemy barely felt it. Haru called out, "Kound!" signaling for help. Kound, seeing the enemy's focus on Haru, chose not to help, believing he had a better plan.

The Dark Elf leaped at Haru, blade falling from above. Haru blocked, but his insecure stance and shock at Kound's betrayal caused him to fall. He landed near Nourttaku, who was in Lattermere's way. The enemy saw the opportunity to impale both with one thrust.

Kound seized the moment to flee. Lattermere jerked, distracted by Kound's abandonment. Instinctively, Nourttaku's magic sprouted from his back to his hands. A shockwave from the release knocked Lattermere off his feet. Nourttaku grabbed Haru, and the strange magic, acting like wings, propelled them out of range of the attack.

Yohain bit his lip, drawing blood to break his paralytic fear. To slow the pursuit, he grabbed onto the Dark Elf and held tight. The Dark Elf quickly flipped his sword to stab Yohain in the back, but Hondou arrived faster, striking from behind.

***

Moments earlier, Freyja and Hondou fought the light-haired Dark Elf. He swung his short glaive at them, and a quick bob of their heads saved them from decapitation. Hondou shoved Freyja behind him, placing himself between her and the enemy.

The Dark Elf raised his left hand, and a black light began to form around it. The fire of the magic changed from eerie black to violet as it matured. Hondou muttered three words under his breath, as if recalling something not quite known by heart. When the Dark Elf shot out the power, it stopped in front of Hondou as if hitting a shield. "Even we humans can learn to shield against magic, and you happen to be fighting one of the best."

The Dark Elf smiled. "Then I suppose I am lucky to be among the best in my class as well. Dederom Maullia is my name, and yours is?"

Hondou gave him a single look that conveyed his refusal to answer. Dederom's eyes caught a fast movement, and with a mere glance and a feeling, he thought, "Kound."

The Dark Elf's lemon-colored hair lifted, defying the heavy rain, with a sudden surge of power. His eyes grew brighter until they resembled small golden flames. In a yellow flash, he vanished, sprinting expediently.

Freyja and Hondou were bewildered. The unexpected departure suggested the Dark Elf had seen something he didn't like. They searched briefly, trying to discern what he saw or if he was truly gone at all, but the rain was too thick. They could only hope he wasn't there. Their questioning halted quickly as they needed to find their companions.

Freyja could sense their life forces, making it easy to locate them. Hondou, moving swiftly, saved Yohain from a deeper injury. Yohain, who had resigned himself to death when he grabbed the Dark Elf, was relieved to be wrong.

After cutting down the enemy, Hondou checked to see if Yohain was fatally wounded; he wasn't. Freyja knelt beside Yohain, who softly said, blood dripping from his bitten lip, "I thought I was going to die for sure. I knew it. I've never been so happy to be wrong."

"Freyja, get him up. We need to get out of here." Hondou soon spotted the others. "And Nourttaku, I don't care if you're hurt! Suck it up, or we'll leave you behind!"

Nourttaku glared at Hondou through the pain. His body gradually turned shades of grey, blue, and black from bruising. He pulled his arms tight against his chest and stood to follow.

"Come on," Lattermere said to Haru, grabbing Nourttaku's arm and pulling him up to drag him along. Haru tried not to think about how strange it was to see wings sprout from a body too small to house them.

They raced over the rocky, slippery terrain and into the forest. Running was exhausting. Nourttaku was the first to fall, and Lattermere had to start carrying the weight of two.

Seeing Lattermere close to collapsing, Hondou stopped and muttered to himself, "Not again!"

"Should we stop?" Freyja asked, deciding to question him further at a better time.

Hondou plucked Nourttaku from Lattermere. "No, we're too close and too cold," he replied.

They said no more, too out of breath, but continued running to the town. By the time they reached it, none of them could move any longer. Those who might have kept going couldn't once they saw the others fall. It was pure luck that someone spotted them and ran to get help.

They were brought into Jien, a small town filled with good people and simple housing. The rain had stopped, and dawn was breaking. The smell of hot soup filled every room in the house they lay in. Freyja woke to the pleasant aroma and savored the peaceful thought that they had reached Jien. She assumed it wasn't a dream.

When she finally opened her eyes, she found a pair of bright brown eyes staring into her blue and green ones. The man looked as if he had just discovered she was alive. He was surprised and delighted.

She immediately turned bitter and confused. This man was right in her face, wearing a leather floppy-eared hat in a warm house. He also wore a house robe and furry slippers. Was this man crazy? What was he going so close to her?

He smiled and said, "Don't be startled. My name is Suruki. I am your doctor. And yes, I know who you are and what happened to the capital, Onferwel."

Freyja opened her mouth to respond, but he placed a finger over her lips. "Save your strength. You will need it for the near future. Your food will be brought in shortly." He turned, saying, "I'm checking on the others."

Freyja watched the dark-haired man walk away and join two others. "What should I do now?" she wondered, staring at the ceiling with bright, bewildered eyes. She hoped her brothers were faring better than she was. At that moment, hope seemed futile. Shaking her head, she banished the negativity. "There is always hope when fought for."

Why let herself think so hopelessly? Why lose faith in them and herself? Freyja took a deep breath, savoring the air. "I'm warm," she stated simply, then wondered about the others and her family. Two overpowering emotions surged within her: wonderment for her brother and hatred for her father.

After eating, Freyja got up and asked for the owners of the house. When she found the lady of the house, she learned that her son had found them and quickly brought help.

Freyja inquired about Onferwel, but the mother looked down and did not answer directly. "We are moving," she said, pausing as if forced. "When we heard of the attack, we knew it would be best to get farther away. I'm sorry we can do nothing about it. We are too small a town. I am also sorry for making you travel again so quickly. We, as a town, are leaving tomorrow early morning." The woman then bowed to Freyja in apology.

"Actually, I wasn't planning on staying long. Since you are leaving, I must move quickly and gather some of your men. We are on a mission to save Prince Ashtion Airslen. We need more hands and supplies for the road ahead." Freyja smiled. "And I'd like to meet your son to thank him for saving us."

The woman felt honored that royalty would want to thank her son, so she called him immediately. "Ain, Ain, come here!"

After a short while, a young boy ran into the room. "Yes, mother?"

Freyja smiled at the child, who was around ten years old. She lowered her head to him. "Thank you for helping us. You must have very keen eyes. I would like to know who you are so that, in the future, I can give you proper thanks, Ain."

The boy, nervous and happy and frozen in panic, said nothing. He almost jumped up and down, yet his eyes darted everywhere. He tried to speak but ran away instead.

Freyja tried to make sense of what had just happened. The boy's sweet and different personality made her smile, reminding her of Lotus. He had a similar innocence, always thinking well of people.

The mother of the child apologized. "I'm so very sorry. He's just shy. I'll call him back to apologize for his rudeness."

"There is no need for apologies. I loved the way he handled it. It was refreshing after this journey's interactions. I feel the need to apologize because I want more. I need a detailed map of the northwest, medical supplies, food, water, and clothes. I will also need capable hands for the mission." The woman nodded, and Freyja left to join the others.

Haru and Hondou were busy packing and gathering items. Hondou was also making a list of what they needed. Nourttaku, on a couch, was weaving back and forth, drinking tea, and trying to fight a severe headache. Lattermere attributed the headache to depleted magic, lack of food, warmth, medical care, excessive movement, pain, mental stress, and depression. Nourttaku's torso was completely bandaged.

Freyja walked in and quickly asked, "So what happened to Kound? I'm guessing he's dead." Haru's gaze shifted to the corner of the room. He started, "He…"

"Look at me when you talk to me!" Freyja scolded.

Haru did so and restarted, stronger than before. "He ran. We were in a skirmish with the enemy. After an attack, I countered and asked Kound to act, but to save himself, he ran!" The bitterness in his voice was palpable, his body shaking with rage.

Hondou replied, "So he ran? I wonder if he's the one our Dark Elf pursued."

Haru looked up in surprise. "The Dark Elf ran away?"

Hondou's stern expression never changed, but he noticed Haru's fluctuating emotions. "Get some rest, Haru. You're becoming overbearing and unstable." He walked away.

Passing Freyja, he added, "You should rest too. You're losing your strength. At this rate, you couldn't even beat me, and I'm not only speaking of physical abilities. You're losing focus."

Freyja glared as he walked out. She realized he was right. She had lost her strength and was getting upset over every little thing. But even knowing this, she wondered how to calm down. It wouldn't be easy.

The doctor came in and approached Freyja. "We have to talk," he said. Freyja shook her head. "I feel too dizzy. I'm going to take a nap." She went off to bed, and he allowed her to go.

A brief time later, she woke up, forcing herself to do so. Luckily, the doctor, who greeted her when she awoke before, had already gathered what they needed. Hondou's assisted in every step, it had to be perfect. He also received the map from the lady of the house.

Freyja was relieved to hear this, but her mood dampened with the memory that the doctor wanted to talk. "What was it you wanted to speak with me about?" she asked reluctantly.

The doctor shook his head. "I decided not to tell you right now. Go back to sleep, for we all leave in the morning."

In the morning, the town started moving on. They were all outside with their most precious belongings and food. The town, left well stocked with water and food, was deserted by its residences. They only took what they needed; the rest was for Freyja and the others staying.

Yohain was leaving with them because of his wound and because he was not a soldier suited for this mission. It was farewell to the company Yohain had grown to admire. Freyja bowed her head and said goodbye.

The company now consisted of Freyja, Hondou, Lattermere, Nourttaku, Haru, and three new, skilled experts. The eight were close to their destination. The plan grew to having a protective rally point expecting them after the mission. A message sent by a hawk yesterday ensured the city within the mountain range would be watching for them.

Freyja felt a surge of energy as her worry and excitement grew. Having a city watching and waiting for them made the mission seem more hopeful.

Gazing at the mountains, she marveled at their towering, lifeless rock masses stretching into the clouds. They represented the barrier to the most dangerous, unruly place on the continent—their haven. The world was twisting around, causing every known fact to be questioned and every myth to be considered reality. Freyja was in the middle of it all, powerless to stop the chaos, forced to adapt.

CHAPTER 14

The Light of Hope Remains

Damp darkness surrounded him, and it was cold where he lay. The ground was stone and rough, but he wished he could feel the texture fully. He hunted for a different focus, something bold enough to overshadow the bright pain of his current thoughts. The pain shooting from his leg through his body was comparable to the war inside his mind, altogether crippling him.

When he opened his dark blue eyes with bright centers, Ashtion saw he was in a prison of some kind. He soon remembered the road here and what had happened before. Wanting to grieve for his mother, he found himself too defensive. This place and too cold for tears.

"Why? Did staying away so long make me this distant from Mother?" Ashtion asked himself, trying to remember if he felt different before his last adventure. "I should feel the grief clearer. Did my love grow cold."

No.

He had always been in love, passionate about his family. When he and Freyja saw their mother dead, he had wanted to forgo escape just to grieve. What had changed from then to now? The cold, uncaring feeling was unsettling, though not frightening. By his reasoning, it should frighten him; he evaluated the situation until he found an answer.

"There was that mirror Father found so exquisite. He tied it against my back. It hurt. I couldn't even sleep, for that thing was always trying to get into my mind. I don't know if it ever did. All I remember is trying my hardest to keep it out. Father tried helping the horrid feeling the entire way here. Wherever *here* is, and however long it took to get here." Ashtion could not bring himself to think any more about it. It was too upsetting.

He looked outside his cell and saw it—the blasted mirror that haunted him so much. It just sat there, staring at him. The mirror wasn't touching him anymore, so he no longer felt the helplessness it provoked before.

His hand pressed into his stomach; eyes clenched shut in concentration. Opening his eyes, he glared at the mirror keenly. His pupils shrank to nothing, and the brighter color of his eyes broadened. In a moment, pressure grew in front of him, causing wild, irregular winds. Once the pressure grew enough, a powerful blast of air shot from him and punched the mirror. The chair it sat on shattered against the wall behind it, but the mirror remained, floating in the damp, mildew-scented air. It was a costly failure.

"Drat!" he yelled, slamming his hands on the ground in frustration. Gradually, he relaxed his tense body and began to breathe deeply.

"Calm down. No matter how hard it is, you will be better off remaining calm," Ashtion muttered to himself, hoping the words would anchor his thoughts.

His mind leaped chaotically from one thought to another, sensible ideas mingling with impractical ones, while negative feelings attacked him relentlessly. Memories of his mother's death, his last perilous journey, and the painful separation from his sister Freyja flooded his mind. Amidst these scattered recollections, he wondered about the fates of Freyja, Laithrum, Adeyas, and home.

He trembled violently, consumed by fear and confusion, yet unable to cry or mourn, which only deepened his frustration.

"She's causing you strong worry. Next time you see her, if she is alive, don't fail her!" Ashtion glared at the mirror. "Get out of my head. You are a ridiculous sheet of glass! What are trying to say?"

He knew it was futile to speak to the mirror; he had learned that well enough on his journey here. "Why?" he asked himself, too bewildered and exhausted to form a coherent question. What did he truly want to know?

Ashtion's golden blond hair was now matted, tied back loosely, and filthy. He was a complete mess: physically, mentally, emotionally, and situationally. He glanced down at his hands, the burns from the ropes reminding him of his struggle during transport. The ropes had left burns around his waist, hands, and feet.

Attempting to rise, he fell back to the floor, his right leg refusing to support him. Frustration mounted as he clenched his teeth, helpless against the pain. He had no allies. His vision was blurred with fear and worry. Slowly, he managed to sit up, staring at his leg, which had received no care. He dreaded what he might find.

After a deep breath, he inspected the wound. As he feared, it was filthy and hot with infection. The wound was severely infected, the skin dark purple, greenish-yellow, while the rest of his body had turned pale.

"Why? Why is father…" he shook his head, rejecting the word, "…Niejill trying to kill us? If this isn't taken care of, I will die." He shut his eyes tightly, trying to comprehend how this could happen.

***

Neijill stood before a group of four elite men. Two hailed from Thuthairryon, another from Seintroven with a red mark at the end of his left eyebrow, and the fourth, with brown hair, did not appear human.

"Why did you four want to see me?" Neijill inquired.

"Because you can make a decision final, sir," said the Seintroven, the leader of the small group. The taller of the two Thuthairryins spoke next, "There is an evil that creeps in the shadows outside the base. It is powerful. Our mixed-blood companion sensed it, and he is elite in that ability."

The Seintroven man spoke again, "We need to take action, but the decision is yours."

Neijill dismissed them to ponder the matter alone. The king did not care about threats outside. Angered at Neijills negligence two left immediately, the other two men remained. They chose to wait for Neijill's return.

Neijill descended to the prison. Ashtion winced at the sight of him. "What is your reason for coming down here?" he asked.

Neijill ignored him, plucking the mirror from its spot in midair. Ashtion dreaded what would come next.

Neijill stared at the shattered chair, confused. "What happened here?"

"I have not the slightest idea," Ashtion replied, his words dripping with sarcasm yet restrained. Neijill smiled at the pain on Ashtion's face.

"Ashtion, my son, please stop thinking what I am trying to do is a bad thing. It might take some time for your infant mind to understand." Neijill's smile never wavered. "I did not come to see you, though. It was this I came for," he said, lifting the mirror. "I hope you might learn to love this as much as I do."

"Never. That thing has no value. It is evil, and I will not let something so wicked have any part in my life. The value you speak of is nothing more than trickery. It exists to deceive. Things that encourage treachery and betrayal have no value to me," Ashtion argued, though his words held no hatred toward Neijill. He despised what his father was doing but wasn't fully convinced it was him. It might even be more than the black magic of that mirror.

Neijill retorted, "Do not think yourself good; no one in this world is. You are just as wicked as me. You are not as strong as you pretend. You are already falling apart and would commit any erroneous act if you thought it would lift the pain or get you out of here."

Ashtion knew there was truth in Neijill's words. He couldn't think of much he wouldn't do to end this pain and leave this place.

"You are a hurt bird in a nest of snakes, fearing the moment one of them gets hungry," Neijill said, knowing he was right. Ashtion knew the truth in his father's words but didn't want to accept it. He was too weak to fight back and knew saving his remaining strength would be wiser. Holding on to the control he had left was his only hope.

Ashtion's head bobbed slowly, his face swelling with heat and tears fogging his vision. He thought, "This cannot be happening. I need to stand strong; it could help father come back if he's even alive." No positive thoughts seemed to work. The same feeling he had on the ride here was returning. He couldn't help it. There was no hope.

Neijill laughed, his head dropping suddenly as if held up by strings that had just gone slack, then slowly lifted. "Just listen to your father, and the pain will leave, I guarantee it." He left the room, taking the mirror with him. When the mirror left, so did the insensible feelings that had caused Ashtion to feel so hopeless.

"It was that mirror," he muttered to himself. "Does it have that much power over me now?" Terror gripped Ashtion as he pondered, "If just by holding it, Niejill wielded such power, what else could he do? What could that thing make me do?"

After retying his hair, he lay back to rest. This would be the only chance for sleep he would get. Once that mirror returned sleep was too dangerous. Even through the pain and intense thoughts, sleep came instantly.

In a dream, he saw another man enter after his father left. Cloaked and with a friendly voice, the man spoke through a thick haze. "Prince Ashtion Airslen, be strong, for you do not fight alone. Friends are here for you. I am sorry we cannot free you now, but we brought some medicine. Please take it." After drinking what the man offered, the dream ended, and Ashtion awoke.

He woke on the cold, hard floor, chilled to the bone and stiff. The prince had been asleep for what felt like only an hour or two, but in truth, it had been more than a day.

Ashtion's blonde hair was a mess again, strewn around his head and over his face. He worked to fix it, but when his tired eyes opened, he saw two figures—thin and tall, cloaked but without hoods. They blended perfectly with the gloom of the stone walls. Their presence eerily like the mirrors feeling.

Ashtion's vision was still blurry from his long sleep, though it was improving quickly. He sat up, realizing his right arm had fallen asleep. With his other hand, he pulled the hair away from his eyes to see the strangers clearly.

"It seems like the little kid has finally woken up," said one of them, a woman's voice.

"Indeed, he has. Should we do something about it? He could prove to be a nuisance," said the other, a man with a deep voice.

The woman whipped her arm and struck him across the head. "Of course not, you moron! You know what we're here to do! For now, the human stays here," she hissed, trying to remain silent.

"Who are you two?" Ashtion asked, now able to see them clearly. He noticed their pointed ears and felt the eeriness of their presence. The woman had dark red hair and dark green eyes full of hate and violence. The man's brown eyes reflected the same, but his hair was light yellow, and his skin was at least three times as dark as hers.

They didn't answer but stared at him intensely. Despite his intimidation, Ashtion continued, "Are you Dark Elves? For that is what you look like. My main question remains: what are you doing here? If you are after that black-magic mirror, Niejill Airslen has taken it back. If I had that thing, I would gladly give it to you, even though it would probably bring more problems in your hands."

They laughed at his words. The female, seemingly in charge, replied, "We know; our master was the one who gave that gift to the king years ago. I'll answer your question about what we are doing here. Nonetheless, I would have to trust you not to tell anyone about it." She paused. "So, how can I trust you?"

Ashtion thought for a second and, with a smirk, replied, "Who would I tell? My father or one of his men, or maybe another who belongs to your group? I will tell no one about you or your motives," Ashtion assured.

She studied him with her dark green eyes, framed by long red hair, brushing her index finger over her lower lip. She waited, rating his honesty.

"Of course, I will not tell anyone," Ashtion repeated plainly.

"We are staging an attack on this base. Then we will take someone. The reasons for our actions… I will not reveal… yet," she said, her piercing eyes framed by dark face paint.

"Attacking with Dark Elves?" Ashtion asked. They shook their heads.

"No, most of the Dark Elves went to your capital. Even though we are few, we are still a force to be reckoned with," the male said with an arrogant smirk and a soft grunt. The female coughed, as if suddenly sick. "We'd have more people if it wasn't for Kound."

"Kound?" Ashtion asked unintentionally.

"A man who started a group with the mission to kill mixed bloods and anything unpure; Us." she paused. "But that group has been recently taken care of. Just like the one we're here for. They worked for us, and now… the plan has changed." And with that, they vanished without a trace, leaving no evidence they had ever been there.

Once out of Ashtion's sight and hearing, the woman said to her partner, "He looked quite bad, injured. He wouldn't want him to die—he has a job to do."

Unaware of the smile creeping onto his face, Ashtion thought of the impending attack on the base. He felt better already, as if treated by medicine. He remembered his dream; he had been given medicine. It really happened. It came from a Dark Elf? Why?

He needed some kind of proof. Quickly he looked at his leg wound. It was healing. How could so much infection be gone already? Why would he receive help from them?

The recent events were too much to comprehend. His father's betrayal and assistance from Dark Elves seemed flipped. Reality seemed to have turned upside down, and now life was new and unfamiliar.

After Ashtion settled and slept, the Dark Elves returned with more medicine and medical assistance. She told him to get ready because the stage was set. Everything would be better soon.

He knew that "better" meant "different" because how could a Dark Elf's version of better mean anything good?

***

Outside, after just arriving, Freyja finally saw the base. It was built into a small cliff. It looked small, so she assumed it extended deep into the earth. The roots of the woods provided great cover; she and the team traveled underground for over a mile. Memories of the tunnels made from roots and filled with spider webs made her skin crawl.

Worse than how the bugs made her feel, was her suspicion. The doctor, Suruki, knew about the underground paths from his childhood explorations, or so he said. This sounded highly unlikely.

Nightfall was moments away. Suruki and his male nurse, Altham, seemed very confident in the plan. Too confident, Hondou and Lattermere thought. Freyja was unsure who to trust. The medics' confidence influenced her, and her mind reasoned with the soldiers. In the grand scheme of the strategy, neither argument mattered. Only the mission mattered.

CHAPTER 15

Acting on Hope Alone

Darkness fell, and the group split into two teams of four. One team's task was offensive movements through the base; this team named Alpha. They slipped inside without resistance. The other team was to defend the first team from behind and secure the escape route; this team named Bravo. The night was perfect for them—cloudy with a strong, noisy wind.

The underground tunnels through the steep hill provided perfect cover and allowed constant surveillance of the base.

Haru, Altham, Suruki, and Nourttaku formed Bravo. Haru's greatest strength was his keen attention to every possible change. He noticed that the wind, in the last few minutes, had started spiraling inward toward the base. The gentle, steady spiral was subtle, hidden by the natural strong gusts, but Haru's sharp senses caught it. He wondered why the wind moved this way; since the terrain offered no explanation, he assumed it was some type of magic.

Haru glanced toward the Ring Mountains, suspecting black magic. "Something else is here," he whispered to his companions.

"What? Did you see something?" Nourttaku inquired softly.

"Yes, the wind is acting unnaturally. There is magic changing the directions. I can't guess the purpose for this," Haru sighed thoughtfully. "And Alpha is already in the base."

...

Hondou led the Alpha group with Lattermere as the rear guard. Entering the base felt like a long time ago, given the tense yet uneventful entry. The entrance was well hidden but unguarded. An unprotected entrance usually spelled out a trap, as there was never a time when a base's door went unmanned. Yet, it was not a trap, and there were no enemies. Alpha was safe, and the path remained clear.

Neither Freyja nor Khan noticed any signs of life. Marks on the floor, walls, and ceiling caught their attention. Lattermere and Hondou exchanged looks, noting the evidence of struggle. Their group was not the only one to enter this base; they were not the first. Alpha team followed an unknown force, an enemy both stealthy and powerful.

Hondou stopped before crossing a door; Khan closed the already narrow space between them. Hondou grabbed the knob and rocked forward once, twice, and on the third movement, they both shot into the room. With swords ready, they surveyed the area. "Clear," Hondou said. "Clear," Khan echoed.

At the signal, Freyja and Lattermere entered, with Lattermere gently closing the door behind them. The shutting made no sound. They continued in stealth.

"We have to talk," Hondou said quietly. "We are clearly not alone. Something is ahead of us, erasing the guards and patrols. We are in more danger now. We could end up fighting against two enemies. Being only two teams of four our odds are suicidal. We should turn back..."

A burning glare from Freyja pierced Hondou. "Princess, I don't want to do the smart thing either, but it..."

"At what point was this mission ever smart? From the beginning, it was impossible. I'm not turning back just because it becomes even more impossible."

Lattermere nodded, ready to follow her. Khan, however, had been distracted by a sense of impending doom for days. He regretted joining this rescue mission, which now seemed more like a suicide mission.

Hondou smiled. "Then let us continue and defy rationality."

Lattermere pulled out a sketch of the base that Nourttaku had created. "We are close," he said, pointing to their location and the destination. "We need to move in…"

Suddenly, the earth shook. They gasped, alarmed at first, then frightened as a foreboding wave of wind flooded in. Spinning around in confusion, Freyja looked to Hondou for advice.

"Let's move," he responded, running toward the door. Khan followed, then Freyja, and lastly Lattermere. Before stepping out, they paused. Hondou clarified, "The plan is the same, but we move at double-time."

***

Responding to the earthquake and ominous wave, Ashtion pulled himself up using the bars of his cell. Barely allowing himself time to wince from the sudden pain. He asked his newly acquired guards, "What was that? This area seldom has earthquakes. What is happening outside? I'm guessing the base is scared, because I now have you two as company."

The guard turned, equally confused. "Quiet, we…" A sword pierced his chest, and an arrow from a crossbow struck the other guard down. The two guards lay on the ground, silent, still, cold… dead.

Ashtion waited impatiently for whoever was going to enter. Another enemy or a rescuer? It couldn't be a rescue; who could have found him? So, it was an enemy. He grabbed his stomach and focused sharply on the doorway.

A shadow of a female figure appeared. It was that Dark Elf again, Celle! Ashtion felt both relief and fear. She looked at him presumptuously. "Tell them to take the front door out," she commanded. "Quickly!"

Her hand radiated a dark purple glow. Forming it into a ball, she threw it at the cell. The black magic melted the bars into a bright-orange puddle. Ashtion, leaning on the opposite side of the cell. The heat from the steel filled the formerly cold room. His breaths fluttered as he wondered what could possibly be happening.

"Ashtion!" He heard a familiar voice. Freyja stared at the darkening puddle of steel in confusion. She refocused on her brother again. Her heart raced with urgency, gladness, and anxiety.

Ashtion felt a similar urgency but remembered the Dark Elf's command. "Lay that table," he ordered, pointing to the guards' side table, "over this metal." Lattermere acted swiftly, obeying without question.

Using the table as a stepping-stone, Ashtion hopped short distances on his one usable leg. Lattermere and Freyja caught him during the last hop, offering support. "I got him," Lattermere assured Freyja, not wanting her to strain herself further. The haste, exhaustion, and stress were taking their toll. Her expression was transforming to how it was during the ambush—the memory filled him with fear. He needed her to stay calm before she went berserk again.

"We will take the front door!" Ashtion commanded.

"What?" exclaimed Hondou.

"It is what I was advised to do! And so that is the route we will take!" Ashtion argued. Lattermere needed no further reason; he would obey the prince's command without question. Ashtion and Freyja had his unconditional respect.

Khan grabbed Ashtion's other arm to help. "Come on, Lattermere. Let's run!"

Hondou took the lead, heading the team to the front door against his better judgment. The ground shook hard again, causing them to stumble and slow, but this quake was deeper and more focused. The tremor originated from within the base. It was not magic but movement. Hondou could only reckon two creatures large enough for such a physical force: Dragons and Earth Beetles.

As they regained their speed, Ashtion heard a voice in his mind, "Niejill has issued a self-destruct to the base. Get out now!" His eyes widened in panic.

"Quicken our pace! We must get out!" he urged, as a musky smell filled the air.

Hondou reiterated Ashtion's command. "Hurry!" he paused in fright. "It's an Earth Beetle!"

. . .

After the first earthquake, Haru began exploring the base's escape routes. Despite his lameness, Nourttaku helped hurriedly. The two medics moved casually, perhaps distractedly; their pace was slow, and their eyes were glued to the patches of visible sky. They were waiting, watching for something. Haru wanted to pay closer attention to their actions but couldn't spare the focus.

Altham grabbed Nourttaku's shoulder. "Come with me to check on the rear entrance rendezvous point." Nourttaku nodded and looked to Haru to ensure he knew where they were headed. Haru nodded and gestured for him to hurry.

The shrill sound of bats echoed loudly and suddenly. The black sky started to move turbulently. The rapid sound of wings mixed with the gusty wind. Then, feet started pounding above them, running. The ground shook, and dirt rained down, but the thick roots kept the ground firm. The base was being stormed, but by whom? The bats moved with breathless speed toward the base, and the feet soon came into view. Many figures were charging, storming the base. What did they get into the middle of? This was terrible luck.

Haru scrambled for his sword, but it was gone! Where could it have gone? The second tremor hit. He looked at the base, sensing the tremor's origin. He looked at the front door, feeling an inexplicable need to do so. His intuition was right. Alpha team appeared.

Hondou fought vigorously against the bats, dreading the moment the enemy would get close enough. Fortunately for now, the base's soldiers mistook Alpha for allies.

Haru turned, "Suruki, we must help them!" But the doctor was gone, nowhere in sight. Haru had no time or desire to search for him.

Haru leaped out, grabbing an enemy and taking up his sword. Charging down to Alpha team, he realized these enemies were a small race. Being large even for a Thuthairyon man, he plowed many down as he ran. The hill seemed more like a bluff when descending it. It was so steep it felt more like falling than running. He could barely keep his footing.

Nourttaku spotted Haru and traced his path to Alpha. Altham quickly spoke, "We should get to the front escape point. It's the best we can do for them."

"Best? Escape will be pointless if they are dead!"

"What would be the point of living long enough to get there and having no escape?" Altham took hold of Nourttaku's shoulder again. "You will make it, and so will they. Trust me. Few of us have anything to worry about."

Although confused by Altham's words, Nourttaku changed his focus and followed him to the front entrance rendezvous point. Altham's confidence and bravery baffled him.

Freyja felt the surges. She was more an enemy to herself than those around her. This time was worse than the last. She was losing the fight. Everyone looked like an enemy, even her friends and brother. She shook off the thoughts as best she could.

Then the storming men arrived, and two plowed into Khan from the side. Khan was supporting Ashtion while Lattermere defended them. Lattermere engaged the enemy who had surrounded his comrades. After striking those men down, the ground shook terribly. The quake didn't stop; it only grew stronger until the ground cracked under Lattermere's feet.

The crack lasted only a moment before collapsing into a sinkhole. Ashtion, Lattermere, and Khan were quickly twenty feet lower than they had been. They struggled to free themselves from the dirt but were too buried. In a moment, Khan cried out in fear and pain as he was pulled underground.

Freyja didn't wait a moment longer and jumped into the sinkhole. She landed firmly and recovered quickly. Lattermere's fear shifted toward her as she grabbed him and Ashtion to pull them out. Ashtion was lost in wonder, too bewildered to respond. She was too strong; this was impossible.

Freyja held onto them roughly, carrying them, one in each arm. After running back up the side of the hill, she threw them onto the hard ground. Freyja looked at them intensely. She knew them; she knew that she did.

The beetle burst from the ground behind her. She sprinted out of the way, leaving her brother and Lattermere. The beetle crashed down, and Hondou shouted as he saw the creature smash into the earth. There was no way they could have survived. The Earth Beetle was fully grown at ten feet high and thirty feet long. They would be crushed under its charcoal grey body. The dust filled the air, and they could only see the blaze orange spots of the beetle shell.

As it rose on its black and orange legs, Hondou saw no remains of his friends. His attention was soon captured by a near collision with another figure. Was the man thrown by Freyja? Hondou dropped his blade's tip but managed to hold the handle.

Who was this? Once, this woman was his princess, a Thuyon woman of firm and strong kindness. Now, he saw a berserker with eyes turned black and pupils slit like a cat's or a lizard. Her strength and ruthlessness paralyzed him. "A… demon?"

"HONDOU!" a distant voice shouted. "Hurry here!"

He looked up, lifting his blade. It was Lattermere? How had he not been crushed under the raging Earth Beetle? Hondou didn't care enough to ponder. His dash attracted the Beetle, which charged and struck him from behind. Flying forward, Hondou landed close to Lattermere.

Lattermere watched as the Beetle's attention was redirected by Freyja. After he deemed the moment safe, he fell to Hondou's side to help. Hondou had landed face down. As Lattermere turned him over Houdou grabbed his shoulder.

Hondou spat out blood before speaking. "I'm going nowhere, Seidei. When you see Laithrum, tell him I did believe in him. He is a good man and raised himself to be one."

"Tell him yourself, I—"

"No. It's over. My body is dying, so take what I can still offer. Laithrum is the one this land has been waiting for. It's disgusting that he's a Weresync child from an affair, but that doesn't define him. I learned you can't know a person by their race or birth…" He saw the last image of Freyja in his mind. She was violent, blood-stained, and had abandoned her brother and friend.

"Freyja… bring her back. Save her from this…" His eyes faded, and his skin grew cold. Hondou had passed on. Lattermere wanted to agree to all Hondou's requests but couldn't make sense of them or imagine how to accomplish them.

"Lattermere," Nourttaku called as he was pushed along by Suruki, "we must run!" Lattermere paused for a word of prayer for his comrade and his princess, both of whom he would soon leave behind.

When Lattermere caught up with the group, he asked, "Where did he go? Where is the man who rescued us from under that beetle?"

Ashtion responded timidly, "He said he had to finish his mission."

Suruki chimed in, "We must go. We'll see him again."

They followed hesitantly, the line between friend and foe blurred beyond recognition. In a matter of weeks, the ability to discern a person's nature had vanished, leaving life in chaos.

The company now consisted of five: Suruki, Altham, Nourttaku, Lattermere, and Ashtion. Nothing could surprise them anymore. Their mourning for Freyja was brief, because she was brought back. The man who had rescued Ashtion and Lattermere from the beetle returned with her.

Freyja was unconscious and injured from the beetle, but the extent of her injuries was unclear. Ashtion, Lattermere, and Nourttaku feared her too much to get close. She was covered in blood—hers and her victims'. Guilt overwhelmed her comrades; they didn't know how to react. When she woke, who would she be?

The team had lost three at the base but gained two. But who were these two?

Ashtion was the only one who knew. He sensed their presence and saw enough of their covered faces. It was the two Dark Elves again: Celle, the female, and the male whose name he still did not know. But why were they helping him again?

Their journey was fueled by pure adrenaline. The city inside the mountain range, Amarine, had scouts searching for them. Soon they were found, but as they reached the gates, the two strangers disappeared, leaving Freyja with the doctor, Suruki. Suruki soon discovered that Freyja wasn't merely asleep or unconscious—she was in a coma.

CHAPTER 16

Victory Over the Dark; A Shadow Remains

Light was still hours away, and Laithrum lay awake, pondering what was to come. He searched for glimpses of the future but found nothing. This worried him; it had never been this hard to see a piece of the future before.

Remembering where he was, Laithrum sat up, moving into the light streaming through the crack of the door. His eyes met the light, a warm shade of gold.

"Laithrum…" The prince was startled by the sudden whisper, was someone calling his name. He looked around to see if someone else was awake. He knew he wouldn't find the person who spoke to him; it was the same as when he was still at home, the same as how Onlortrens first spoke to him. But this wasn't Onlortrens. Whoever or whatever it was sent chills down his spine and a feeling of suppressing, dark fear. It was the same as well in the meeting.

He placed his hand on the back of his neck and started to rub. He was sore, tight, tired, worried, and now scared. Laithrum looked around and frowned, realizing he would soon have to be alone again. Who in this team was trustworthy? He thought about his friends positively and didn't want to be suspicious.

The light from the door was soon blocked. It opened a little wider, and the sunlight framed the person, highlighting the color in their hair. Linus' bright red, wild hair framed his face.

Laithrum carefully rolled himself off the bed and picked the Ellovast off the floor. He carried himself out the door. Linus' half-lit face grinned, amused at Laithrum's tired expression and unsteady gait. Once outside, Laithrum shielded his eyes, letting the light in slowly.

"Follow me, please," Linus said, closing the door behind them. Laithrum complied, trailing after Linus. As his eyes adjusted to the light, he noticed they were headed to the back of the ship.

Once they arrived, "Why are we here?" he asked slowly.

Linus shrugged. "I just wanted to ask you a few things. Location didn't matter if it was privet. Right now, I just want to stand here and think about how to phrase my questions." The redhead tried to clear his mind. The sea air hit his face; this usually helped calm him down, but he could smell the storm.

Laithrum could easily tell something was troubling Linus, but he didn't want to pry. Linus seemed ready to share without prompting.

"How are the others? Have you seen any of them today?" Laithrum asked, trying to get him talking.

Linus faced Laithrum, showing the respect the prince deserved. "Yes, I saw Lotus at sunrise. Soon after, Dowen came and led him off somewhere. A while later, I came to wake you." He finished relaying and then asked, "How did you sleep?"

The prince smiled. "Poorly, but the rest was good." He sighed, guilt weighing on him. "I spent too much time in heavy, restless thought," he paused, "and I couldn't find what I was searching for. I'm very discouraged right now."

Linus groaned loudly, hanging his arms and head over the rail. He flinched as he moved his left arm, the wound still too fresh. Laithrum knew Linus was beyond frustrated. Everyone has a limit to how much they can take.

Amused, Laithrum said, "What's your problem? To make a noise like that, you must need to tell someone what's on your mind."

"Remember last night when you came out after I received that letter?" Laithrum nodded. "Well, it told me to do something. It would seem right to someone with little or no personal experience." Using his good arm to rest against the ship rail, he continued, "I know my father. He wouldn't tell someone to do this kind of thing without a very good reason. That he has, kind of, but even though he has a reason, do I do as I'm told?"

Laithrum thought for a moment and replied, "Was it an order or just a request? Did he order you to do this?"

"No, but he said I must do it," Linus mentioned, blind to any hope.

"Jobs can be quit, and *'musts'* need reasons. I think you need to go to the one who sent the letter and get some answers. If you need an escape, I will order you not to complete this task. I outrank your father; I will reveal my identity to the whole fleet if I must."

Linus was speechless. He wouldn't let Prince Laithrum's mission be undone by revealing himself to the ship commanders and captains.

Soon, the deck began to fill with people, and Linus pursued the answers to his questions. After Linus left to see his father, Laithrum went to Onlortrens.

Laithrum wanted to ask the elf why his visions had been blocked. At least he could see that a storm was coming. He could easily smell it in the air. Since leaving the palace, his senses seemed to have grown stronger. The whole time he had been out of the palace, Laithrum felt both free and clueless. Needing to find shelter, ration food, face physical danger, and rely on friends were all unfamiliar experiences to him, yet strangely, they felt more natural.

Laithrum wondered what could have changed to block his foreseeing. Was it the results of an enemy? One or both people who spoke in his head early.

"Hey, who are you?!" a man yelled threateningly at Laithrum, the man stood among a group of about fifteen irritated people.

Laithrum, disliking the look and feel of these men, kept his reply short. "My name is Laithrum." He knew they wanted more information. "I was originally stationed on Derdin, but it sank in battle. I'm friends with Commander Dowen Kackveriage, and he can tell you I was born and raised in Thuthairryon." He stopped talking when he saw the men sneer as they got a better look at his face.

Guessing what they sneered at, Laithrum became defensive and started moving away. The prince knew they saw his gold-colored eyes and now viewed him as a problem.

"So where are you going, demon?!" one hissed loudly.

"And who are you talking to? Not me. I said my name is Laithrum, remember?" he said sternly, making the group furious. Laithrum knew he shouldn't have said anything; he might have had a better chance of avoiding an attack. Now, it seemed inevitable.

"I'M NOT GOING TO LET ANOTHER EXIST IN THUTHHAIRYON'S ARMY!!!" exclaimed the man as he charged forward, drawing his sword. Laithrum moved to run but his legs collapsed under him. Two swords clanged above him. Someone rescued him. To his surprise and interest the rescue came by his brother.

Adeyas pushed the man back into his group and yelled, "WHAT IS GOING ON HERE?!"

The men quickly realized who they were facing. None could say a word. Adeyas spoke for them. "Let us just kill him, because he must be like the other one. If that is how you'd answer me, then you are wise to keep your mouths shut." He paused, his glare intensifying. "The only ones who can participate in judgment are those who know the backgrounds and facts. Do any of you know what kind of blood mixes don't work? Or what the other races look like?" He waited for a reply.

One man stepped forward, his chin low and voice shaky. "No, sir, we do not know either."

"Then get back to work, and use better judgment," Adeyas commanded. He waited until they were far away before speaking to Laithrum.

"That was one group looking for Lotus. We need to keep Lotus away from any battle until he's at full strength again. Don't worry, Laithrum, Dowen is watching over him, so he'll be fine."

Laithrum's gaze hit the deck floor, his mind drifting back to when Lotus explained what happened in the battle. He remembered that Lotus had left out pieces of the story. He bit his lip, not wanting to ask but craving a glimpse of what happened. Adeyas could read his little brother like a book.

"His blood started to boil…art least I like to phrase it that way. Lotus went crazy, totally lost control. I don't know what he is. A Weresync with certain blood becomes like a berserker, but he's different. That's why mixed-blooded people have started being called Demons. What Lotus is, I do not know." He hid the constant fear he had that Lotus might lose control again and harm those around him.

"What about me? What am I?" Laithrum asked. He hoped for good news. But his goal was to divert the conversation.

"You're half IseamA, Yiyumiss' race," Adeyas replied. Seeing Laithrum's surprise, he continued, "Your mother was an IseamA from a wolf-like branch. Just as humans come in different colors, sizes, and shapes, so do they. They can learn to shape-shift and are born with physical traits resembling cats, wolves, rabbits, and other animals, as well as humans. Despite their obvious differences, they are the most similar to humans."

"Thank you for telling me. I've always wondered… and it's because my two races are similar that I'm stable, right? What mixes aren't stable?"

"Elf mixes more commonly turn Dark, making them unstable. Julrainzak usually can't have children with humans or IseamA because they are made of too much magic. Their form is more magic than flesh, so all mixes are unstable and unlikely. Thithes don't come to this continent, if they even exist, but they are said to be unstable in and of themselves. So, any mix would likely be unstable." Adeyas sighed. "And then there are curses and magical tampering that cause issues too." He remembered the classes taken to become a competent leader. They seemed worthless at the time, but now he wished he'd learned them better. "Laithrum, I need to leave soon to visit the leadership; do you have another question?"

Laithrum sighed, knowing his brother would find another question annoying, but he asked anyway. "Brother, do you know where Onlortrens is?"

"Why can't you ask how my day is going? Or where to find good tasting food around here? You know, something I have answers to. But the answer to your question is…" He paused, watching Laithrum grow impatient. "I don't know."

This response made Laithrum feel like he was being teased for amusement. He wouldn't complain, though; this light-hearted harassment was a valuable piece of home.

***

Linus crossed over to the ship with his father and hastily made his way to the quarters. This ship, much like Derdin, had intricate markings and carvings on the wood, and the sails were numerous and grand. The vessel's craftsmanship was artistic and welcoming. But as he passed by the deck, all he could see was the damage from the battle. The damage was a shame yet fitting. War has no appreciation for beauty.

Linus knocked twice at the door and waited for a reply. "Come in," came the quick response.

Makoto smiled when he saw Linus. His son's distraught expression soon provoked a frown fallowed by a question, "What is the matter, Linus?"

Linus' stomach tightened, and his mouth went dry. He felt scared but knew he was only nervous. Not nervous about what his father would do after hearing why he was there, but nervous at the thought that his father could truly wish death upon someone just because of their blood. His light green eyes closed tightly, and he tried to take a deep breath. His breath ended short as he said, "I didn't do what you said. I won't avoid Lotus, and I will protect him as a friend." After finishing, he reopened his eyes, now carrying a hard stare. He prepared himself for anything, or so he thought.

Makoto's eyes softened and closed as a smile crept over his face.

"Good." That was all Makoto needed to say about his son's decision. He reopened a book that was laying on his lap.

Linus felt a wave of relief wash over him. He brushed his hair back with his fingers and chuckled. "That went better than I imagined. So, this isn't an order then; I can continue as I have been. But what about the others?"

"Don't worry about them," Makoto said softly, gesturing for Linus to come closer. "The search is for someone who won't cause trouble unless provoked. There's no rush. The leaders are preoccupied with the coming storm and the prisoner trade. Once we reach land, the Lotus matter will escalate. I'm hoping to find a way to distract everyone, so they forget or dismiss that mission. We need a better plan."

Linus nodded in agreement. "I would like to know how dangerous Lotus is when he goes berserk because of the mixed blood."

"He'll be too dangerous for anyone here to handle. Remember, your father is smart. Lotus does not have mixed blood. If you move back that shaggy hair, you'll see ears that are longer than ours and flat-topped, much like a rectangle. This is normal for his race, and yes, as you guessed, I'm not going to tell you what he is. Other than that small detail they look human; until transformed."

Linus accepted that this was all his father would reveal, and it was more than enough. With the confusion about Lotus settled, Linus turned to new matters. He walked closer and sat at his father's feet. He noticed his father had been injured, perhaps from the previous engagement with the Seintroven or the struggle against the black ship. Linus gave his father a worried look, questioning if he was badly hurt.

His father shook his head. "I'll be alright. I'll be taken back to the capital after the storm passes. It should be here shortly, and I think you should return to your ship to help your friends when they need you." Makoto's eyes drifted to his son's left arm, which was in a cast.

"So, are you returning as well?" Makoto asked, never lifting his gaze from Linus' arm. Linus smiled and shook his head at the memory. "Usually, events that put your life at risk cause anxiety, but..." He paused, recalling the incident. "It was a Julrainzak. I was unarmed and down. He swung his sword at my head and... missed completely. It's not like I was far away or moving. He was simply pathetic with a sword. What made it worse, or more laughable, was that my arm was scarcely hurt. The shallow cut barely wounded me."

"So, how did you defeat him? Even being terrible with a sword still gave him the advantage over an unarmed man." Makoto asked, growing curious.

"I didn't. An IseamA girl named Yiyumiss came, but in the end, he escaped." Linus remembered the Ellovast and knew he should tell his father about it.

"Did you know that, for some reason, Onlortrens had the Ellovast, the red-stone sword?" He stopped when he saw his father's expression change to gladness.

"That's wonderful. He found it," Makoto exclaimed. Linus nodded, giving his father a questioning look. Makoto explained, "It's something I asked him to do for me. I heard it was stolen and was on one of these ships." He paused for a moment. "We need to get that back to the capital as soon as possible!"

Makoto then started to crawl out of bed but was quickly and almost forcefully pushed back down by Linus.

"No, you should stay in bed. I will go and tell Vander about this, and then I'll head back to the other ship," he said, bidding his goodbyes. The two parted on good terms.

CHAPTER 17

The Clouds Turn Black

As a light rain began to fall, Laithrum found Yiyumiss, who was searching for the others. They were soon ordered inside and told to stay put to avoid getting in the way. The ship's top cabin filled with the sound of rain, which grew stronger as the waves outside swelled.

Yiyumiss, with her sure feet and abnormal strength, was an obvious candidate for outside ship duties. While she worked outside, Laithrum helped manage the inside of the ship.

Laithrum heard shouting from outside and used his mind to search for what was happening. The ship and a Seintroven vessel were dangerously close to colliding. Someone ran up from outside and grabbed Laithrum's arm. "We need help outside!" the man shouted over the noise.

Laithrum responded swiftly, "What do you want of me?!"

The man looked around before focusing on Laithrum. "Your eyes! What are you?.. How keen is your eyesight?"

"I am human and IseamA. I see most everything!"

The foreman brought Laithrum to a vantage point to watch for rocks and debris. Opening his mind to the future waters and watching carefully, he knew what the path looked like. The watchmen used light signals to communicate by code. Grow rocks and empty cans were used to create flashes, directing what was coming and where to go.

Laithrum's ability as a seer proved extremely useful. Right beneath them was a rocky ridge that, with the dropping of the ships due to water displacement, would cause a collision. Laithrum lifted his light and started guiding. The light was seen not only by the Thuthairryon sailors but also by the Seintroven ships, which observed the chosen best course.

A Seintroven soldier, performing the same job, noticed that Laithrum could see something others couldn't. He gave his ships the same instructions with necessary modifications due to different angles and vessel designs. As the ships drew closer, they observed the rocky points of the ridge breaking the surface.

The cold gray water splashed up, hitting their faces and jostling their bodies. Many were fastened by ropes to prevent falling overboard; others used the ropes as holds while moving.

Despite being wet, tired, worried, and cold, Laithrum performed his task with gratitude, knowing he had prevented both ships from becoming wrecks. A band around his head held his hair back. The band prevented his eyesight from being blocked by his thick hair whipping in the wind.

He watched as some ships ahead entered the protected area and said to those around him, "Keep sailing straight; we are almost there!"

Some strained to see the entrance, but most could not discern any sign of their destination. A few sailors were familiar with these waters and the shape of the rock ridges. They identified where they were.

The opening was narrow, allowing passage for only a couple of ships at a time. Anxious feelings and drawn-out worry hastened their movement through the passage.

At the haven's entrance, a recklessly steered ship struck the side and got stuck. The waves twisted the ship to block the entrance and the large hole torn open beneath it began to fill the ship rapidly. The sinking ship's crew panicked, they raced and tried solving this colossal problem.

Laithrum's ship and the Seintroven vessel next to them were next to enter, but the entrance was now mostly blocked. They were flying forward with little control as is. This would become a pileup of ships. No one else would get through.

Laithrum knew he couldn't move the broken ship. Fear began to spread among the sailors. Onlortrens emerged from below deck, dragging Raven with him.

They scanned the scene and quickly understood the commotion. Spotting Laithrum at the front of the deck, they rushed over. Raven dropped beside Laithrum and teased, "Nice to see you're still being useful after the battle. Does this mean you have some natural talent?"

Laithrum, puzzled by Raven's detachment, chose not to respond.

"Onlortrens, can you do anything about this?" Laithrum asked.

"Yes, but I need to get over to that ship," Onlortrens replied with a smile. "Oh, Laithrum, did you notice what's behind us?"

Laithrum turned and squinted into the distance. Huge creatures swam close behind them. "Two Sea Dragons!" he exclaimed. "This couldn't get worse! What are you planning?"

Onlortrens only smiled and gripped the rail tighter. The ship tilted dramatically, sending two men overboard, saved only by the ropes tied around their waists. Onlortrens moved to help pull them up when he heard Yiyumiss shout, "Just get us safe, elf! I'll pull them up!"

Onlortrens yelled his thanks and turned to Raven. The elf's gaze shifted between Raven and the storm. Finally, he asked, "Are you sure you can fly this? You still have that wound on your back and wing from when we were thrown off Derdin."

Raven's acute glare pierced through the rain. He hesitated and hissed, "Yes!"

Onlortrens remembered the previous day's strange behavior from Raven. Something was bothering him, but what? Perhaps it was related to the theft of the Ellovast? Raven was supposed to inform him of his plan once they reached land. Both were likely reasons for his nervousness. Onlortrens sensed there was something more.

Through the hemmed slits on the back of every layer of Raven's apparel sprouted wings resembling bird wings, but feathers made of chitin and looking like many dragonfly wings. Large, midsized, and small bright dragonfly wings together shaped into wings like a bird. The largest wings, disguised as feathers, were black like his hair. A black darker than night, with a floating, colorful, fluorescent shine leading into a pale blue, they were purely magical.

Raven grabbed onto Onlortrens, who was much larger than him. Onlortrens looked slightly nervous and held on tightly as they took off. Flying into the rough sky, they battled the hard wind, heavy rain, and extra weight. Wings flared rapidly trying to stay on route. The winds pushed and spun them, the falling water blurred their sight, and the spray from below knocked them off their path multiple times.

It was grueling work for both of them. While Raven struggled to fight the wind to their destination, Onlortrens focused on not falling. He used his magic to navigate through the storm. Together, they reached the trapped and sinking ship.

Their landing was more of a crash. Laithrum watched them intensely, relieved to see them both standing on the deck.

Onlortrens closed his eyes, and a green light enveloped him. The elf called one of the dragons to him. It took longer than the sailors wanted, and Raven tried to calm them down and keep them from disturbing Onlortrens. Raven, not adept at calming people, resorted to flapping his glowing wings forcefully. A couple of sailors were minorly injured, but he hoped it would scare the others away. This plan only delayed and distracted them.

Onlortrens needed time because sea dragons were not inclined to help easily. He had to find one willing to assist. The men grew tired of Raven and struck him down. They then ran over, grabbed Onlortrens by the shoulders, and shook him awake. The elf blasted them back with a surge of power.

"What were you thinking? You shouldn't have touched me like that!" Onlortrens yelled, looking behind him in panic. The dragon that had agreed to help was now lifting its head above the water, anger burning in its eyes at seeing the elf attacked.

"RAVEN, GET OFF!" Onlortrens warned.

Raven hastily picked himself up from the tilted deck and started to run out of the crowd of men.

The dragon grabbed Onlortrens between its two immense knuckles. It then plunged back under the water and shot up from beneath the ship, shattering it into pieces. Raven had already taken flight but was caught by the upward blow. The chitin-made feathers and skin tore around the base of his wings, causing intense pain and forcing him into the water.

Raven surfaced, gasping for air. He painfully retracted his wings and called out while trying to stay afloat. "Onlortrens, Onlortrens!" He looked around, seeing only the churning water and debris. Distressed and dizzy, he muttered, "You left me…" then screamed again, "HELP. ONLORTRENS, WHERE ARE YOU?"

Laithrum and the others on the ship watched in disbelief. "Is that what the elf tried to do?" one man worried.

"He'd never!" Laithrum stated. "Something obviously went very wrong. We can't know what happened for sure until they get back." Laithrum fixated on the word "they." Onlortrens had been taken by the sea dragon, so his fate was unknown. And Raven had disappeared in the explosion; was he alive?

Laithrum looked around frantically for them. He protested when the ship started moving through the remaining debris. Men lined the rim looking to spot any survivors. No one wanted to accept more loss of life. Although hopeful they quickly realized that more people would die trying to search the waters. They needed to get out of the storm's winds.

Linus and Dowen were called to help spot survivors, earlier. They stayed hopeful. The plan was to pull victims from the water as they passed the wreck. Due to his injured arm, Linus was only tasked with spotting. He quickly tied a rope around himself for safety. Linus spotted someone in the water and as advised, first looked to call over Dowen, who was helping another. With no choice, Linus quickly jumped in himself.

Dowen, with help, pulled himself and the rescued man up the rest of the way. The two men assisting them took the saved man away, leaving Dowen. Leaning on the rail to catch his breath, Dowen never stopped looking for Linus. Before the men got too far, Dowen grabbed one by the shoulder, eyes fixed on a downed rope. "Who was there?" he asked.

The man glanced at what Dowen was staring at. "I don't know, but the person needs help getting up!" he exclaimed as he and Dowen ran over.

Dowen took position closest to the rail, his partner just a step behind. They prepared to pull at Dowen's command.

Linus finally reached the man but felt his rope tighten. He reached out as far as he could and grabbed hold of the small frame. Linus cringed as he pulled the man into his chest. When he opened his eyes, he saw the hair. "Raven?" Linus questioned, knowing Raven had been on the same ship. How did he get so far out here? Was he thrown from the ship?

"I'm glad you're so puny, Raven. Your small size makes this doable."

By the time Linus was pulled back up, the ship had already passed through the entrance, and Onlortrens had returned, courtesy of the Sea Dragon. He ran to meet Laithrum, who was still standing in the rain. Instead of looking for hazards, Laithrum was amazed at how calm the water was. The protected area stretched like a long hallway, leading to a small stretch of flat land for docking.

"Laithrum, do you know if they found Raven?" Onlortrens asked from behind.

Laithrum spun around to face his friend. After seeing him, he gave the elf a hug. "You almost died, and you come up to me like nothing happened." He let go and thought about Onlortrens' question. Laithrum shook his head. "I don't know about Raven."

Linus was lifted onto the deck. Raven was quickly grabbed and laid down. Dowen gripped Linus by the shoulders and lightly shook him. "What were you thinking?" Dowen asked, his worry still evident.

Linus smirked. "I couldn't just let someone drown after seeing them. But..." he sighed, preparing to joke, "if I had gotten a closer look when I was up here, I would never have jumped. Putting my life on the line for Raven; yuck."

Dowen knew Linus well enough to recognize the joke, even if it was a bad one. He turned and watched his assistant with Raven. He started coughing up the sea water, he would be alright.

Dowen moved over and placed his hand on Raven's back to support him. Breathing deeply to calm himself, he asked, "Why was he...? How did he get in the water? He wasn't on that vessel."

Linus shrugged and knelt beside Dowen. "Well, let's get him inside and ask him after he's been treated," he said, knowing Raven was unlikely to answer. He'd probably have to ask Onlortrens why Raven was there; the elf seemed to know everything.

General Vander of Thuthairryon pondered two pressing matters: the prisoner trade with the Seintroven and the information Linus Lounlyossa had brought about the Ellovast.

Earlier that day, he consulted the ship's weather expert and learned that the storm, known as the Wet Circle, always appeared around this time of year. The Sea Dragons accompanied the storm to explore on land. This storm lasted two or more weeks, meaning they could likely reach the capital on foot to return the sword days before the ships could, due to the storm's delay.

Vander called the other commanders and captains together to discuss these matters. They decided it would be best to send a ground company—a small platoon to return the sword to its rightful place. According to legend, the king was supposed to reveal himself any time now. Vander disliked giving up men for this tale—even if true, "soon" could mean years.

The group was to be formed during the prisoner trade. The number of people to send was the most debated part. Some leaders argued for a large group for the sword's safety, while others insisted on a small group to avoid weakening their forces.

They discussed for a long while before a Seintroven commander appeared in the doorway. "I know a good way to decide," he said.

"Who let you in?" Vander spat.

"I let myself in," the commander replied, stepping further into the room. "After hearing that you have the Red-stone sword here, I decided to make myself known." He flashed a brief smile. "My name is Evayrai Norkora. I was glad to learn that you are not planning anything underhanded. Now, regarding your company problem, we can send men as well. Of course, both of us would only send people who aren't in crazy hatred of the other side.

The biggest calming agent we should bank on is the Legend. Since it's for all of us, not just Thuthairryon or Seintroven or any other race. We all want to see it done. Both our sides are responsible for it, so both our sides should sacrifice for it. Or am I wrong, and Seintroven shouldn't help?"

"Why are you really asking this?" Vander asked, now very suspicious. Their eyes locked, and the stare told them neither was trying to pull a dirty trick.

"Should we vote?" Vander asked Evayrai. Without much thought, Evayrai shook his head. "It will only be Thuthairryon people if we do that. The Seintroven commanders will pull out their men because it's

Thuthairryon's problem, and Thuthairryon leaders will accept based on distrust of the Seintroven men and leaders. There will only be fighting among the group. You are the leader of the Thuthairryon ships, and I am the leader of the Seintroven. What we say happens. Decisions need to be made quickly and in absolute authority." The others in the room were shocked at his presumptuous commands, but they knew he was right. It was the best course of action given the shortage of time.

The two leading commanders took charge of the prisoner trade while other commanders and captains formed the group. Their first challenge arose when they found the members possessing the sword: Onlortrens, Laithrum, Linus, and Dowen.

"You're Linus Lounlyossa, right?" one of the captains questioned.

Linus nodded, though the look of surprise never left his face. The commanders and captains themselves were taking on the responsibility of searching for the Red-stone sword. What was this sword, really? He thought it was a symbolic heirloom.

A captain continued the discussion. "At this moment, do you know where the sword is?" Captain Iindra Hiishlore asked respectfully.

"Yes," Linus answered vaguely but honestly. He did not trust them enough to reveal more. He glanced at Onlortrens, Laithrum, and Dowen looking for support. They were all alert and suspicious of the situation.

Captain Iindra smiled approvingly. He turned to the commander. "I'll handle the rest from here. Go and tell the others that we found Linus and the sword." The commander took Iindra's advice and left.

"So, tell me your terms. Do you want to come with us in returning it?" the captain asked, outlining the plans. He could tell that Linus, and the company he was with, didn't trust them.

"No and yes," Onlortrens replied. "We want every member of our group to go."

Iindra's face showed his shock. If these people became too troublesome, he would have to take the sword by force. His aversion to unnecessary violence was why he was chosen for this job. Iindra would keep the conflict low. "Will you tell me the number of individuals in your group and their condition?"

By asking this, Onlortrens realized Iindra was a patient man who preferred thoughtful decisions over hasty commands. He wanted to make this work.

Laithrum unlatched the Ellovast from his back and held it in front of him, folding back the fabrics. It was uncovered for the first time. The hilt was beautiful yet plain, wrapped like a braid. Cords of leather woven in a spiral adorned the stone hilt. The three cords were silver, dark blue, and pale green. The butt of the sword resembled a faceless coin, the same color as the hilt beneath the cords. The color was dark, not black, and shifted hues randomly. The handle-guard had blank coins on it, and around its base were three images: a tree, a flame, and a white square.

Laithrum felt the urge to unsheathe the sword but refrained. He only needed to show that he wouldn't hide it. They needed to know the sword's location. He wanted to draw it badly but wouldn't… shouldn't.

"Our group numbers eight. One is currently in the hospital due to the storm," Laithrum answered the captain's question with authority, not deference. This irritated Iindra, prompting him to ask the black-haired youth, "Who are you?"

Onlortrens stepped in. "The one who'll be carrying the Ellovast. His name is Laithrum."

Dowen sensed the captain's confusion. Was Laithrum a renowned warrior? No, not at that age. Was he someone trusted by the royal family? Iindra dismissed the thought as unlikely. Refocusing on the matter at hand, he felt relieved that their group wasn't very large.

"Well, yes," Iindra finally said. "You and your friends can come, but only if none of you harbor uncontrollable dislike or hatred for the Seintroven people. They will be traveling with us as well."

The Thuthairryon soldiers were too surprised to respond, but Onlortrens quickly replied, "That's wonderful. Now our Seintroven companion, Raven, will be able to talk to some other Seintrovens."

Linus turned, confused. "He said he was fighting on Thuthairryon's side!"

"He lied," Onlortrens stated simply. "Did you really think Raven was fighting for a side? He's fighting for his own goals. Whatever those goals are, I do not know."

"Is he a spy?" Dowen asked, still unsure.

The elf smiled and shrugged. "I don't know his goals. But he is not a spy from Seintroven or anywhere else because he'd have to be part of a 'side'."

Iindra nodded, relieved to hear Raven was just a random nomad. As troublesome as people with no commitments can be, at least they don't typically hate one warring side over the other.

This group was going to be trouble, but time was tight. "You should get your friends together and ready to go. We will be leaving for land right after the prisoner trade, and every member of the traveling team will be together on this ship." He smiled and added, "If you don't show up, I'm going to hunt you down." He looked at Laithrum. "You're coming with me. That sword is not leaving my sight."

Dowen chuckled at the threat. "I've heard that threat before…" Iindra was again irritated by these people's strange claims of authority. Their positions were unmarked in his memory and unexplained by them.

"My name is Dowen Kackveriage, commander over niento dragon matters."

The captain's eyes widened, surprised to hear that someone like him was coming along. "Are you coming as well?"

"Yes; I've become invested in these strange people. I understand you are leading this company; consequently, I will not disrupt your command," Dowen informed, which made Iindra relax a little more.

Before leaving, Laithrum looked to Onlortrens for guidance. The elf just shook his head. "It seems life just threw us in a strange, unexpected direction." He looked at them. "I'll gather the others and get ready to go."

They knew not to argue with the elf, but they wondered what they were getting ready for.

CHAPTER 18

Winds Blow in a New Direction

After the Thuryon and Seintroven regrouped and readied their equipment, they set out for land. The weather urged them to wait before initiating their mission, but the commanders chose to ignore the desire for comfort. The men needed to face the elements. There wasn't time to wait.

The rain fell hard and unrelenting. The tall cliffs surrounding them blocked the wind. The ocean view was obscured by rain, visibility reduced to ten or twenty feet. The chaotic weather persisted for hours, with large waves shattering against the stone walls and the wind carrying sheets of water over the ground. The colors were a blend of grays, blues, and greens, creating a dark, dull, and cold atmosphere.

The crew, clad in hooded wet-weather coats, swiftly descended the ramp as soon as it was laid down. Motivations varied—some aimed to reach Seitrova, others Thurthairryon, while some focused on recovering the ships.

The company heading to Thurthairryon consisted of thirty-one Seintroven, including Raven, and thirty Thuthairryin, including Yiyumiss, Onlortrens, Linus, and Lotus. The presence of other races and a wearsync became more noticeable in the small unit.

Onlortrens tapped Laithrum's shoulder. "You wanted to say something, or ask a question maybe?"

Laithrum paused before replying, "I heard a voice earlier this morning. Someone said my name while I was trying to see what was to come. I wanted a glimpse, but nothing, not even a picture. Just that voice, seemingly intentional. You don't know me well, but this is unusual for me."

Onlortrens appeared almost scared. "Yesterday you said you heard or felt someone else's feelings or thoughts."

"Yes... do you think the two are related?"

"Yes, I do. Don't talk to anyone you don't know, because I think we have a spy among us. I have no doubt they made themselves part of this group. I will keep my eyes open for them. I suggest you do the same. Honestly, I was expecting this. Thank you for telling me about those voices."

They walked back into the heart of the group. Dowen turned to them, noticing Laithrum's cautious expression. "Is something wrong?"

Laithrum shook his head in denial, though his eyes confirmed the answer was, yes. Dowen, trained in observing thoughts and emotions through body language, decided not to press further. Laithrum must have a personal or important reason for keeping it to himself.

"Commander Dowen Kackveriage," a Seintroven soldier called, running up. "There is a leadership meeting. I was told to inform you so you should attend."

Dowen mused, "Is this an invite or an order, really?"

"I honestly do not know, sir."

"I'll come because I like to know what's going on," Dowen replied. "Laithrum, don't you want to come too?" He teased, knowing Laithrum was looking for an excuse to join.

"I'll accompany you with gladness," Laithrum answered, appreciating Dowen's kindness. As they walked closer, each step Laithrum took felt heavier. He recognized the feeling—so many choices affecting their future, it was dizzying.

Upon arriving, they saw the leadership assembled. Iindra Hiishlore, the Captain responsible for gathering the company members, was present. They also met Evayrai Norkora, the leader of the Seintroven side from the past battle, along with Captain Motoko Lounlyossa, Onlortrens, and Prince Adeyas. Dowen found the leadership both over-the-top and fitting for the mission.

"Thank you for joining us, Kackver—"

"It was an order, sir. There's no need to thank me," Dowen interrupted Iindra as respectfully as he could, still expressing his annoyance. Iindra understood the irritation. He had placed Dowen as a squad leader without informing him first. Dowen had a right to be annoyed, but the presence of the young dark-haired soldier worried him.

Having the sword in sight again eased their worries. But the unknown carrier was a concern. Iindra even asked Captain Motoko Lounlyossa about him, who only informed that Onlortrens had added him to the crew right before leaving port. Motoko was very annoyed that this was all he knew about someone he needed to trust so greatly.

Adeyas grinned broadly at his brother. Laithrum, once again, snuck into an important meeting while remaining a, considered, insignificant individual.

"Time for us to begin," announced Adeyas. "Please introduce yourself briefly and clarify your responsibilities. We'll start with Evayrai Norkora."

"I am the Seintroven General of the Seintroven Alpha fleet and Second Prince of Seintrova. I'm responsible for the thirty-one Seintroven individuals in this company and for seeing to the completion of this mission. I am also responsible for the individual who fought among you, Raven. My mission is to safely bring the Ellovast to Thurthairryon's capital, Onferwil."

Laithrum and all but Iindra were surprised to hear that he was part of the enemy's royal family. He was the second prince, like Ashtion was for them. Glimpses started forming in Laithrum's mind. This man knew Raven's name well before this mission. Significant events involving them had occurred before this adventure. What happened remained unclear because of the mysterious block plaguing Laithrum.

Iindra replied, "I am a Seintroven captain often trusted with public relations. My responsibility is to act as a liaison between the two sides of this unit. If anyone needs to report an interpersonal issue, an equipment issue, or any possible plot against others, they come to me."

"You all know who I am," started Adeyas. "You may not know I have a death sentence in my country. My responsibilities are to take the most dangerous road, defend Thuthairryon until death, and oversee the Thurthairryon side of this unit." This statement shocked the two Seintroven leaders. The Thurthairryon leaders were saddened, remembering this official duty of their prince.

"You're what?" Evayrai asked, concerned. As a fellow royal, this came close to his realm of reality.

"Don't pry and judge as if you're not guilty of anything! We'll continue the introductions," commanded Adeyas. Evayrai sank down, feeling the weight of his own guilt. The events of his past that had led him to this lifestyle were less than honorable. Memories nagged at him constantly. Every move he made reflected his shame. And now his guilt felt worse. The person that he wronged person was there, in the crowd, helping them.

He had no right to judge Adeyas; he was guilty of worse.

"I am Captain Motoko Lounlyossa. I was a fisherman twenty-five years ago when I saved a Thuthairryon vessel from sinking in a storm. I started working closely with Thuthairryon and eventually became a captain in their army. My responsibility is to communicate the plans devised by Adeyas and Evayrai to the whole unit and relay information from the unit to our leading princes."

Dowen looked over to Iindra. "And what am I here for?"

Iindra grinned guiltily. "You are responsible for guarding the Ellovast." He quickly glanced at the mysteriously important Laithrum. "You, Dowen, will be holding onto the Ellovast."

A harsh vision flooded Laithrum's mind, and in unison with Onlortrens, he said, "No, he is not taking the Ellovast!"

"Who are you?" Motoko asked before even Iindra or Evayrai could. Motoko had known Onlortrens for a long time; the elf had even agreed to escort him during this mission because of his injuries.

Motoko trusted Onlortrens, but Laithrum was a mystery. This individual seemed to have more authority.

Laithrum hesitated, but so many images flashed into his mind that he didn't care about his situation. "I am Prince Laithrum Airslen."

"He is my brother," said Adeyas casually.

"He is my highest responsibility," stated Onlortrens, worried about not hiding Laithrum. The spy complicated things.

"And he's my friend," added Dowen, feeling glad to have known before this moment. He wouldn't have wanted to share the expression of astonishment radiating from Motoko's face or the look of confusion from the two Seintroven.

"All this time I…" Motoko said under his breath, not noticing he didn't finish. Not even noticing he said it aloud.

"And…" started Laithrum firmly, yet ending in some confusion and uncertainty, "we are not going to Thurthairryon."

"WHAT?!"

Even Onlortrens was surprised. "Then where are we going?"

"Give me tonight to clarify things. We must do everything discreetly, and you know why, Onlortrens," Laithrum said, referring to the spy. Onlortrens nodded, more worried than before; he guessed the destination Laithrum would reveal, and no one, not even himself, was ready for it.

"Why are we listening to this child?" complained Evayrai, who felt no need to respect a prince born at a lower position than himself. Laithrum was the third born and had mixed blood. He was of little importance. Evayrai didn't realize the relation he had with Laithrum until now.

"Because he's abnormal in useful ways," started Adeyas harshly. "Laithrum is a seer. He glimpses pieces of the present and the most likely future."

Dowen was unaware of this and looked at Laithrum in shock.

The young prince's body trembled with the weight of his stress. Though he successfully hid his anxiety, his identity, abilities, future, and safety felt scattered. He had to lead because no one else could, but how could he? He was no leader.

Onlortrens asked, "What do we do until morning, Laithrum? We must tell the men something."

"Tell them to get ready to travel in the morning. They should rest and pack tonight because after breakfast, we move."

"Yes, sir," Dowen replied, supporting this new directive. He was confused and frightened by Laithrum being a seer. The ability to read the present and future was both freakish and intimidating. However, knowing Laithrum as a person, the fear was short-lived. Coming from Laithrum, those abilities didn't seem terrifying. Furthermore, his respectful brother revealing it and the noble Onlortrens confirming it made it seem like a skill rather than witchcraft.

"Can he see the past?" Evayrai questioned shakily.

Laithrum nodded and was about to speak about not invading people's lives, but the prince and general stood up and started leaving.

Iindra stood quickly to follow, then stopped and said, "We'll meet again tomorrow morning early. It must be before sunrise." He looked at Laithrum. "But I guess it's up to you." He felt contempt toward this youth who always seemed to claim command without earning the right to lead.

Laithrum had no experience, yet he had taken command. He had just revealed his comparatively undistinguished name and taken control of these sixty-one lives. What did he plan to do with them?

Laithrum responded to Iindra's question, "Yes, before sunrise is the best decision. Captain Iindra, it is true that I have never led before. You have the right to worry about the lives, which include your own, and that is why I need all the leaders' trust. I need your trust because I need the troops' trust. I can't do this by myself."

Iindra appreciated Laithrum's humble words yet was unnerved by how precisely Laithrum responded to his thoughts. And with that, the meeting ended. All were troubled and confused and somehow had to address their men with confidence.

After talking with all the team leaders and many of the men, Motoko went to his son. Linus told him the whole story of how

Laithrum became a member of his crew. Linus started with Freyja and Laithrum's hunt for answers to what was plaguing his mind. Then he explained how he snuck on board and was given armor, clothes, and weapons. Finally, he ended with how he was given the Ellovast and how it healed his wounds after the battle.

Motoko listened intently and said very little. He finally had these questions answered, nevertheless, what about the story of getting the sword? Who stole it? How was it retrieved? What happened to the thief or thieves? Why was a dragon made into a ship? And why did that dark ship come at all? Motoko left his son with more troubling questions than he had come in with.

That night was hard for all the leaders. So many questions, most of them deflating their confidence. They had so little understanding and control; feelings of vulnerability spread through them. One meeting had never done that to them before. The air in this forest felt crippling, unnaturally so. Laithrum did not sleep for a moment. So many questions were answered that night for him. In many ways, he preferred the sense of reality before he knew the truth.

CHAPTER 19

Clarity Within

First, the wind back at home, then the odd ship, and now a spy. After the vicious wind at port, Onlortrens told me it was meant to kill me. Was the purpose of that dark ship to kill me too? Laithrum shook his head gently, ending the thought. It wasn't a question—it was a certainty. I am a threat because I can figure out his plans. That's why I am a target. Even though this all made sense, none of it felt true. He was missing the intent, somehow.

The voice is from the person who is after me, but how? I heard his voice both late at night and in the morning three days ago.

Laithrum turned his head to see who was next to him. There lay Linus. Linus felt the stare and looked to meet it. "What? Is there a problem, Laithrum?" he asked, his voice noticeably more energetic than Laithrum's.

"Honestly, I was just looking to see who was next to me." After replying, he decided to ask, "How did your meeting with your father go? I'm guessing it went alright by how you've lightened up. Since you received that letter three days ago on the ship, you had been uneasy."

"Yes," Linus remembered, "That was the last time you and I had a one-on-one conversation, wasn't it? To think it's already been that long.

Just now, I felt an air of strong thoughts from you. If you don't mind, will you tell me?"

Laithrum thought for a moment before answering. "No, I cannot talk about it." This came as a surprise to Linus, but he guessed it was either very important or very personal.

"Did you know, Laithrum, that you've been driving my dad crazy for weeks?"

Laithrum shook his head, feeling sympathetic toward Motoko.

"He came to me earlier, after you let out your secret. I told him how you got onto the ship. I apologized every two words for not telling him who you were. Anyway, please, Laithrum, be easy on my dad because he is injured. He hides it very well and insisted on coming with us after hearing that I was going with Lotus. My dad is smart, but he worries a lot, so tell him stuff, okay? He's trustworthy."

"I am trying my best. Keeping this team safe is a deep concern of mine, and I will be less secretive. I won't be as annoying, I hope." Although Laithrum agreed with Linus, that Motoko was a trustworthy man, he may not be able to speak with anyone. The spy overhearing was far too dangerous. He started meditating on the actions to take and the precautions to place to reach their destination safely.

The morning meeting ended; the information was vague, but the first destination was given. The rain lightened at times but never stopped—not even once in three days. The forest around them was dark and filled with water. The attitudes of most travelers were pessimistic, and many were struck by strong hallucinations, which started fights and other trouble. The events were escalating into a dangerous environment.

Raven hadn't really spoken to anyone since he woke up after almost drowning. He seemed very distracted and upset about something. He also noticed they were traveling in the wrong direction to go to Onferwil. He should have been around people more in the last few hours; perhaps he would have known what was going on.

Onlortrens felt that Raven was avoiding him, but the elf wouldn't allow himself to dwell on it. Most importantly, somewhere in this crowd, there was a spy. The spy was more urgent and important than

Raven's troubles, which seemed never-ending. What Onlortrens found interesting was that Raven was still with them. What had he decided?

Captain Iindra and Captain Motoko led the company, though it felt more like two separate groups since they were divided by their wartime allegiances. The captains knew this division was problematic but struggled to find a solution. Forcing them to merge could end in disaster.

After identifying the least aggressive soldiers, they paired them in groups of two—one Thurryon and one Seintroven—and sent them ahead to scout. Strengthening these pairs could help the individuals bloom into team members. The scout teams worked, and hostilities between sides seemed to decrease. However, new conflicts arose within the sides, and some men experienced troubling illusions. Despite these issues, Motoko and Iindra found the overall situation better than before. Teamwork remained a challenge until they reached the Turwin village.

As they neared the village, just half a day away, the company remained on edge. Distrust and short tempers grew. Some men became especially irritated seeing their comrades talking with the other side, suspecting them of trading secrets. Suspicion was high, and trust was thin.

In the mass of people, Lotus remained alone, contemplating their camp. Strategically sound, the watchmen were twice as many as he expected. And at night the patrol grew in number. The air was thick with tension. Lotus fidgeted with the sword at his waist, becoming more aware of his weapons: the longbow on his back, the sword at his side, the dagger at his belt, and the two throwing knives. His previous bodily limitations were completely gone. Ever since he woke with the Neintoe dragons, he was fully healed. This worried him more than it encouraged him. He knew where they were headed and the enemy's plans.

Dowen and Onlortrens walked next to him, sensing that Lotus shared their thoughts—there wasn't a warm welcome waiting ahead.

"The tension is thick. Do you have any clues why?" Dowen asked.

"We have a spy. He's among us."

Raven had just returned from the woods, anxious. In pain, he spun to face a nearby thick patch of trees. "Someone was there." He hid the sudden pain cause by his fast movement.

"You could sense him that easily?" Onlortrens asked, remembering that Raven's abilities would be useful in this situation.

"Yes, I could."

Onlortrens continued, "I realize I don't know much about you. We first met a little more than a year ago. You seemed to be running from something or someone; I never asked about it. I'm sorry if that offended you. We re-met just before boarding the Thuthairryin ship, and you said you'd help me as repayment for helping you that time. That was two years ago, right?"

"That's right. Why are you recapping this?" Suspicion swelled inside Raven.

Onlortrens emerged from under his cloak, his eyes piercing Raven's. The air grew thick with authority. "Raven, I need your help with something. I have a few questions that need answers."

Raven's expression soured, and the glow of his eyes brightened. "What are they? Or should I guess?" he retorted bitterly, his eyes shifting anxiously, unable to hold Onlortrens' gaze.

Onlortrens waited, but Raven's eyes never settled. He gave up trying to maintain eye contact. "I'll ask the questions, but I'm sure you can guess them." He paused. "First, what is bothering you so much?"

"Well, it took me a while to get over almost drowning and knowing that it was Linus who saved me is disturbing." He groaned almost playfully.

The elf replied, "Does that mean you haven't even thanked Linus for risking his life to save yours?"

Raven shot him a glare of annoyance. "Does that count as one of your questions? I'm only giving you three more, but I'm not guaranteeing I'll answer everything you ask."

This reaction was expected. Onlortrens continued without delay. "What is your plan now? You remember me asking you that during the battle, right?" As Raven's lips curled into a smirk, Onlortrens quickly added, "And that was only one question. The second was just verification that you understood the first. I don't care if you answer the second or not, as long as you answer the first."

Raven frowned, missing the chance to dismiss two questions easily. "I'm going to the village with everyone else. After that, I don't really know. I'm torn between two places, and if I tell you either option, I fear you would… do something."

"And what would I do?"

"If I told you, you'd know what I'm planning. Anyway, I'm sticking around here for a bit longer." He then muttered to himself, "No. Hopefully, I won't stay much longer."

Onlortrens noticed Raven was talking more to himself than to him. The elf pondered Raven's indecisiveness, which was unusual. Onlortrens thought about the last question. "Raven, I'm going to bring up a past event. When we first met, who were you running from?"

Raven pressed his lips together, forming a straight line. "Seintroven soldiers. I robbed them of something." He knew the vague metaphor or abstract perspective could be considered a lie because it was meant to deceive. He was willing to be called a liar this time.

Onlortrens understood it as a lie, though he knew it was partially true. The last question was the only one Onlortrens planned to fight for the entire story. He asked firmly, "Why did you steal the Ellovast?"

Raven's eyes widened, hoping this question would never be asked again. Why couldn't the elf ask something insignificant like how his injuries are healing? Facing the Ellovast situation would be too much. Then both Onlortrens and Raven's concentrations turned as an arrow came into view. It landed so close but hit no one. "Thank you," Raven thought outload to the arrow or the one who fired it. It rescued him from that question. The elf spoke before running off, "I'll be back for the answer so do not thank the enemy too much."

One, two, three more arrows came from all directions, missing everyone. Was the enemies aim off because of the rain? In the rush and confusion of the crowd, Dowen knelt near an arrow. After examining its design, he shouted while springing up and away…

"THE ARROWS ARE EXPLOSIVE!"

Those who heard the warning ran, repeating the declaration. There wasn't much time before they detonated. Dowen didn't get far enough away. The arrow ignited, its fiery wave engulfing all within five meters, spreading minor injuries up to twenty meters around. Dowen found himself on the ground with someone on top of him.

"Come on!" Yiyumiss urged, pulling at him to get up. He glanced at her necklace. "We're very lucky to have you wielding that gem—thank you!"

"Right."

They ran off, helping others up and searching for their friends. They needed to follow the crowd to the village, despite the uneasy feeling. The enemy was growing in number behind them. The forest was grey and wet. Many people fell, slipping on mud, water-covered rocks, and slick wood. Maneuvering was difficult. Soon, most of the forest floor was submerged in water, ranging from an inch to three feet deep. The water was too dark to gauge its depth. The rain had been accumulating for more than a week, and it was still pouring.

By the time they reached the village walls, their company was reduced by a fourth, and the enemy… was gone. The pursuit was over.

The group re-gathered—they were now only fifty-two members.

"Halt, who goes there?!" a watchman yelled from the top of the wall.

Adeyas answered first, "We are a company of Thuryon and Seintroven requesting a place for the night." He hoped the recent attack hadn't destroyed their chances of finding refuge.

The man was about to turn them away, but then Laithrum spoke. "Adeyas and I are brothers of Ashtion Airslen. You know him well, correct?" He stated, recalling past events there.

More than just the wall watchmen listened. The gate started opening immediately. "Come inside," the watchman commanded. "Hurry!"

CHAPTER 20

New Greetings

A man dressed in a dark-gold robe and a black overcoat shuffled up. He walked with purpose. People made way for him, regarding him as one of the village leaders. His name was Tain, and he was considered the village host, responsible for all relations with neighboring cities. He was in a hurry to greet them and return to his routine duties. Stable relationships seemed more urgent and important every day.

Tain spoke to the group, "We expected you because of him." He gestured toward Onlortrens. "And we allowed you in because of Ashtion Airslen." He paused, waiting for the company's leader to speak.

Laithrum looked at Onlortrens curiously. The elf explained, "I have not been in contact with this village for months. The anticipation of our arrival has been long-lived, I guess." The explanation did not calm Onlortrens' curiosity; his guard was heightened by their expected arrival.

"Come," Tain started, "I'd rather have you dry up, eat, and rest before we get started. The end from when we start might take a very long time to achieve."

The leaders stayed close to Tain as they followed the main body. They were led to a religious temple of some kind. It was a large building crafted to accommodate many people. It had stone images of winged humans and patterns of colorful stained glass. Rock made up most of the architecture, complemented by hardwood in more complicated structures.

After a change of clothes, formal greeting, and a hot meal, they finally found reprieve. The comfort of sitting on chairs in a dry shelter, with warm food, was invigorating. As they regained their strength, their worries about the illusions and hallucinations resurfaced. Some magical mischief had plagued their minds for days.

Raven remained seated throughout the meal. He was too tired to move but this made it easy for Onlortrens to find him. Raven glanced over his shoulder at Onlortrens. "Here to question me again?"

Onlortrens shook his head. Suddenly, Raven felt a thick, ominous cloud descend over the room. "No. We need to find Laithrum, so come on."

Their attention was captured by a stranger appearing. Almost like a ghost, there he stood face-to-face with Lindra. The figure's magical appearance resembled Ravens but with pastel coloring and gentle expression.

"Who are you? How did you get in here?" Lindra demanded.

"None of you will find a way to leave. You shouldn't have come in." His green and gold-glittered eyes darted from person to person, searching for someone specific.

"We didn't come in as much as we were chased in," replied Captain Lindra. "But once at the gate, the enemy disappeared." The stranger smiled and vanished as if he had never been there. Lindra's breath caught, and his heart raced. "It's a trap then," he said in a raspy voice, knowing it to be true. He ran to a painted window and looked outside.

He couldn't see any enemies, but that didn't mean they weren't there. Understanding the ghostly creature's warning, the group realized the gravity of their situation. They stood and organized themselves to fight. They lacked a clear picture of the enemy's size, weapons, and the methods. The room fell into tense apprehension.

Maybe worst of all, neither Onlortrens nor Raven knew where Laithrum was. Finding him was now a top priority.

Suddenly, the room burst into flames. The bright fire scattered the gathering as they darted to escape the burning. As if alive, the flames chased them, breaking them into small groups. The enemies plan worked effectively. The small teams of teams of three to five became lost in the foreign village.

Laithrum, Linus, and Adeyas, along with two other Thuthairryon soldiers, moved silently, crouching low through the building. They searched for others, trying hard not to be noticed by the enemy. Through the rain, they couldn't see much, but they couldn't stop searching; it was too dangerous for such a small group. Staying alone didn't seem wise, nor did hiding, as the enemy didn't rely on sight to detect their presence. Their disadvantage grew obvious.

Laithrum kept glancing at a small stone building in the distance behind them. He never fully turned his head but always watched it through reflections. Adeyas, paying close attention to Laithrum, became aware of the spy during their travel. They turned a corner, the building now out of sight, and felt the eyes lift from them.

"We're being watched," Adeyas stated, contemplating how to move faster without increasing their danger. A loud crash shook them, though there was no smoke or visible damage. What could have made that sound, and where did it come from?

The place felt like a ghost town, devoid of life. Then the eyes returned, the sensation of being watched growing stronger. The spy felt closer this time, from a different direction. All five of them wondered how this could be. Could the creature transport itself that quickly, or were there multiple sets of eyes?

Logically, it couldn't have been the same person watching them before. It had to be a team, but no, Laithrum knew it was the same individual. They could move that fast using transportation magic. The young prince sensed it was the same person.

Laithrum's golden eyes met his brother's. "He's the same as before. Unlike the archers in the forest, this person is a leader. He's someone with authority, but something doesn't seem right. Is he just watching, or is he planning an attack?" Laithrum paused, looking directly at where he sensed the watcher. "He knows we know where he is, but he doesn't care."

The watcher smiled at Laithrum's discovery. "Perceptive," he said, his voice soft yet filled with hate and boredom.

"What's the point?" one of the soldiers began. "He can follow us anywhere. There is no escape." He pressed himself against a brick wall.

Laithrum gave the man a hard stare. "We'll be in a worse situation if you think like that. We need to stay strong and hopeful to survive this. The likelihood of victory isn't great, but there's hope. Now come on, we must get Prince Adeyas to a safer place."

Laithrum knew this would motivate them to refocus; only the bravest and most loyal had been brought on this mission. He had spent enough time with them to know this was true.

***

In the burning room where they had dined and rested, Raven was grabbed by Onlortrens. After being pushed down, arrows came screaming in through the burning and broken window. The remaining company ran out of the building. The molding and funiture now ablaze in the stone building.

From the inside out there was no longer any protection. Onlortrens and Raven waited inside, using the rest of the company as decoys. "Hopefully the captains and Dowen will find a way to keep them all safe," the elf said.

Raven knew it was hard for Onlortrens to abandon people, so he refrained from joking. Humor always helped him cope with fear, pain, and worry, making them feel less real and important.

"Raven, stay here in the shadows. Help if you can but do so without being seen. Ensure the enemy doesn't get the Ellowvast. And Raven, don't steal it either."

Raven nodded, looking as if he might pass out. Onlortrens worried about his condition, fearing it might jeopardize the mission.

Sensing Onlortrens' concern, Raven said, "Just go! I'll be fine, and so will the sword."

The uncertainty in his voice scared Onlortrens even more, but he had no time to address everything himself. He ran off, leaving his trust and hope in Raven.

Once Onlortrens was gone, Raven muttered, "My mission commences." His light-blue glowing eyes filled with determination and doubt. Before anyone else could get the sword, he had to find it, watch it, protect it, and take it. Only then could he complete his personal mission.

***

Laithrum ducked as an arrow whizzed past him. Adeyas grabbed his brother and pulled him behind a brick wall. The wall was the remains of a house, proving this village has been terrorized for a long time. Adeyas wondered about the people who cared for them when they arrived. Were they being threatened, were they enemies, or, thinking of the illusions, were they even real.

Their backs pressed against the broken wall, and the arrows ricocheted off the brick, sparks flying over their heads. If the rain wasn't still coming down these magic tipped arrows would have everything ablaze. Arrows struck the ground besides, in front of, and behind them.

Adeyas looked at the three others with him, then at Laithrum. "We cannot stay here. That much is obvious." He checked his surroundings again. "The enemy is only at our backs right now. We must move before they surround us." Then they felt those eyes on them again, this time even closer and directly ahead. Laithrum strained to see.

"There," he whispered, but Adeyas heard. "Laithrum, you actually see him?"

Laithrum nodded, then took hold of an arrow and strung his bow.

"Well, brother, you said we needed to move, and it looks like we won't be able to sneak out of this." He prepared the arrow and sprang up to fire at the enemies behind them. Adeyas smiled, amazed at how much Laithrum had grown.

Pulling out a mirror to spy on what was behind, Linus said, "Two of you go ahead. The three of us will cover you. Prince Adeyas, you go first with Denhain. Once on the other side, help cover us as we cross." Looking through the mirror, he noted the enemy's location.

He signaled to Laithrum, who was waiting with a strung arrow. The two shot up, turned, and fired once, then dropped back down. "Hey, you," he said, looking through his mirror again while speaking to Laithrum. "You missed completely. What's with that?"

Linus answered for Laithrum, "He hasn't been using the bow or sword for very long. It's almost unbelievable he made it through the last battle."

"I won't miss this time. It matters too much to miss," Laithrum said to the man, who stared at him, baffled. What was his purpose on this mission? Laithrum continued, "What is your name, so I know how to get your attention later?"

"Yayn," he answered, giving the two a signal to run. They nodded and prepared for the dash.

"But wait," Denhain said, "aren't we running straight into that fast-moving spy?"

"Yes, so be ready for anything, but you have to go," Laithrum instructed. As Denhain looked ahead, enemies began falling from the sky. Whether they jumped that high or were flown overhead was uncertain.

The rain suddenly intensified, obscuring their vision. After colliding with the ground, many enemies charged at them with blades in hand. Adeyas and Denhain readied themselves, and Linus stood with them. Yayn turned and shot one of the approaching rogues. Laithrum grabbed the mirror from Yayn and looked behind them.

"That won't work; the rain's too thick!" Yayn lectured. Laithrum's piercing yellow eyes silenced him. Yayn waited to see what Laithrum would do. "Send the others ahead. The enemy behind us is shooting aimlessly. They can't see us, and they think we can't see them, but I can. Cover me and lend me some arrows when I run out. Alright?"

Yayn nodded and ran to relay the plan to Adeyas, Linus, and Denhain. They acted quickly before the next wave of men fell upon them. As Linus and Denhain started running, Adeyas grabbed Yayn by the shirt. "Take care of my little brother, got it?" he commanded. Yayn nodded, fully understanding Adeyas' words and Laithrum's command.

Laithrum stood, straining his eyes to see and picking off enemies. When some got an idea of his location, he moved. Yayn ran up behind him and refilled his quiver. "Come on, it's not safe for us to split up for long."

Laithrum agreed and followed, saying, "You'd be proud. I hit more than I missed." Yayn marveled at Laithrum's composure. Laithrum was alarmed by the realization. He moved on instinct alone. but he felt he had to do more. Pure determination allowed him to think clearly past his fears. Still, he knew he wasn't without fear for his own life and for the main body of the unit.

"Laithrum, stop!" a voice called out. Laithrum tried to stop, but Yayn pulled him out of the path of an arrow. Breathing heavily from the adrenaline rush, Yayn kept pushing Laithrum in front of him.

Laithrum recognized the voice. It was the same one from the ship all that time ago, and it had just tried to get him killed. Who was this?

Laithrum tried to refocus, but the voice lingered in his mind. Adeyas looked back and saw Laithrum's pale, distracted face. Adeyas swung his arm forward and struck him.

"Wake up!" he yelled, knowing that if Laithrum stayed that way, he'd get himself killed. Laithrum regained focus and was grateful his brother had snapped him out of it. Adeyas sighed in relief that his action had worked.

They ran through a small stone village house. This home was still in one piece but in bad repair. The village was in terrible shape. Almost through a long hall, they abruptly stopped. The man who had been watching them stood at the other end.

A woman emerged from behind the dark figure. She had dark red hair and dark green eyes. The man, Dederom Maullia, had brown eyes, light yellow hair, and much darker skin than hers.

Laithrum scrutinized the enemy's appearance, noting ears that were longer and more pointed than those of an average human. They resembled an elf's ears, but he couldn't be an elf. Laithrum's eyes drifted to his brother, who was staring intensely at the figures ahead.

"You're Dark Elves, right?" Adeyas asked the one in front. He appeared calm, though his insides churned with anxiety. His main concern was getting Laithrum out of there, but he could only speculate how. This was not an even match.

"Exactly!" answered a voice, not from the Dark Elves in front. Who said that? Everyone, even the Dark Elves, looked confused. Without wasting time, a wave of green magic shot through the wall, hitting both Dark Elves.

The residual magic pushed and shook the five-man team as well. The female Dark Elf regained her composure and, using magic, sank into the wall as if through water. No trace of her remained. Dederom fixed his posture. He wanted to stay and fight so he waited for their attacker. The challenger would pay for this humiliation. He had no intention of retreating until the lady's arm came back a pulled him along.

CHAPTER 21

A New Team

Raven watched the sword Laithrum now wielded, carefully. Enemy contact was imminent, but he waited patiently. He would let Laithrum or Onlortrens act first. This would be the wisest move because the Dark Elf might return. Or maybe not; there was still the spy. Somewhere, the spy was hiding. Raven could feel him and almost see him.

"Laithrum, no one will come for you," said an airy voice on an unnatural wind.

Laithrum replied, "Who are you?" He looked around, trying to find his opponent. He listened carefully to hear where the voice came from next. Adeyas, Linus, and the two others looked at Laithrum as if he were crazy. "Who are you talking to?"

Soon they were spoken to as well and transported elsewhere. Adeyas found himself running across a beach covered with starfish and edged with palm trees. He stood in shock but felt joy deep in his heart at the beautiful sight. What was going on?

Linus was now standing in front of a table adorned with food, surrounded by people laughing and talking loudly with high spirits. Laithrum watched as Yayn lay down to sleep and Denhain started flailing on the ground.

Laithrum heard a sigh in response to his question.

The voice soon said, "Why is that always the first thing people ask? Why is it important to know who I am since you're about to die?"

Laithrum's sight then returned to what he remembered as normal, and there was Onlortrens standing next to him. "Laithrum, I need to teach you how to fight someone who can use magic, don't I?"

"Yes, I guess so," Laithrum said, still scanning for the enemy. "But Onlortrens, why can't you uncover where he is?" Laithrum's eyes widened as Onlortrens swung his sword at him. He ducked just in time, and another Onlortrens appeared, kicking the first one back. Laithrum watched as the new Onlortrens set the other on fire. The flames were green and gold, yet without heat. Laithrum's golden eyes lifted to Onlortrens. Had the real one just arrived? Was this one a fake too?

"Laithrum, calm down," this Onlortrens said. "This opponent you found is good but still too inexperienced to outmatch me." Green magic swallowed the surrounding area, undoing all the spells cast. The team recovered and regrouped their thoughts. Onlortrens' weapon was lowered, indicating that hand-to-hand combat was not expected.

Laithrum moved in a circle, looking all around and ending where Onlortrens was staring.

He saw nothing. "Do you see him?" Laithrum asked.

"No," the elf answered. "He's hiding his exact position well. If he moves, even a little, I'll know where to shoot." Onlortrens knew the enemy realized this and was staying still for that reason.

"Does this mean he is trapped?" the prince continued to question.

"No, he can still use his magic, and that's all he needs. If I don't find a way to defeat him now, I could get stuck in one of his webs." Onlortrens slowly strung an arrow. Laithrum whispered back, "All he must do is move, right? Watch for him carefully. I'm going to follow your eyes." Laithrum drew out the Ellovast, its blade red and ghostly.

The sword didn't look like metal; it resembled a chiseled, glowing-red stone and, at times, faded almost out of sight to everyone except Laithrum. To his eyes, it always looked like a red stone with a sharp blade on one side.

Suddenly, the illusions vanished, and Laithrum came face to face with a pair of bright-green eyes. The enemy intended an assassination but fell in pain before he could kill Lairthrum. After jumping back, he saw the enemy's leg impaled by a throwing dagger. Only after revealing the enemy with the dagger, Raven moved toward them.

The enemy toppled over his cut leg, then sprang up clumsily to attack. Onlortrens leaned back to avoid the first strike. The injured leg shot up with a second kick, but Onlortrens easily grabbed it. Both his hands gripped the foot and twisted it, flipping the enemy onto his belly with an irritated grunt.

"Don't kill him!" yelled Raven, revealing his hiding spot. Onlortrens moved on top of the enemy, striking him hard with his sword's hilt, rendering him unconscious.

Blood from a deep cut on the right side of the enemy's head painted his white hair red, soaking through his braid. He wore two braids, one on either side of his head, to hold back his hair. The right side was fully saturated with blood, dripping onto his long white overcoat that reached his knees. The coat had virtually no sleeves, stretching off the shoulder by an inch or so, and was closed only by a wide dark-blue cloth sash tied around his waist. His shirt matched the color of his belt, with sleeves that went down three-quarters of his arms and were very loose. The neck of the shirt came up high at the back and sides but was open in the front, remaining open halfway down his chest. The shirt's collar was silver-etched, and a similar pattern, though subtle, adorned the rest of the shirt.

Laithrum wondered who this boy could be, and why would anyone wear should clothes in battle. This was the man who showed up in front of Lindra at the dining hall. Was this the spy from the woods too.

"Raven, why are we keeping him alive?" the elf asked seriously as he continued to bind the enemy's hands and feet.

"I'll try to explain after he does," Raven said, running out. "He's not Dark. He shouldn't want to hinder us at all. He shouldn't even want to fight. Furthermore, he's a diversion. We need to find the main body, or they will die!"

Onlortrens didn't like being confused but managed to refocus and picked up their new prisoner. Adeyas wasn't so composed. He grabbed Raven and pressed him against the wall. "I am tired of your games! Tell us what's happening!"

Laithrum, using his seeing capability, searched for the rest of their group. He gasped at what he saw. An image of the imminent future sent chills through him. Adeyas dropped Raven. "Laithrum, are you alright?!"

"I am, but Raven's right. We need to help the main body!"

***

"Yiyumiss," Dowen called her over. When she arrived, he continued, "I want you to leave us and go there." He pointed to a large building across from them. "The enemy seems to be coming and relaying to that location. I want you to blow it up," he said, handing her a large cluster of explosives.

The bomb was rectangular, about three feet long, and very heavy. "I stole it from that broken weapon store across the road. I don't like sending you, but you're one of the strongest among us. And you are protected by the gem around your neck. Three others will assist you."

"I'll go," she replied with enthusiasm. "Don't let them follow me too far. It's far too dangerous. I want to stay out there and survey our enemy before coming back." She smiled. "Always remember, I have this stone that will protect me." After assuring Dowen she would be alright, Yiyumiss ran off to do her duty.

Lotus spotted someone creeping around in the shadows. He surveyed the area to see him again. A solid wooden fence blocked the view. Lotus didn't feel that the figure had hostile intentions. They must not be an enemy.

Raven noticed he was spotted by Lotus. He revealed his face over the fence, then sank deeper into the darkness and stayed still. He wasn't going to risk someone following Lotus' eyes to him. He signaled to Laithrum and the others that they had found the main body.

Near where Lotus spotted Raven, he saw the enemy crouching across a hill, hidden by the slope. One appeared, then another, and another. He tapped Dowen's shoulder and signaled for him to follow.

Both signaled, gathering more people to join. Dowen took the lead, and Lotus switched his weapon to a sword, falling back toward the rear. Something didn't feel natural. Something churned inside him.

Even if it was looked at as betrayal, getting away from this battle was top priority. Lotus actively searched for a chance.

Raven realized the enemy's presence a moment too late. As he glanced behind him, he saw a jagged blade descending upon him. In a swift motion, Dowen blocked the enemy's blade with his own. Lotus appeared, standing protectively in front of Raven while another soldier secured the perimeter.

Unnatural feelings filled Raven and Lotus. Just as Raven jumped up from the ground, Lotus was attacked. A dark figure swung a wood-chopping axe at Lotus, who easily dodged. The enemy quickly retaliated, hitting Lotus with the axe handle. Lotus' strength surpassed that of the enemy, a Dark IseamA. Lotus jumped back, nearly colliding with Raven, who had started running away.

More creatures flooded in. Laithrum knew the Ellowvast had been found by the enemy. The protectors were being overwhelmed. Raven had to leave Dowen and Lotus to fend for themselves. He sprinted toward Laithrum and the sword.

The Dark IseamA soon fled from Lotus to retrieve the sword. In an instant, it transformed into a wolf-like creature, double its human size, and raced toward Laithrum. Raven was delayed, and the creature seized the sword in its mouth. The IseamA struck Laithrum in the chest with its paw, knocking the breath out of him. The large animal, having secured the sword, darted away from the battle.

The creature's speed was greater than Raven's. Flying would be faster. Raven took to the air, flapping furiously to catch up. Once he did, he dove straight down toward the transformed IseamA. Raven swooped low, knocking the sword from the animal's mouth as he crash-landed. Striking against the ground, he skidded and tumbled, using his wings to recklessly change direction. Raven managed to reclaim the sword. Once he held it, he tossed it back to Laithrum, who was in pursuit.

Raven then realized he had given up his chance to escape with the Ellowvast. He sighed, ashamed of his hasty decision, but accepted that he had failed.

After regaining his sword, Laithrum faced the creature again. It distracted him that he was related to this creature. Could he change shape as well? They were both mixes of the same races, so how much were they alike?

***

Linus ducked under an enemy's strike and raised his sword to cut him down, but Yayn killed the enemy first. Linus yelled, "Where's Laithrum?"

Adeyas began searching for Laithrum. Denhain lay on the ground, holding the bleeding stump where his arm used to be. Denhain knew he would only get the others killed in his condition. He managed to stand up and started planning a way to get them out of this mess. He circled around, counting their enemies. He shut his eyes tightly and clenched his teeth. They were sorely outmatched, three to one, and that was counting him as still in the fight.

The enemy charged at Laithrum, knocking him to the ground. The Ellovast fell on top of him, separating him from the beast with its magic. The sword acted as a shield, but Laithrum didn't know how to wield its power. All he had learned was not to let go again.

Linus rushed over and attacked the enemy, pinning Laithrum. As he arrived to help, a blast of magic blew him away. Raven, having risen again, flew to catch Linus. In the process, both crashed to the ground. Linus quickly looked back at Laithrum, dreading what he might see.

Adeyas had rallied the main body together. They were there to help, but was it too late for his brother?

To Linus' surprise and Adeyas' dismay, Lotus had stopped the huge beast from devouring Laithrum. With one hand, Lotus halted the creature, then twisted its head, snapping its neck. The beast lay dead, and the enemy seemed to flee, but their situation had worsened.

Lotus' fierce red eyes watched the scene around him. Memories from his life flashed before his eyes in an instant. He was losing himself quickly. This was right and this was wrong! No matter what misery would prevail.

Laithrum was frozen by the feeling emanating from Lotus. It was the same as the wind in the capital, the dark ship, and the cloud blocking his visions. It was pure darkness.

Dowen, unaware of what had happened, ran to Lotus. He touched Lotus' arm. "Are you alright?"

Lotus was in shock but seemed to be recovering. Dowen looked fearfully at his bright red eyes. A moment later, a Dark Elf's magic grabbed Dowen like teeth made of fire and thrashed him into a nearby wall. He was knocked out by the blow. Lotus watched in slow motion as blood was drawn out by the magic's bite, and pain flashed across his friend's face. Following Dowen's body thudding against the wall, Lotus lost control.

Laithrum took a moment to see if Dowen would move. He didn't. The only movement was the blood dripping from his shoulder and head. The manifestation of Lotus had fully changed to one of violence and a thirst for blood. He had to handle this himself.

Lotus' eyes grew brighter, a red that would fit only in a brilliant sunset. His hair went limp and turned as white as snow. His spirit formed a feeling of darkness, a heaviness that petrified their lungs. His arm moved through the damp air, decapitating the already dead beast. The thirst for blood now poured from his eyes.

Lotus' sight turned to the movement outside, and a crooked, toothy smile appeared on his face. Without further delay, he darted toward the first of the company to kill.

Yiyumiss, still in the shadows, heard the battle worsening. She ran to an opening to see.

"What!" she exclaimed, remembering the past event when this had occurred. The sight froze her.

"No. Lotus, not again!" she thought as her body and mind began to shake. Pain would follow this for everyone. For Lotus and for everyone else, if anyone else would survive.

An arrow from above struck Lotus, piercing his chest near his heart. He pulled it out without flinching, though Yiyumiss could see the pain in his eyes as he searched for the shooter. She knew a piece of her friend was still in there.

Yiyumiss hid her face, avoiding eye contact to prevent him from hunting her down.

The Thuthairryon and Seintroven were distraught. In less than a minute, Lotus had killed seven men and was still fighting their enemies.

They darted away, feeling hopeless. Laithrum, relying on his IseamA side, dragged Dowen toward the fleeing company. Onlortrens soon appeared to assist.

Running to them in panic, Linus shouted, "WHAT'S GOING ON?!" Raven, equally panicked though not confused, was with him. He limped and stumbled quickly in determination.

Onlortrens looked at Linus with intense dark-blue eyes. "A demon emerged, something so strong that material weapons don't harm it." Linus looked bewildered.

Adeyas, recognizing the description, screamed to the group, "Keep running!"

"Lotus…" he worried for his friend, trembling with fear of what he had become.

"Laithrum," Adeyas called, panicking, "Come with us! You can't help him! You will die!" Overcome with worry, he sprang forward, pulling Laithrum and the unconscious Dowen with him.

Raven, surveying the land as he hobbled, spotted Lotus. Laithrum was his target because of the sword. Raven wouldn't reach him in time. Lotus lunged at Laithrum, but Yiyumiss dove in the way.

The red light from her pendant shone, stopping Lotus briefly before he broke through, his hand crashed into her chest, brushing against her lung. Traumatized by her blood, he pulled his hand out but couldn't stop. Laithrum was next.

The prince's gaze locked with Lotus'. Raven finally arrived, plummeting down, with the last strength in his wings. He grabbed Laithrum before Lotus could. Lotus' hand grabbed one of Raven's wings, tossing both him and Laithrum roughly. Tumbling over the rocky surface, he managed to wrap his wings around himself and Laithrum for protection.

Raven's wings were badly injured. Broken wing-feathers scattered about. When they finally stopped, Raven couldn't move. He was awake, but the pain and shock paralyzed him. His magic drained, his blood following suit. Soon his life too would be snuffed.

Laithrum, almost unscathed from the crash, looked at Yiyumiss, then back at Raven, and finally at Lotus. He understood now. The sword had helped heal him before. He bent down and grabbed his sword. "The Ellowvast belongs to me," he convinced himself, pulling it from its sheath. Stepping forward to face Lotus was the last thing Laithrum remembered.

Onlortrens arrived just in time to see Lotus, badly injured but still conscious. Lotus called forth spikes from his back. Four spikes, like those of Nenotoe dragons, transformed into wings, and he flew away.

Onlortrens wanted to smile but couldn't, given what had just happened. "So, he is the king from the legend. He can use the sword's magic, yet he still can't control it."

Adeyas, leading the group in search of survivors, was amazed and overjoyed to see Laithrum alive. He ran to his brother and caught him as he collapsed from shock. The others rushed to assist Yiyumiss and Raven.

The battle had finally ended, and their company of sixty-one was now reduced to nineteen, many of whom were injured.

CHAPTER 22

Off to the Ring Mountains

Finally awake after what felt like an eternity, Laithrum confronted the current reality. Losing Lotus had granted him the glimpses he had sought for so long. Learning all he did was both overwhelming and reassuring. He knew where he needed to go and who had to come with him, though he didn't understand why. Somehow, Lotus' prevented this ability.

Finally, the rain had stopped, and the standing water started receding. The sun was out, and it had been so long since he had seen this much light. It hurt his eyes but warmed his spirit.

Laithrum stumbled out of bed. He wasn't hurt, yet moving proved difficult, as if he hadn't moved for days. Stretching his stiff back he looked around. As he tried to find out where he was, he noticed the room was nice—large and clean, with bookshelves, extra furniture, drapes, and plants. He examined the pictures and writings in the room. He was still in the Turwin village, which he considered a good thing and a surprising thing.

Laithrum meandered to a window. It was warm and busy outside. He had to continue the mission. He stepped into the brightness, guessing late morning. The ground was firm again from the drying earth.

Many people were working on construction tasks, fixing buildings, fences, and even the roads. Others were engaged in landscaping and groundskeeping in the ruined gardens. The men he had traveled with had started fixing the village immediately after the battle as a helpful distraction.

"Laithrum!" Adeyas called, running over to him. With hands on Laithrum's shoulders, he continued, "I heard interesting things, brother. You were able to use the Ellovast's magic and defeated our enemy. You were out cold for three full days. How are you feeling?"

The two brothers stared at each other for a moment. Adeyas was impatient, while Laithrum was surprised by his brother's reaction and the remark about missing three days. The time unconscious explained why he could barely walk when he woke. And how the rain stopped long enough for the ground to start drying.

Finally, Laithrum responded, "Physically, I feel stronger now than ever before. I'm a bit wobbly from not moving for so long. Mentally, I'm overwhelmed with all I learned in these three days."

"What did you learn?"

"When you were captured and ended up on the dark ship, did you ever wonder why you were the only one?"

"Yes, I wondered often. I was treated better than I should have been—nicely fed and never harmed. Why was that? I assume you now know."

"Lotus is our enemy. Or rather, a side of him is." He paused for a moment. "You were protected at sea by being made a prisoner. Ashtion, when he was here, was given three magic stones. The cloaked woman who gave them to him advised him to swallow them and call on them if he needed extra power. She was the Dark elf we met as an enemy three days ago, Celle. Lotus told her to give him those stones. He told the enemy to save you on the ships. He's having trouble killing me because of the reason he saved you and Ashtion. It's Freyja. He doesn't want any more of her siblings to die."

Adeyas was in shock. "How did we not notice? He was a good friend, right?"

"I saw the history of many in our group. It explained a lot. I don't know everything—not even close—but I know what we need to do." His golden eyes shone brightly as he raised his face to the sun. He felt he wouldn't come back… that return wasn't possible for him.

Adeyas wanted Laithrum to rest, but matters were too serious and urgent for any of them to rest. "We should call a meeting. All the remaining leaders and our group will attend."

"And the captive needs to be there. He will be helpful," added Laithrum.

***

Adeyas wasted no time and denied all excuses. The group proved difficult to rally because they had all distracted themselves with solitary activities. The tight group that Laithrum was part of seemed disbanded. Being close to each other provoked conversations and memories. They weren't any different from anyone else. No one wanted to talk yet. Nevertheless, all the leaders were gathered. This gathering was indeed over half of the survivors in the company.

Iindra Hiishlore, the Captain responsible for gathering the company members, was lost in battle. Evayrai Norkora, the Seintroven prince, was there. Captain Motoko Lounlyossa was present with Onlortrens and the prisoner named Oshei. Dowen could not come because he was still unwell from the past battle.

Along with the leadership, Adeyas brought the rest of the team. Linus, who remained well, Yiyumiss, who had her chest wrapped from her injury. She was too stubborn and excited to miss the meeting. Seeing Laithrum up and around was reason enough to go. Raven, pale and sickly—too stubborn to keep his wings hidden, was willing to drag himself there. Yayn invited himself as Adeyas stole his patients from the hospital.

While the others were being gathered, Laithrum sorted out his thoughts and the glimpses. The plan seemed unlikely. It was too simple and impossible, but it made sense why he was considered such a threat.

He looked at the gathering. The wounded, the worn-out, the curious, and the irritated made up this group. They all came but only two had any enthusiasm or hope for the mission left. Not surprising, it was Yiyumiss and Onlortrens that remained optimistic. As Laithrum rated the team's abilities, the future looked promising, but the present needed a lot of work.

"Greetings. Thank you for coming; I know it wasn't easy," Laithrum began. "I want to tell you about our next mission. Oshei knows the enemy and will brief us on them."

As Yiyumiss and Linus' eyes shifted, their exhausted expressions turned to shock. The world seemed so much smaller now. Seeing this guy again was beyond reasoning.

"YOU!!!" Yiyumiss exclaimed.

Linus added, "You're the one we fought on the Dark Ship. The guy who was terrible with a sword!" He still hadn't recovered from the experience. There was no logical reason for Oshei to have missed him.

Oshei wanted nothing more than to protest helping them. He could hide in his mind with an illusion and escape this terrible reality. The embarrassment, pressure, and risks were too much for him to handle. He knew hiding would not be wise, so he acted as if nothing had been asked at all. He simply looked from one person to another, pretending someone else was supposed to start talking. This made the bystanders even more perplexed, entertained, or severely irritated.

Onlortrens threatened him with a hostile stare. After a hard, nervous swallow, the boy's green eyes grew brighter with magic as he began to explain. He unleashed magic to show them his artistic rendition of the historic event.

"Laithrum, you just wanted history and identification of who the enemy is, right?" Oshei asked, already tired of working with them.

"Yes."

"First, I'll start with Pierrah. He came to this continent fifty-some years ago and started taking over the Ring Mountain area. As you know, there was a small war. Toward the end of the one-year war, the Legend of the King was found or made. The legend was the reason the fighting stopped, because of the promise that he'd take care of the problem in the future." He paused, changing the direction of the story.

"Why did he come here? I don't know, and I don't care. Pierrah came with or was possessed by a powerful gem and was already a powerful Thithe. He also took a child here to raise as an assistant in taking over the land. The stone was red... just like that one," he pointed at Yiyumiss' necklace, "and Laithrum's sword. Coincidence? I don't know, but I kind of care. Anyway, he was too powerful to go unnoticed. A group of powerful individuals from over the waters, living in the mystic land where Thithe are from, acted."

"I'm going to show you the fight from the past when he was defeated." Oshei cast an illusion over them, bringing them to the past battle.

Pierrah was tall and strong, but his look bleek, and the feeling he gave off made Laithrum uneasy. Pierrah was a High Thithe with red, arrowhead markings at the corners of his eyes. This team of five individuals put a seal on Pierrah, using the necessary amount of power. Already worn from battle, a bright light swallowed the High Thithe. When the light faded, Pierrah vanished, seemingly destroyed. The child he brought went unaccounted for. The team, mostly women, all went home, I believe. One of them stayed behind and gave the sword to Thuthairryon. That blade is made from a red stone. The hope of someone who could use it coming along was her doing. Thus, the legend was born.

After the vision ended, Onlortrens asked, "Is that all you know? You never even said who our enemy is." The elf was irritated and confused, as Oshei acted as if he had truly answered the question.

"That's because I'm not sure. I believe it's the Thithe that Pierrah brought here," Oshei shrugged.

Laithrum was caught up in the vision Oshei had cast. He wondered if Oshei really knew what they looked like. The individuals in the vision were all like Onlortrens—magical and captivating. He looked at his brother, who sat next to him. "I now know who the second enemy is." He continued to the group, "Thank you, Oshei. Our enemy is two individuals."

"No," interrupted Evayrai, "we have a third. He's the king of Seintrova, my father. He's been morally ill for seven years now, affecting many people."

Raven glared at him, remembering his escape three years ago, but feeling too ill to respond physically. He shifted his eyes to Laithrum and the Ellovast. He still needed that sword, but his condition had destroyed his hope and his body. His anger smoldered inside him. Revenge was all he had left.

Evayrai glanced at Raven, feeling a strong guilt from the past and a responsibility for the present. He didn't know how to apologize.

Laithrum, aware of this issue from his glimpses, said, "You have to work together to fix this."

"NEVER!" Raven yelled. "This man and his family can't be trusted. They use people and take until there's nothing left. Parasites!"

"He has the right to hate me. My father and I used his magic without permission or regard for his well-being."

"And…" Raven continued accusingly, overwhelmed by guilt.

"We're currently using his sister in the same way. They are twins who were kidnapped. She was light like opals and was kept as a decoration… like a pet. After Raven escaped, we had to use her instead."

Onlortrens grabbed Raven's shoulder to hold him down. "She's too ill now to be useful, right?"

"She's not good at adapting to the Seintroven people like you were." Evayrai said, expression filling with shame and disgust.

"You make it sound like a skill! I'm so honored that I can adapt to being robbed of my spirit. Thank you for pointing out this great strength of mine." Raven spat, wishing he was strong enough to move and finally kill this man.

Onlortrens had to restrain him carefully. Thankfully Raven stopped quickly so his wounds weren't reopened. This surprised both Raven and Onlortrens because there was so little aggression in comparison to before. The pressure Onlortrens applied caused Raven to collapse in pain. He tried hard not to yell or faint. The situation just kept getting worse.

"What's the matter?!" Evayrai stuttered, his concern provoked by guilt.

Staying by Raven's side, Onlortrens answered, "He'd be fine, if he'd let his wings out. People could treat them so they could heal." Laithrum then remembered how badly they were broken during the fight with Lotus.

"He's fine? And Wings?" exclaimed Linus, completely confused. The company shared his bewilderment.

"I've known Raven long enough to know this is not 'fine,'" Linus continued. "And I heard of someone with winds.... but it was him?"

Onlortrens began to explain, "He's from a sensitive race. But they can heal very well if they let themselves—right, Raven? But they need extra help."

Raven sneered at the thought but surrendered to what he knew was right. As he set his wings free, they revealed a mass of broken chitin, dripping with black and purple goop. The musky smell filled the air, and the formerly beautiful shine became faint sparkles.

No one expected the sight. Linus was the most surprised and fell over in shock. Staying seated on the ground he stared at the sad, disgusting sight. Onlortrens used his hand, coated in magic, to brush the goop from the surface. This was sure to be a theme—one surprise after another.

Yiyumiss exclaimed before Oshei could, "How could he be a Jurainvel? His attitude is punishing, violent! And he's good in combat!"

Raven glared at her but remained silent. When the goop hit the ground, the infection evaporated into hot steam, vanishing.

She continued, "How can you be the same as the useless Oshei?" The comment warranted glares from both Jurainvels.

Onlortrens sighed and admitted, "I can't explain him."

"I can," Evayrai interjected. "He got the combat capacity from me. I was dying from a disease that infected my entire body. Father and I used him to heal me by pulling his magic out of him and into me. In return, we gave him my disease and, unexpectedly, some behavioral traits not natural to his race. That's why Raven looks like a Seintroven.

Following my healing, the king, my father, used his magic to make his body younger. He and I appear the same now. How he accomplished this, I do not know."

"It's disgusting," Raven proclaimed.

Evayrai responded with a positive observation, "The red line near your eye, that Seintroven mark, has faded. It's almost gone. You are less malicious. I believe you'll be back to your own self very soon."

Raven retorted loudly, "But I needed that aggression and Laithrum's sword to get her back! That's the only reason I came with Onlortrens on this mission!"

Laithrum smiled at the confession. This annoyed Onlortrens some and relieved him greatly, because he nearly begged for that information for years. It was finally released, suddenly and willingly. Raven, annoyed at his own disclosure tried hiding in his frustration.

Laithrum then responded, "All this leads us to where we need to go."

He stood up. "I need to get Dowen to train us to ride Nientoe Dragons. Four for the first team: Raven, Evayrai, and Yiyumiss will go with me to get Raven's sister. We'll need her.

"Onlortrens, please call the Nientoe Dragons, and I need you to go ahead to the Ring Mountains to the village. Take Oshei and Adeyas with you; there's something we need them to do. And if anyone else volunteers to go, we will need help."

Linus raised his hand. "There's no way I'm not finishing this; I'm coming!"

"This is time-sensitive, though I don't know why," Laithrum said. "Motoko, I don't know how many leaders you have left, but you'll oversee the rest of our mission's team. Stay and help rebuild this village or go home—it's up to you. But expect peace soon."

Adeyas stared in awe at his little brother's growth and authority. He stood and announced, "You know what you must do! Pack lightly for the trip, stay close to your team, and once those Dragons get here, you will leave immediately! No extended conversations or sleeping! You have work to do!"

Adeyas went over to Onlortrens. "What must we do when we get there?"

"I have no idea, and neither does Laithrum. The Ring Mountains have a fog around them that makes it impossible to foresee anything."

Oshei was very anxious about going to the Ring Mountains, but he truly didn't have a choice. Onlortrens had too much experience with his type of magic; he was helpless against the elf.

Laithrum soon woke Dowen, and they started the instructions. The mission would come sooner than any of them were ready for. None of them knew how to prepare for such an end.

Chapter 23

WHERE MAGIC GATHERS

The mountains cradled Amarine, and large rock walls protected the borders. The village was mostly farmland. Tinny growing plots tired all over the rock bluffs. Extended families living together in one home to conserve space. Trust was paramount because surviving depends greatly on one another. Consequently, the people never trusted outsiders. They only let them in because of a past agreement. Only Suzuki and Altham knew the details of.

It was in two rooms of the village hospital, where the company of five stayed. Their supportive "enemy", Nourttaku, was still watched but was quickly gaining trust. They still watched him dutifully, but they considered him an ally and brother now. Nourttaku understood and accepted that he wouldn't have any alone time. He wasn't upset about it anymore. He couldn't get home by himself anyway; he needed them.

Freyja stayed in one room, and the other five in another. A person having their own room was unheard of there. Hers was a special case, and no one seemed to know why. Not even the rest of her company could visit. Rest was needed, but now that they were rested, they started to become restless.

There was never any privacy, and they weren't interested in deepening their relationships. The time spent together was more than just awkward; it was irritating. The people of the city didn't like them wandering out; therefore, they were stuck in the same general location. They felt trapped.

Looking out to the mountaintops from their assigned room's balcony, Lettermere stood with Nourttaku. He watched the former prisoner and pondered over the events of their journey there.

"Nourtaku, you're a mixed-blooded Julrainvel, right?" he asked, recalling the magic Nourtaku wielded against the dark elves.

"No. Julrainvels can't reproduce with humans. Kon was mistaken. I was infused with magic from a female Julrainvel for our mission. It was meant to help me retrieve a special sword. Why do you ask?"

"I was hoping you could help Freyja. Maybe wake her up. Julrainvels are known for their healing abilities, aren't they? We haven't seen her for over three weeks."

Nourtaku nodded, understanding the enticement of magic, but he didn't know the details. Before he could respond, Ashtion approached from behind. "I feel the same," he said. "She saved me, and I haven't even thanked her or heard her story. I don't even know if she understood why she… had those abilities."

Ashtion and the others had cleaned up, no longer wearing weapons or armor. They felt safe. Despite this, Ashtion had kept to himself, haunted by the mirror's influence, and taking time to mourn the many losses. His mother's death, the capitals fall, his father's betrayal, and his sibling's life's being a mess. These days were cleansing and hard. Facing the heavy emotions was so much harder than running away from them. After his thoughts felt normal again, Ashtion came out of his hiding to confront the team.

"I've seen the doctor coming out of her room more often," he continued. "He said she's coming out of her coma and returning to normal." His demeanor remained somber. The darkness and mystery still lingered. Who was she now? He had no idea what to think or do.

Lattermere replied, "I don't know what the princess is, but I want her back. I miss talking to her and I want to apologize for being so cold since the battle outside Thuthairryon. You weren't there. It's when she first went berserk. I'm very sorry…"

Suruki appeared from behind. "She might hear you soon. The magic that caused her to go berserk and gave her that strength is centralizing rapidly."

"Magic… do you know what she is?!" Ashtion asked, still grappling with the revelation that Freyja was his half-sibling.

"Yes, I do, and so do you. She's human. She's your sister; you share the same parents."

Lattermere and Ashtion's memories stirred disbelief. They had known her for years, yet what they had witnessed made them question everything. Their torn thoughts needed clarity and direction. Suruki needed to stop being vague and tell them straight out before they aggression became any higher.

Nourtaku watched the three quietly. He remained the most ignorant of them all. The emotional detachment to Freyja, or any of them, made this situation less charged. He had seen too much to assume anything. He could believe anything after using Julrainvel magic and witnessing Freyja power at the capital.

Suruki continued plainly, "She had a romantic relationship with someone who wasn't human; that's all."

"What! What do you mean?" her brother shouted, a mix of shock and anticipation in his voice.

"Lotus, the one who worked in the palace. Their relationship resulted in a child. The magic has left her flesh and is now focused on forming the child. She won't go berserk again. You could say she's back to normal."

"Did he know this would happen?" Lettermere growled defensively, while Ashtion laughed, feeling a mix of joy and amusement. He never would have guessed this behavior from Freyja. She was the most responsible person he knew. His carefree spirit shielded him from reacting angerly, but as he chuckled, a painful prompting tore away his amusement. This would be very difficult for his sister. A mission, urgent and given by the same magic as the mirror, pressed on his mind. He had to plan carefully.

The doctor started to explain, "Most likely, the possibility of a child never crossed his mind. First children don't come easily to Thithe… that's what he is." He changed to a cheery tune, "Who of you wants to see her?"

Ashtion started walking to the entrance, pensively. "Well, come on, let's go see her."

Lettermere followed swiftly, dragging Nourtaku with him. Suruki stayed behind, knowing they'd have to wait for him to enter her room. Once alone, Celle jumped down onto the balcony, landing next to him.

"It's already time for the mission's end, but you seem unmotivated. What's the matter?" she asked with an uncontrolled smile. Their victory was so close she could feel it, and it was glorious to her.

He didn't answer. The same happiness was far from him, but doubt, or maybe fear, overwhelmed him. He remained in thought until changing the subject. "We are about to have company. The elf Onlortrens is with them. We'll have to move quickly once the time comes, because our situation's complications have just doubled."

"We'll be fine. I have a surprise for them." She kept a straight face, but her eyes shifted to distant thoughts. She was troubled by something, affecting her confidence greatly. She still had full faith they'd win, but this thought was more personal. Suruki recognized this because he felt the same way.

She left as quickly as she came, and Suruki returned to his role as a friendly doctor. He joined the company waiting to see Freyja.

***

From their vantage point high above, the landscape of Seintrova unfolded, a water-laden expanse of wetlands and rivers. Sparse trees dotted the scenery, while tall grasses almost rivaled them in height. Due to the standing water, most houses were built on stilts and tall platforms, connected by bridges that served as walkways between commercial buildings and homes. The trees, with their thick roots stretching above the ground, mirrored the houses. Their bases provided homes for various wildlife.

Riding a Neintro Dragon demanded bravery from the two teams. Typically, the training and bonding process spanned months, but in this case, it took only a few days. Onlortrens facilitated introductions between the riders and dragons, fostering quick trust. However, as with any new relationship, miscommunications were frequent. During this flight, the dragons occasionally snapped at their riders out of sheer irritation.

Laithrum, accompanied by Raven, Evayrai, and Yiyumiss, arrived at their penultimate destination. It was his first glimpse of Seintrova, having never seen even a picture before. The palace, like the rest of the city, stood high above the solid ground. Water ways meandered through the thick stone stilts holding the foundation. The architecture, designed as a maze, had built in garden boxes of flowering trees, shrubs, and groundcover plants interwoven amongst the stone.

Tall iron fencing surrounded the palace separating it from the nobles' houses. Different social groups lived in proximity, creating distinct visual villages throughout the capital city.

As they flew over the fencing, arrows shot upwards at them. The attack failed as the projectiles were swallowed by the red magic emanating from Ellovast and Yiyumiss' necklace. Eveyrai called out to a guard, who quickly recognized him and ordered a ceasefire.

Upon landing, they were greeted by numerous guards. Archers were strategically positioned around the winding building, watching while staying covered. A patrol of Sinjar came around the corner because of the commotion. The man who had called the ceasefire approached them swiftly.

Laithrum turned to the group, who doubted the success of their approach, and exclaimed, "The king is controlled by the same power that controlled my father and now influences everyone inside these gates. Because we know this, the mission will be swift."

Raven shrank back from the group, hiding his face and healing wings behind his dragon. There was a chance the guard wouldn't recognize him, as his facial markings had vanished and his body had reverted to a Julrainvel's form, but he doubted it. "Laithrum," he began, "Can I stay here? I'm too much of a Julrainvel right now. I've lost my nerve for combat. I'm a useless pretty, little, magical flower now. It's embarrassing."

"You'll be fine. It's too easy," Laithrum reassured him. Turning to the second prince, "Eveyrai, keep an eye out for your father. He'll be the only one to try and stop us."

They all looked confused. "Oshei explained that our enemy is directly opposed by this sword's magic, and that will be our advantage. The king is the wielder of the enemy's power. His obsession with it has paved our way because everyone here is affected by it. And I have greater power so now I'm in charge."

He realized that if he wanted to, he could overthrow the kingdom on this mission alone. That was too much power for one person to have. "The king has placed his kingdom in a terrible situation."

After Laithrum's explanation, he drew his sword and addressed the warriors, who had become receptive to his words. "Take us to the Julrainvel woman."

They started leading the way immediately. Raven leaped from the Neintro Dragon and followed nervously. He reacted at any sudden movement, but there was never an attack. It couldn't be this easy. He hoped no one noticed his skittishness; his condition was so humiliating.

Laithrum spoke the plan to his team as it unfolded in his mind. "Yiyumiss, you're our defense here. If anyone not possessed by this dark magic attacks us, it's your job to hear them and defend us in time. Eveyrai, I'm hoping your father attacks us so I can break whatever is controlling him and set this place free. You'll take over the rule over this kingdom, so you won't be following us to the Ring Mountains."

Eveyrai looked both confused and overjoyed. "Hope can be solidified by good planning and action, Laithrum." He turned to one of the men leading them and ordered, "Go inform the king that I need to take Vega on a mission."

After the man ran off, he explained, "He'd never let that happen. He'll show up once he figures out what's happening."

Raven shook his head in disbelief. "I fought Onlortrens, stole that Ellovast, and stressed over this for years. Now I stroll through without resistance. I just don't know how to accept this, but since it's in my favor I will."

Laithrum agreed. "Me neither. I have no idea what I'm doing. Honestly, I'm just telling you what comes to my mind. Most likely, it's the Ellovast directing these movements."

At last, the team arrived and saw her. A large birdcage stood in the center of the room; its floor covered with pillows. Vega lay on and under many fluffy pillows, hiding from everyone around her. They only knew she was there because of a foot and a hand protruding from the colorful pile.

Suddenly, across the room appeared the king, who looked remarkably like his son in both appearance and age. Furious was the only way to describe his expression. He was ready to fight to the death with a sword in his right hand. As expected, his left hand gripped harder. He secured a drinking cup that transferred the black magic, controlling him.

"Leave her here!" he reproached.

His load voice woke Vega. She pulled her hands and feet inward to hide better, but she was too curious. Vega's face slowly peeked through the pillows.

Raven could not restrain himself. He drew his sword and beat the lock off the cage, damaging the weapon beyond repair. She started fervently crawling out of the fluff. Her silky silver hair sparkled with colorful light, draping over her body. She wore a white lace dress that flowed over the ground. Raven tossed aside the sword and ran inside to embrace his sister. He dragged her out before she could even get over the shock of being free. Her blue eyes, like her brother's, were bloodshot and tired from her weakened state.

Laithrum raised his sword at the king's prompting. He was intimidated by this opponent. Not because of the lack of skill or training but because of the need to not harm Eveyrai's father. Gaining peace was too important.

He knew that his fast adaptation to combat wasn't nature. He was lucky or protected by his… fate. Somehow, following his calling set him up to have all he needed for success. Just like all the times before, he faced his fear and plunged into the unknown. This should be fine; they shouldn't even have to fight. He had to trust again.

The king charged at Laithrum. Laithrum raised his sword, and the charging king fell to the ground. The metal drinking cup glowed red and melted into a hot puddle next to the king.

Laithrum remained in a battle position for a moment in shock but slowly straightened and stood plainly. Strange things were going to happen from here on out.

Eveyrai ran over to his father. He checked for breathing and injuries, but everything was fine. The guards realized what was transpiring around them and grew confused and defensive.

"Don't worry," called out Eveyrai. "Everything is going to be fine. I have very good news that I will announce shortly. Keep it secret until I formally announce it, but… I am the king now, and the war is over!"

CHAPTER 24

Trauma Where Magic Gathers

Entering Freyja's room was hard for all of them. They didn't know who they'd meet or what they'd see. The room was bright. A large window on the far side funneled in the sun's light. The glass was very clean and the room strangely empty. She lay on a large bed with plain blankets. The foot of the bed faced them.

Freyja's hair was tied back and well cared for. She looked completely healthy and had no marks from injuries on her arms nor on her face.

"Freyja," Ashtion gently called out.

Her eyes shot open at the sound of her brother's voice. Pushing herself up, she was weighed down by her stomach. Confused, Freyja grabbed at her surroundings. She screamed in shock as she wrestled with her pregnant belly. Ashtion ran over and held her hands still so she wouldn't hurt herself or the baby.

"What's going on? How did this happen? When…?" She cried in confusion and grief. Her mind raced through her memories, hating what she saw, yet none of it explained her condition.

"Lotus is the father. No stranger did this. You're going to be alright." Ashtion gently kissed his sister's head and let go of her shaking hands. He didn't go far.

Lettermere approached and knelt beside her bed. "I'm very glad you're awake again."

She looked at them in turn with her bright red, teary eyes. "How long was I out? This all happened so quickly… and I'm pregnant now." She brushed back her hair tightly against her scalp. "I'm lost. I can't handle any more."

"Freyja," Ashtion started, "thank you for coming for me. I'm alive and well because of you and this team. You don't have to worry about going berserk anymore, because the troublemaker is centralized." He said cheerfully, referring to her belly.

She allowed herself to calm at her brother's light and carefree spirit. "You know how to make things seem very insignificant. Thank you, the positivity is appreciated. I am going to be fine, right?"

Suruki then spoke, "Good strength of character. You'll need it for giving birth. Any day now."

"What! How long was I asleep?"

"A few weeks only!" answered Lettermere, still no calmer than she was.

Suruki explained, "She's not having a human child. It'll come out as a soft-shelled egg and harden in moments." He said with a glow, almost like he was the parent at his child's birth. The expression in his eyes was magical.

Conversely, Freyja couldn't handle it and started crying loudly. Cupping her face in her hands and leaning over her large stomach, she yelled, "Lotus, I'm going to kill you! Then I'll hide in a cave alone. Never come out. NEVER! This is just too much!"

Ashtion rubbed her back and consoled, "Oh Freyja, you don't mean that. If I tried to hurt him for this, you'd become very angry with me. That's how I know you don't mean it. And don't even think of leaving us. This family needs to stay together for once."

"But I really mean it," she exclaimed through her tears, knowing he was right. Freyja started petting her hair to calm her mind. They took good care of her. She was grateful.

Lettermere looked at the doctor. "Why would you say that? Even if true, it was bad timing!"

Suruki shrugged. "I was never taught human sensitivity. This is a fantastic event for me; so beautiful. As a doctor, only physical ailments are my concern. Labor won't be hard, unlike if it were a human child, and the baby isn't as fragile."

Ashtion questioned, "Does that mean Lotus hatched from an egg?" The doctor nodded. "That's so weird."

"Much too weird," Freyja exclaimed. She remained crouched over, petting her own hair, but stopped crying. "This has been an adventure for sure. A truly awful experience. Some wonderful things happened, yes. Like getting you back, Ashtion, and Laithrum escaping the palace. I wonder how he is. I've tried not to worry about him since he left, but I think about him often."

Ashtion held his sister. "You've done so much for us as your little brothers. Just let us take care of you. Alright? But with that said, Freyja, I need to tell you…" He leaned in and whispered in her ear.

Her body tensed even more, but soon relaxed. The chaos wasn't going to end, at least not soon. Not giving up the fight she sat up straight and refocused on her surroundings. She looked around the room, at its plainness, and at the large window facing the mountains. The light streaming in from the undraped window. It was warm, much warmer than she was used to. It wasn't early spring anymore; it was summer, and she was in the Ring Mountains, a place where people are told never to go. She knew she would soon experience why.

That night, Celle informed Suruki that Onlortrens and Oshei were soon to arrive; consequently, he needed to speed up the birth of Lotus' child. Suruki and Celle set up the room for the delivery and prepared for the arrival of the elfin prince by gathering their own team. Altham and Dederom Maullia joined them. All four prepared to leave the village that night and finish executing their plan.

Resting in the next room was Ashtion, and the remaining of Freyjas companions. They considered Ashtion the fifth and last member of their team even though he wanted nothing to do with them. He expected them to come any night now.

A Dark elf stealthily entered the room. Ashtion, ready to wake at the arrival, abruptly opened his eyes. He knew this feeling. His time with that treacherous mirror had educated him on many evil things. As expected, Celle stood over him. After she saw that he was awake, she leaned over getting very close to speak softly, "I'm confident you remember when you first met me." No one else would wake up from such silent communication and movement. She was like a ghost.

"You were the cloaked figure. You gave me the stones to swallow in the Turwin Village. And you helped me escape the prison when Freyja came to rescue me. You gave me this magic to use as defense, but what did it take away? You want me to steal Freyja's child, but why? Because you are forcing me to do this, I need to know why."

"We as Dark creatures won't be able to hold it for long. Our energy would hurt the child. We need to bring it to our master. And what we took away from you, by those stones, was your freedom. You were mesmerized by the power and didn't even ask what it would cost. Now you know."

Ashtion felt shame and regret of his impulsive decision. He had failed then, but he'd at least face the consequences now. "So, you all want the child to hatch with him. Why? It doesn't make sense for a tyrant to want anything so innocent and weak."

Celle smiled broadly and held back a laugh. "The first child of a Thithe doesn't appear human or Thithe and is, definitely, not weak. Where do you think the large dragons come from? They don't have nests or sexes like the small Neintro dragons do. The large, winged dragons and the sea dragons are all firstborn children of Thithe. Train them from when they're hatched, and they are your ally forever. He made sure to provide her with medicine early on, to separate the magic from her, when he found out she was pregnant. She must have stopped eating, considering how berserk she went during this pregnancy. He was trying to take care of her, but they sent him to war to protect her brother instead."

Ashtion clenched his fists, his knuckles turning white as his mind raced for a solution. "Please don't do this," he pleaded. "I don't know if you have any compassion inside of you, but please don't send the child to him. Don't take more away from my sister. My father because of the Black magic mirror tried poisoning her after Lotus left. He failed to plan that well."

"Don't cause so much death by adding this weapon to Lotus…" He struggled to say Lotus because it didn't make sense that such a nice guy could be part of anything malicious.

"You waste your breath. Lotus isn't alone. Neijill's job was to dismember Thuthairryon so Freyja wouldn't be trapped as royalty. But he wasn't the one giving the orders. I don't have a choice either. She'll have her child tonight, and you'll take it; the end."

Earlier, Suruki ensured Ashtion would have an easy entrance into and out of the room. Freyja, informed about the mission by Ashtion earlier, remained calm. She had been preparing her mind for this ever since Ashtion told her. Doctor Suruki spoke the truth about the birth. She physically felt nothing. A dizzying fog came over her mind as if she were about to faint, although she was very alert to what transpired around her.

Freyja watched as Ashtion came in with Celle. He looked as if he were sleepwalking or under a spell of some kind. He made himself emotionally detached to not make silly decisions.

Nearby stood the Dark Elves: Suruki, Altham, Dederom Maullia, and Celle. Only Ashtion touched the egg. It started as a soft sack with a harder form in the center and quickly filled out to become a perfectly round, dark red, hard ball about eleven inches in diameter.

After making eye contact with Ashtion, Freyja sight went black. She wouldn't wake until morning.

…

Through the night air, in a formation like geese, Onlortrens, Oshei, Linus, and Adeyas rode their respective dragons. Onlortrens, who took the rear behind Oshei, was struck by a message.

His expression transformed. An earnestness came over his thoughts. Laithrum was right about their need to hurry, but the depth of their flight training and the dragons' abilities would make them late.

There was a threat greater than he knew. They needed help. Would he be able to help turn this around with effort and planning? The consequences of tardiness would be boundless.

"We are going to be a day late," Onlortrens informed the group.

"A day late for what?" called Linus.

"Intercepting the enemy's next move. I'll have to call for assistance."

Curiosity about the assistance filled Linus, but he let Onlortrens work. Linus then reported up to Adeyas, who held the lead. Adeyas was frustrated by the communication. It was difficult and slow because of the distance and air movement between them.

CHAPTER 25

Help When Magic Is Given

The end was coming. Laithrum could feel it. Knowing why he felt this way was an unanswered plea that he pondered and searched hard for the answer. Before leaving on this adventure, he floated through life. No direction or purpose. Not even clear thoughts about day-to-day things. Hondou Unrey, the last Crowned Knight Thuthairryon, was worried about the king's decisions when he sought out Laithrums advise when still in Onferwil. His worries were warranted but no one knew what to do. Laithrum wondered rather he made the right decision in leaving. Onlortrens thought it was right for him to leave. Maybe there was no better choice to be made. He was headed to the right place now. He knew it.

They were flying again. This time without the Seintroven Prince, Evayrai, and with Ravens sister, Vega. Raven and Vega were together since the time of the cage breaking. Vega had gained back her strength, and the redness had left her eyes. Even now the two of them rode on one dragon leaving the extra dragon to fly without a rider.

In the dark of night Laithrum heard from Onlortrens. The voice in his head wasn't like it was in the palace. Not subtle and resembling a feeling. It was bold and sounded as if coming from right next to him. The shock woke him quickly.

Onlortrens continued talking. "The enemy has taken the asset they needed from the Ring Mountain City, Amarine. I'll be able to get you there at the same time we arrive. Once we get there I'll be without a plan. Have you had any glimpse that could direct us?

Laithrum turned his thoughts outward in hope of catching an answer. He had his dragon move him next the Raven and Vega.

"You two, if you try, will be able to sense the enemy. When we move past the border of the ring mountains, I need your help. After we find their location, we need to head straight to them. Rest well now because we may have to fight Lotus again very soon."

Ravens' expression turned to shock and disgust, "you're not placing my sister near him! I'll go but…" he stopped because he didn't want to not be with her. He couldn't decide what was worse.

"I'm alright with going." She said over her shoulder at Raven, "I want to help and together we have more power than if we were separate." Where his hair was darker than the night with eyes that glowed, Vega was light exceptionally light. Colored emulated off her with colors like an opal. From a distance she looked like a star.

Though still hesitant, Raven excepted Laithrums mission for them. He felt the need to question, "we are days away so why do you say *very soon*?"

"Onlortrens is sending us a boost. We'll be there tomorrow with him."

Not long after their planning the sky behind them grew red. A fire like a storm cloud raged quickly toward them. Soon they were burning in the magical fire. Yiyumiss clung onto her dragon. She would just have to wait until they were gone. Fairies irritated her greatly.

"Fire fairies!" exclaimed Vega in excitement resembling that of a small child. Her excitement was hard to contain. Raven remained silent as he enjoyed having his sisters' company again. He focused his resolve to prepare the best he could for the unforeseen and ominous future.

Laithrum reached out his hand as a fairy flew in front of him. The dragons felt irritated at the invasion of these magical insects so it flew away from the leader so she couldn't land on Laithrums outstretched arm. The fire all around them and running through them and empowering them was both fantastic and frustrating for the Neintoe dragons. No dragon liked to get help nor did they like strangers close to them.

Raven and Vega used magic to calm the beasts so Laithrum could chat. It worked quickly so Laithrum could soon have the conversation. The fairy was able to land into his hand.

"Are you on the mission to get us to the Ring Mountains by tomorrow?" he asked politely.

"Yes. Did Onlortrens tell you about us?" the lady fairy asked curiously.

"He did not tell me about you, directly. He said that he was sending a way to get there at the same time as them. Not even with all my foresight can I think of a faster plan. You and all the fire fairies are our only hope of arriving in time."

The fairy puffed up her chest in pride. The thought that her fairies were such an imperative part of this important mission brought her much joy. She raised up her arm and rallied her little troops. They were going to catch up with Onlortrens and make the elf's time of arrival sooner as well.

And so, it went as the fairy's planned.

With the mountains only now in view, Onlortrens noticed the closeness of the fire fairies. Linus, Oshei and Adeyas both turned their gaze back to look upon an incoming fiery cloud.

As planned, when they all crossed the mountains mist border Raven and Vega searched for the enemy and pointed the way. The fairy's assignment was over, so they turned around and left. They were now a team of eight. This small team were expected to survive and win over the one behind this game.

. . .

The woods were thick and seemingly empty of wildlife. The tree's bark was covered with colorful fungi and the woods floor was busy with broken branches and tangling bushes. Lotus sat on a downed tree comfortably amidst all the mess. He still had straight white hair and a sinister expression. His rectangular ears were finally visible through that flat straight hair. His eyes were no longer glowing since he had become calm.

"We finally have a way home."

The bushes behind him moved. It was not anything physical, the magic was sent as a reminder to continue his mission. He stood and started the journey to the rendezvous point.

The sky was hazy and bright, it acted in a way that enhanced the colors below. A company of five trudged through the woods.

Ashtion, holding the hard-round egg, walked as loudly as he could. He snapped every stick, kicked every leaf, and sang any song that came to mind as boldly as possible. Ashtion grew tired of doing this, but not nearly as tired as the people around him. The irritation growing over his companion's faces was motivation to persevere in his antics.

Celle, as irritated as all the times before, exclaimed repeatedly, "No one around would assist you in escape! That is, if there was anyone out here at all to hear this! Only we can hear you! Consequently, shut up and stop making so much racket!"

Suzuki, and Dederom Maullia the partner Dark elf to Celle, ached for him to listen to her plea. Altham was enjoying the chaos of sound and movement. All this racket was led by the desire to harm those around him in whichever way he could.

Ashtion looked sternly at them and responded. "Why should I? If there is no way I can escape, and no way I could defeat you then way not do what I can against you? My loudness and annoying behaviors are my revenge!"

Ashtion looked down at the egg. "And after we deliver the egg, my safety has ended. Will you use me again or kill me?"

A new voice spoke, a familiar voice, "we won't kill you if you just leave peacefully."

Ashtions company froze and looked frighten. Was this their leader? They looked around for his location. There were so many large trees and organic mess that he could be hiding anywhere. Ashtion noticed that no one else searched for him. He soon reached the conclusion that his enemy was not hiding at all. He casually stood just on the other side of a tree.

"Bring that egg over here." He commanded.

Ashtion did as he was told. He was reluctant but wanted to see this individual too greatly to deny going. Around the tree he saw him. Hair, dark and crazy with loose waves. His head rose from its downward gaze showing his face.

Lotus.

CHAPTER 26

Birth of a Legion

The misty barrier around the Ring Mountains swallowed their sight and soaked their bodies. The humidity was suffocating creating a greenhouse effect. Heat increased as the water coated their skin, becoming seriously uncomfortable.

Infused in the moist haze was barrier magic, blocking their foresight and tracking. Only after crossing the border could Raven and Vega, reluctantly, point in the direction they sensed Lotus. The two were committed to the mission, even though the energy behind their determination was weak. In contrast Laithrum's focus stayed absolute and immediately he followed the direction.

Moving past the mist they could see all the green. Lush forests waved over the hill and mountains. Random patches of fields and bogs. As far as the eye could see, even from the high vantage point, there were no people or animals.

Soon, Laithrum was contacted by an unknown voice. It wasn't foreboding nor would he call it friendly or tender. The voice called him by name, commanding him to come to…her.

The woman's voice called to him, again. Though they needed to hurry, this encounter felt crucial. The Ellovast shone brightly, urging him toward the voice. He knew to trust the swords promptings.

"I'm being called, this way," Laithrum said, redirecting the Neintoe Dragon downward. The forest canopy approached quickly. The others followed him questioningly. They broke through the beautiful treetops into a chaotic landscape of fungus, moss, and broken sticks. The ground waws a textured mess.

In the large patch of moss sat a large dark mass with bright yellow eyes—a beautiful dark wolf with silvering fur from age. She sat still with an unwavering stare, waiting for them.

They landed carefully, dragons struggling to maintain formation in the disorganized woods. As they started to walk the sticks snapping under their feet frustrated them. Was stealth something obtainable in these woods?

"I'm here to help you succeed," she said as they approached. Her voice full of urgency and her a snarl showing her teeth in anticipation. Her golden eyes contrasted sharply with her black, brown, and silver fur. There was something familiar about her.

Behind her lay a woman, face down and filthy. The wolf looked at Raven, Oshei, and Vega. "Heal her and wake her. In that order!" She commanded, her tone assertive and unyielding.

They hesitated, distrustful of the animal. These siblings and Oshei looked out of place, they shone brighter than the surrounding mushrooms and their gentle expressions clashed in the tension. Even Raven had regained his natural demeanor, his previous aggression seemingly impossible to muster. The wolf snarled fearlessly at his attempt at a threatening gaze.

"Don't hesitate! When people pause out here, they die!" the wolf scolded.

"Trust her," Laithrum insisted, staring in disbelief. Her golden eyes matched his. They were related, he felt it.

Raven took the lead. Vega clung to his hand as they moved. Neither made a sound. Linus followed them closely, making as little noise as possible, but even his stealth skills couldn't find a quiet path.

As they approached, they realized it was Freyja! Her eyes were partially open, staring at them, but she couldn't move or speak. She was overjoyed to see them, but exhaustion from pursuing Ashtion had taken its toll. Once she woke, she ran out to find him.

As they knelt to heal her, Raven teased, "It's nice when you're too tired to be sassy, princess."

Both his sister and Linus glared at him. Laithrum perked up in joyous surprise.

"Freyja," he began, running forward, but the wolf bared her teeth, stopping him.

"I am already taking care of her! Listen to the mission, boy!" the wolf sneered.

"You were called and targeted from the beginning boy. They put you inside me to give your success a level of likelihood. Your father was your father because of timing. It took one-hundred and thirty years for the timing to be right." She was clearly bitter having to wait that long.

The wolf continued, "I didn't know why Lotus didn't kill you before, but now I understand. The Dark One, a Thieth, fell in love with your sister. He kept you alive for her, but he weakened you from poison, using Niejell. You are still controlled though, like your father and the Seintroven king. At least you're too powerful to be crippled like them. Don't take that as a compliment. You are disappointingly useless. Lotus did a great job at sabotage. The Ellovast has been healing you, but you remain handicapped. We'll try and fix you soon enough."

"Inside you," Laithrum echoed, fixated on that statement. "You're my mother, aren't you?"

"That is the least important part of all this! But yes, and I am glad to finally meet you. We needed you close to the sword to grow up correctly after birth, so the king was the best choice. Now follow me and make yourself useful by helping your sister!" Laithrum's mother looked at his companions.

"I like the elf and, of course, I like you," she said to Yiyumiss. "I am excited for you dragons." She paused in pleasure at the sight.

"But the rest, I'm not sure about. You all seem troublesome." The wolf then trotted away, expecting them to follow.

Freyja stood with Vega and Raven's help; Oshei stood by and refused to help. "Don't treat me like a burden!" she sneered at the immense wolf.

"I'll stop the treatment, after you stop the meriting." Retorted Laithrum's mother.

Freyja accepted the wolf's observation because she knew it to be true. The hike through the woods to find Ashtion proved too much for her weak body. Going from the strongest in the company to the weakest damaged her pride. She refused the temptation to not fight. Her resolve would not fail so easily.

Trust for this wolf was low. There was no reason to think she cared about their lives. The whole team could be a means to an end, or a meal. What was this wolf's purpose? Was it the same as theirs?

The nine moved quickly through the woods until they reached a cave blocked by oversized mushrooms. As the wolf burrowed through the fungus, they saw the cave was made of tree roots and rocks. It expanded deep into the earth possibly having multiple cavities connected by the tunnels. It was very spacious. How many creatures could be down here? If this was a trap, and the tunnels were filled with enemies, it would be their end.

Onlortrens kept to himself, using every iota of concentration on gathering magic, planning, and surveying the area. He would need to work harder than he thought possible, because the situation was dyer.

Freyja wasted no time. She tended to her cuts and scrapes, refitted her shoes and clothes. She dressed in nursing clothes stolen from the medical room in the village. The room was attached to hers, so it made sense. Many sizes were available to choose from, but sadly, she ended up with males' clothes because of her unusual height. This was her first time wearing pants.

Adeyas knelt beside her. "And where do you think you're going?" he asked, firmly placing his hand on her shoulder to hold her down. He had no intention of letting her leave the safety of the cave.

"I need to find Ashtion and… my child." She hesitated, the thought of the egg still making her sick, and yet, she still wanted it.

"Your child? Ashtion? What are you talking about?" Adeyas asked, bewildered.

Laithrum looked at his sister with sympathy. "I believe we are all on a similar quest, Freyja. You are not alone, and we are more than willing to help you."

Their line of sight was soon blocked by the wolf's fur. She stood, irritated by the small talk. "No, *we* are not willing."

"Stop your chatter. You can deal with your personal wants after we save this land. Millions of lives are at stake, and you can only think of yourselves. Disgusting." She lay down, exhausted from days of fighting.

The wolf's ears perked and her head rose in excitement. She was filled with excitement.

"We finally have leverage. That woman—your sister, Laithrum— is Lotus' weakness. We have a piece to play against one barrier."

She lowered her head again, realizing, "But the one pulling the strings has no emotional weaknesses. It's too simple to create new ideas or connections; and everyone else involved is just a tool for it to use."

The wolf plotted alone, "I will take Laithrum to the boss… thing. And the pretty twins."

Raven hissed, "That is not my sister's and my new title!"

"Yes, it is!"

Raven smiled through his frustration. "Laithrum, your mom is sassy. I think…I like her a lot."

Onlortrens finally spoke. "I don't want to be apart from Laithrum during this crucial time. I was sent by the wisest and most powerful of our people to retrieve him, rescue him from the palace, and train him. I was to guide him into his purpose. Don't take my mission from me. I have too much invested."

The wolf smiled kindly. "I should have guessed you were the one to thank. Call me Methrum and consider your mission complete. He's here, and this is the time, but he needs help because he is pathetic. This is not your fault. But now we must make up for it."

Methrum looked seriously at Onlortrens. "The other team needs more power. You should stay with them."

As much as Onlortrens disliked the plan, he knew it was the best option. He thought thoroughly about his team—Adeyas, Oshei, Freyja, Linus, and Yiyumiss—and began speaking with Oshei.

Yiyumiss didn't like the team being split. She knew it was necessary but didn't care. Being separated from Laithrum hurt; surprisingly it hurt a lot. And she liked the 'pretty twins' more than the creepy Oshei. Her body shook as she forced herself to except the plan. Maybe she could plan well enough to have fast victory and fight beside them too?

She walked over to Freyja and lifted the necklace over her head. "You've had a rough journey; this has made mine easier. I will give it to you. Never take it off," Yiyumiss said reluctantly. Freyja didn't know what the red gem was, or its significance, but reached out to accept it. Oshei stared at it jealously, having tried to steal it for years.

Freyja placed it around her neck. "I want to return this to you after the mission. It's too special to you. I can tell."

Yiyumiss' eyes watered at the thought of giving it away, and at the thought of getting it back. She enjoyed the power, but, sometimes, the responsibility caused more burdens than she wanted. She looked intensely at Laithrum, wondering how he felt; the entire world depended on him. So much responsibility is on him; it must drive him wild inside. The stress could cause complete insanity. She resolved to take as much of the load as she could. But why did she care so much?

Methrum nudged Laithrum to step away from the others. He sat down, and she cuddled around him, her fur soft and comforting.

"Pull out Ellovast," she instructed.

He did as she asked.

"Laithrum," she began, preparing to teach, "this is not a sword. It's a life form. He will help you fight, and he is very skilled, but without you, he cannot do anything. He's trapped in there, just like Yiyumiss and that necklace she just gave away. I'll talk to her next." Methrum sighed, and complained, "you kids needing to be taught is so much trouble for me."

"I… am sorry." Laithrum responded and quickly focused his mind on the sword… no, person in his hands. The Ellovast was easier for him to use than anything else. It seemed to solve problems on its own, to think critically. It being alive made sense, but other things she said did not.

"Mother, if I'm this king of legion and using this sword proves it, then what is Yiyumiss? The necklace seems special. Special in similar ways as this sword."

"Man was never meant to be alone. She is the queen of legion, and without her support, you will fail."

Laithrum stared at his mother in shock. He knew what it meant; it was clear as day. He and Yiyumiss were meant for each other from birth. But how could this be? What powers dictated all of this? And why were they being placed on different teams?

His mother comforted him. "Don't try to understand it. There are ways of life that transcend all understanding. We are part of something much bigger. You are just entering the adventure. Chat with Ellovast now. He'll help you understand the mission."

Methrum quickly left him to meet Ellovast. She had to explain the gem to Yiyumiss. Then Methrum would get to watch Yiyumiss, awkwardly, ask Freyja to return it. The wolf grinded as she imagined the uncomfortable conversation. The gem wouldn't work for Freyja anyway.

Methrum only waited a few minutes before pushing everyone out on their missions. The fight would not end until victory or death.

■ ■

After trying to hunt down Ashtion, Suruki, and Althen all morning, they came to Freyja's room. Lettermere and Nourttaku opened the room slowly, not expecting it to be unlocked. Stealthily, Lattermere looked around the doorway, "Freyja."

Surprised and aggravated they burst into the room finding it empty. Somehow, Lettermere and Nourttaku were alone and had no information network to consult. Freyja was in no condition to up traveling around even if Ashtion was there to protect her. Their best guess' weren't helpful they needed clues to follow.

Both were skilled trackers, so tracing Freyja's movements wasn't excessively difficult. Especially since she wasn't trying to hide, but she was traveling alone. Where was Ashtion? And she ran hastily right outside of the village.

The villagers' distrust was evident; they let her go; certain she would die. The gatekeepers preferred these outsiders to leave and were open about speaking it. The village was threatened to let them in, so they assigned Freyja and company with negative reputations. The safety of these unwelcome visitors did not matter.

They looked at the gate and the keepers, knowing they would be more than happy to let them out. Nourttaku and Lettermere were ready to go. They felt there was nothing for them anywhere anymore. This feeling lowered their fear of death because what they had lived for was no longer around. Lattermere's country was in shambles and Nourttaku was betrayed by his. Even if they wanted to head home, it was just as dangerous as pursuing Freyja.

Lattermere took the first step forward but was abruptly halted by a very large flying insect. This three-inch bug struck his face, seemingly on purpose. He became frustrated and disgusted in equal portions. It buzzed in front of him, revealing its humanoid shape—his anger receded, it was a fire fairy.

A small group of other fairies joined her. "We were told you should stand guard until they get back."

"Who are you, and what are you talking about?" Lattermere asked, bewildered.

"Onlortrens said this would be the haven. As far as we are concerned, his words are law. Don't worry about the village people. We're here to help you and to protect you. So, hang tight."

After looking to Lattermere for answers, and received only a confused expression, Nourttaku grinned and responded carefully, "We do not know this Onlortrens you speak of. Are you willing to tell us more?"

"He's with Freyja, Laithrum, Adeyes, three pretty and useless people, and man named Linus…" The Fairy spit out all the information he knew, hoping that something would matter.

Nourttku lifted his hands slowly to signal the fairy to stop, "Anything you say, really. We know enough about your allies. We are all together in this. Thank you, all our options sounded terrible, you brought us some positive direction."

Waiting would be easy now that they had allies. Lattermere, guarded gates in the capital for most of his life. The job felt near to his heart, almost like being at home. It shouldn't be long. They would manage.

CHAPTER 27

An Air to Freedom

Lotus moved swiftly in front of Ashtion, his red eyes piercing through Ashtion's mind. The intimidation presented was like nothing Ashtion had felt before. Paralyzed with fear, the prince waited for the next move.

Lotus grabbed the egg and held it gently. The shell came alive with colors and a pattern made by spots. Lotus calmly started walking away. His steps were almost silent through the debris, more so than the stealthy elves Ashtion traveled with.

Even though Lotus told the Dark Elves to let him leave unharmed, Ashtion knew he wasn't safe, his life was forfeited as soon as he lost the egg. Lotus, mesmerized by the egg, would not notice.

Ashtion, calming down, know he couldn't wait any longer, nothing would stop him from asking, "What are you doing? What are you, and how could you betray Freyja's trust?"

Ashtion's questions got Lotus to stop. He chose not to answer directly but responded, "And who are you to ask? Where were you all those years?"

Rage burned inside Ashtion. The guilt from the truth and the terror of the situation caused him to burst. "YOU'RE THE ONE LYING! YOU STARTED ALL THIS DEATH, STOLE FREYJA'S CHILD, AND LIED ALL THOSE YEARS ABOUT WHO… WHAT YOU WERE!"

Lotus' eyes shone brightly, his hair flattening and started bleaching in color. Ashtion froze from the intense aura. His body relaxed slightly as he noticed Lotus wasn't even looking at him but past him.

Celle sprang into action, pulling Ashtion toward a tree. The attack on Lotus began.

Bright lights, fire, and magic came from every direction. The display did its purpose, to disorientate Lotus. He tore through the flames and spells, one arm wielding his short sword, the other clutching his child. Reaching the other side of a fiery wave fire he came face to face with Freyja.

His strike was stopped by the protection of the red gem. Grateful and familiar with this power he glanced around for Yiyumiss. Lotus couldn't see Yiyumiss, who stood back-to-back with Freyja, the gem around her neck protecting them both. He was still self-controlled and didn't want to hurt these friends; not again.

Yiyumiss' planning had just saved Freyja's life, but she knew Lotus could easily push through the magic if he wanted to. They were lucky that he wasn't transformed.

At first, Lotus didn't know who else was there, but soon he felt Oshei's magic. He's cloaking them! The fire was from the Neontoe Dragons. They too were cloaked, but where?

"Lotus," Freyja began, "let's talk through this."

Lotus struggled to look at her. The shame he felt for allowing the relationship and those actions bringing forth a firstborn troubled him. It wasn't his plan. His battle was stirring his rage; he would kill her. Already so close, chaos churned in his unstable mind.

"Freyja, I am very sorry. I know me words mean very little, but I love you and didn't…don't want to hurt you."

Lotus couldn't stay. He sprinted backward like a released arrow, sprouted his four rectangular wings, and bolted. Swiftly, not looking back, he was gone. His only were of escaping before things worsened. He took to the sky, above the tree's canopy, and left immediately, with no intention of returning.

After Lotus disappeared, the battle reignited. The Dark Elves were free to do what they wanted. Celle attacked first, provoking tree roots to grab Freyja's legs and pull her to the ground. The roots, devoid of aggression, her plan was to protect Freyja. The Frayja out of the way she could fight freely.

The roots movement was traceable. Yiyumiss located Celle instantly. After hurling a knife at Celle, she leaped into a tree for cover. Celle managed to evade the knife, but soon realized the enemy was completely hidden. Celle companions were able to retreat underground for protection.

Seeing Suzuki, Althen, and Dederom Maullia down there, she sank into the ground and joined them. Yiyumiss heard the Dark Elf beneath the earth, too deep for her to attack. But she wasn't alone.

Ashtion was left out of both parties because no one knew which side he supported. "Celle," he said slowly, "They won't fight you if you let them go after Lotus." Ashtion petitioned, hoping she would call off the attack. Her past words echoed: *You waste your breath, I don't have a choice either,* from when he pleaded to not steal the egg for Lotus. Was he wasting his breath again?

Onlortrens watched carefully, intrigued at the strategy, hopeful it would work. He marked Lotus for tracking and was eager to pursue him. They didn't have much time and diffeating four strong Dark Elves would take a while. Could they even win? They questioned Ashtion's allegiance, was he friend or foe?

Ashtion, himself, wished he was trustworthy but was unsure if he could be turned against his sister at the Dark Elves' will. The desire to help wasn't enough. If he attacked, his mind might be used against Freyja because of those magical stones. He schemed as he considered all that he understood.

Adeyas and Linus never left Onlortrens side. The elf needed protection while gathering large quantities of magic. The first prince thought protecting the strongest collaborator would put him in the most danger. He had his pride fully committed to his mission; he would die fighting for his people. Linus refused to let the prince embrace that command. It felt undeserved.

Roots shot inward, downward and up from the ground, grabbing three Dark Elves by surprise. The trees were instantly reinforced by green magic from Onlortrens, he couldn't wait for a response.

Celle stood apart from the others so remained free. She emerged from the ground. And read the situation. Her comrades would soon break out and the fight would drag on. They would win easily. After she paused, deep in an intrusive thought, her magic left her and strengthened Onlortrens bindings. "There, Ashtion. Regain your world if you can." She then collapsed, cold and stiff but still awake. "Don't hurt my people. But now we both have a chance to win. It's fair." She passed out. Oshie ran to her, looking for life.

"She's going to die. There's nothing I can do," he said.

"You're a julrainvel, right?" Ashtion yelled. Oshie looked at him curiously. The prince continued, "Keep her alive. If we kill the one controlling them, will she live?"

"Maybe…" Oshie managed to say though very disturbed.

"She's still Dark. Always prone to harm others more than any other creature," Onlortrens lectured. The eight Dragons emerged at the sound of Onlortrens arguing. They were protective of him and always ready to defend.

"I feel I'm the same kind of Dark," Ashtion said. The mirror had changed him. He felt the same Darkness he assumed she always felt. The darkness felt like home and frightened him greatly.

Onlortrens understood partially, he knew Ashtion had to realize he wasn't the same before he could stop defending them. Right now, the prince felt he was related to them, almost like family. Onlortrens knew this would fade in time, but Ashtion only hoped Dark beings didn't have to stay that way. He hoped they could change. The argument rested there. The elf knew keeping hope alive was more important than defeating a few enemies.

Onlortrens freed Freyja from the roots, and Adeyas picked her up and out of the dormant roots. "Ashtion," Freyja began, once her feet touched the ground. She was feeling the same Darkness. "I agree with you. Let's see what happens to the villains when we take away their boss. Give her a chance. I have been given one." She remembered the faces, the screams, the numbers of her victims. She had no control, but she still felt like the worst of them all.

Onlortrens fully understood their trauma and accepted that they would need time to feel…human again. They wouldn't get the time they needed unless they won this fight. Onlortrens began to refocus them, "The woods will be against us. We must move quickly to help Laithrum but we can't leave Oshie alone. He will need protection while watching over the prisoners and caring for Celle."

"I'll stay," Linus said and started creating a shelter for hiding and protection.

"And I'll stay to help him," Ashtion added, "if I go, I may be controlled by the enemy. I would be more use to you all here."

It was decided. Onlortrens commanded three of the Neontoe Dragons to stay and defend them. The other five would follow Lotus. Hastily, Freyja, Adeyas, Onlortrens and Yiyumiss pursued her lover, their enemy, and their friend. The dragons sprinted without regard for stealth or concealment.

***

Methrum carried Laithrum on her back as Raven and Vega traveled on dragons overhead. Guided by Laithrum's foresight and Methrum's experience, they navigated away from the most hostile areas. Raven and Vega had to sense Methrum and every movement in the woods.

The large wolf did not make the job easy as she was often underground running through tunnels. Everything seemed to plot against them—trees tried to trip them, birds dive-bombed them, and enemy scouts actively searched for them. It felt like a miracle but, so far, they were an unstoppable team of four that soon reached the mountain cave.

This was their destination. The most unsafe location in the world. It was no surprise that the enemy had prepared for them; however, the extent of the preparation was shocking. Lined up for battle were the Thurthairron soldiers, taken from the beach before Laithrum's adventure even began. Laithrum vividly remembered the wind and the people who never descended.

A large dark wolf emerged behind the men. Methrum bared her teeth. "You fell into the enemies plans so easily, brother. You made the wrong choice!" She shook for Laithrum to dismount. He jumped down and drew Ellovast. Raven landed beside him with his own sword, while Vega took cover in a tree. She would feed Raven extra magic for strength. Raven wished he was at his best, but the loss of aggression and the injuries still not healed put him in a precarious position.

Large lizards, knee-high to the men and ten or more feet long, gathered around the controlled corpses. The cave's entrance was mostly blocked by mushrooms, but they could see the increasing number of lizards inside. The men drew their swords and strung their bows, preparing for the attack.

Methrum shrank to the ground, sensing a threat from behind. The force in front of them parted. Laithrum saw it, but stood tall, unshaken.

Lotus landed with his back to Laithrum and the others. He tried not to confront them as he walked into the cave. Don't look behind, he told himself.

"Lotus," Laithrum called, "can you not remember that we are your friends?"

"Of course, I remember. My choices kept you alive." Lotus, reluctantly, turned to look Laithrum in the eye. "I could have killed you but made you sickly instead. I tried to grab you and Freyja out of the capital before the attack but only got these." He gestured to the men around him.

"I even harmed myself in salt water to guard you on those ships! Now you want to go against me! If you had just denied the power, we could still be friends. But now, you'll die." He turned and walked inside. The struggle within him raged but was imperceptible. He had a Dark side and a light side. When one was in control, the other felt powerless, yet they both felt like the same person.

Once Lotus was out of sight, the men and creatures attacked. The large wolves were the first to engage, gnashing at each other with strong, sharp teeth, tumbling through the woodland floor.

Laithrum and Ellovast finally worked in harmony. Laithrum saw the future, and Ellovast reacted with hundreds of years' experience. Raven relied on muscle memory and past training to compensate for his lack of hostility, while his and Vega's combined magic made up for his minuscule size.

Injuries from arrows, swords, teeth, and claws were healed quickly. Injury after injury was mended by Raven and Vega's teamwork. However, the constant healing depleted their magic and soon their energy depleted.

The enemy stepped back to regroup. Raven and Laithrum, barely standing from exhaustion, were covered head to toe in their own blood. Their injuries were healed, but the blood loss before healing left them dizzy.

"Laithrum," Raven started, "we could help your body recreate you blood in an instant, but that would be the last we could do."

Laithrum wouldn't ask that of them. They did enough.

All knew they couldn't last much longer. Methrum, victorious but weary, joined their side and devised a plan. Though hurt and tired, she wasn't as worn as the others. Her instincts told her there was hope, and she clung to that with all her might.

Laithrum, filled with determination, spoke up. "We need to get to the real enemy."

Methrum nodded. "You're right. Raven, you and your sister must heal Laithrum completely. If you have any strength left, flee from here. Laithrum, I'll run you through and give you a head start."

Laithrum understood that her plan was likely a suicide mission for herself and for the other two. The plan might not even succeed in getting him to the enemy, but it was their best option. He was too close to the enemy to see far into the future.

"Let's do it," Laithrum agreed. Raven and Vega reluctantly healed him, restoring his strength. Raven sprouted his damaged wings to join his sister. As they flew past the tree canopy, but both lost all strength and plummeted unconscious to the ground.

Methrum carried Laithrum through the enemy forces. At the rear, she bucked him off her back into the cave's tunnel, away from the enemy. He knew not to look back; if he did, he would stay.

Methrum fought fiercely, stomping, and biting at the lizards and remaining humans, but she was soon overwhelmed and brought down. They aimed to kill her, but more teeth arrived in time. The new five Neontoe dragons tore the lizards and people from her, overwhelming the enemy with fire. The dragon raged out of control at their fallen friends that supported Laithrum's team. The riders had no choice other to hold on for their lives.

Onlortrens jumped down to check on her. Methrum was badly hurt and wouldn't wake up. Adeyas ran to check on Raven and Vega, who were no better off.

Three Neontoe dragons stayed with Methrum, Raven, and Vega to guard them as the others continued in pursuit. Adeyas and Freyja rode the other two dragons while Yiyumiss and Onlortrens ran beside them. Laithrum, and the trailing team, still needed to confront the two strongest enemies ahead.

Laithrum held Ellovast tightly as he navigated the narrowing tunnel. The luminescent fungi showed him where to step safely. His foresight guided him down the correct paths, making him feel completely dependent on this power he didn't fully understand.

A rotten smell filled the air, reminiscent of a decaying swamp. The thinning air increased the need for breath whereas the odor choked him as he breathed. Laithrum spurred to move faster the increased hardship was to be expected. He was almost there.

Light appeared ahead, and a presence awaited him. Laithrum ran into the light, facing the figure. To his surprise, it wasn't a person. It was a slimy lump with a bright red center on its forehead. Eyes waved on fleshy pillars atop its head. It was a giant slug. The slug had no intention of fighting. Was it even alive? Laithrum felt as if they had already lost.

***

Onlortrens, Yiyumiss, Adeyas, and Freyja followed the tracker magic placed on Lotus. As they drew closer, their hearts raced. None of them felt strong enough to face him. Onlortrens, the most powerful among them, knew he couldn't protect anyone but himself.

There was Lotus, sitting ahead, waiting for them. His appearance was as they first met him—black hair with wild waves, mahogany eyes, and a gentle expression. This person looked like their friend, but trust couldn't be farther away.

Onlortrens halted the others, aware they couldn't see as well in the dark. Even Yiyumiss struggled, her vision distracted by the bright mushrooms. But she smelled him long before Onlortrens saw him.

"Lotus," the elf began, "what's your plan here?"

Freyja bit her lip, forcing herself to stay silent.

"You make it seem like my plan is still in play. It's not. I won."

"At what cost? What exactly did you win?" Freyja exclaimed, feeling she had lost more than she knew. Was her sacrifice just collateral damage? Did he even care?

Lotus frowned at her pain. "I'm sorry, Freyja. You were supposed to be taken by the wind before the attack on Thuthairrion. I never wanted you to go berserk like I do. You've experienced nothing I haven't. I know how you're haunted by the memories and feelings. Now that the piece of me is no longer a part of you, you're free."

Freyja swallowed hard, wanting to scream. She didn't feel free. Freedom from the terror seemed an impossible blessing. "Answer my question!" she shouted. "What did you win?"

"A way home." His eyes narrowed with guilt and grief as a red light flooded over them. Lotus plucked a mushroom from the tunnel's side. "Freyja, eat this and leave." At that moment, Onlortrens realized they were too late.

***

Laithrum approached the slug, looking into its eyes.

"You're already dead," Laithrum observed. "But what happened?"

The red light inside the creatures' head responded, carelessly revealing the plan. Laithrum gasped as Ellovast burst from the sword and into the red center. The slug exploded, and the light grew larger. Laithrum was overwhelmed by the suggestive power.

This was what cursed the mirror and cup, controlling the kings' minds. This was what surrounded the Ring Mountains, making it impossible to see through with magic. This was the Dark life's root, disease—the enemy.

Laithrum ran deeper into the light, holding onto the center. He saw Peirrah.

"So, you're the one set out to stop me," Peirrah laughed, as if it were a joke. "Maybe you could have, if you weren't so slow and pathetic."

Laithrum realized Peirrah wasn't even there. He was still banished and would remain banished if he could stop the environmental shift. The red light, spreading through and around Laithrum's body, was the cause.

The light moved quickly, touching the borders of the Ring Mountain, then rising from seven points around the land to create a dome. One of the seven points was there. That's where Ellovast went!

Laithrum dove deeper into the light, feeling his life being drained. "Stay back," Ellovast warned. "You'll die too!"

"You won't break in on your own!" Laithrum declared, raising his clear, empty sword to strike the light. As he did, the red light shattered, and Laithrum's spirit stood outside himself. He spun around, seeing his body lying cold and limp in the dark. It was over. Everything went black. They were too late. The mission to save the Ring Mountain residents had failed.

The haze around the mountains had grown, trapping the magic and transforming the land inside. The old life couldn't survive, at least not most of it.

***

Freyja and the others fell to the ground, gasping. Lotus extended his hand toward her, offering the mushroom again. Her instinct told her to eat it, and she did. Good air filled her lungs again. Quickly, she gave it to the others, and they could breathe as well.

Lotus stood up. "I've been trapped on this continent as a cursed being. I waited over two hundred years for a home where I could live without the curse of breathing toxic air. If I influenced this land quickly enough, I'd be able to live here soundly. Neijil, I used to weaken and delay Laithrum. He's five years late in hunting me. The Julrainvel provided enough magic, and humans provided the best border. Your cities and villages have survived because of me. I tried to stop you from having to fight, from the beach, I tried to save you and capture Laithrum. He wouldn't have stayed out of the palace too long, missing the medicine. He wouldn't have regained his magic and purpose. I wanted to save all your siblings, so I kept them close."

He began to walk away. "The war and your sister's death weren't my doing, but it was all done by us. It's only me now. I lost everything too, but we can always start again." He vanished without waiting for their response. They couldn't understand, and he forgave them for that. He had to start over. But now he had a home, and that was a good place to start.

Laithrum woke from death. How was he breathing again? As his eyes focused, he saw Lotus kneeling over him. The peaceful look, backed with deep sorrow. Laithrum recognized this man as his friend. Friend or foe, their relationship had shifted into something complicated.

"Even though I win today, I have lost more than I won," Lotus said to Laithrum, reasoning with his grief. The decision was made, and the action complete. There was no going back.

"Please explain. I truly don't understand."

"Two hundred years of knowing that I could become angry and kill everyone I cared about tortured me inside. When I lost control, I did kill them, and I had to leave that home and start again. It never got easier. And it was only because of the air I breathed. I already had to watch my human friends die from old age as I slowly changed. I had to watch myself kill them too if I became too angry. Other races felt my magic and didn't trust me in their communities. Everyone needs a home, Laithrum." He convinced himself. All he wanted was a place where he could not be a monster.

"You killed millions of lives to create this air. Some lived. I saw them all. Only the ones that ate the plants you grew special in the woods, but so many didn't. They didn't know."

"Go be with your family, Laithrum. It's all over." Lotus stood up, sobbing while holding tightly to his child. As he started walking away, Laithrum rolled up and made a request.

"Will you teach me about the seven points around the Ring Mountains? What was their purpose?"

"To create a gateway for Peirrah to come back." He looked down, realizing how much of his plan was a trick to bring that tyrant back. Lotus fell to his knees. "What have I done?"

Laithrum and Lotus waited for the trailing team to catch up.

Lotus had saved their lives by teaching them about the plant to chew, which corrected the air as it entered their lungs. But the number who died from the change didn't change. The fact was that they had all failed.

Laithrum swallowed hard, wishing he could go home or rest anywhere, but he couldn't allow himself that luxury.

"I understand why I have these talents," he began. "I see the threat more clearly now than I did in the capital. It's not over for me." He looked purposefully at Freyja and Adeyas. "You should go home and start rebuilding. I'm staying here. I need to free people and ensure Peirrah cannot return. I'm sure you two would help." He turned to glance at Raven and Vega, who were barely awake and barely alive. "After helping them, I will hunt down all the other bases still controlled by Peirrah's power and free them. This otherworld expansion is over." He directed his words at Lotus, who agreed to be his hidden ally—an ally only to prevent Peirrah, as he hoped to start over completely.

"I'm staying with you," Yiyumiss said, having grown strongly attached to Laithrum. She didn't want to be apart from him, nor did she want to leave the mission incomplete.

"I wanted you to feel free to make your own choice. I'm glad you're coming," he replied, knowing he needed her by his side.

Freyja argued, "I wish to stay and help you, Laithrum. I can't just go home after all this." She said but questioned if she could handle any more adventures. The thought of facing her memories and trying to live with them terrified her. She wanted the distraction but didn't know if she could emotionally handle it.

"Just go rebuild our home!" Laithrum commanded, directing his words mostly at Freyja. Adeyas held her shoulders in a half-hug, trying to reassure her. He knew she was at her limit. She needed time to grieve, to face the past, accept what had happened, and move forward with life.

"Laithrum," Adeyas began, his voice filled with pride, "what should I tell the others? Onlortrens left to save the other team before they suffocated."

"I already spoke with him. Everyone can go home. Onlortrens sent Fire Fairies to protect some people in the nearby city, Amarine. Sadly, most of the city died, but I saw friends still there to let you in."

Freyja thought about those friends, hoping they were Lattermere and Nourttaku. She had accomplished her quest to save her younger brothers. She should be glad, right?

***

Oshie was the only one still awake when Onlortrens arrived. They soon recovered enough to breathe on their own. Even Celle woke up.

The Dark Elf spoke to Ashtion the moment she saw him. "Look, Ashtion, everyone died anyway. All your effort to do the right thing was wasted."

"No, it wasn't," Onlortrens interrupted, walking up with one of the Neintoe Dragons. "Laithrum stopped Peirrah from coming back. It has been a victory overall."

He looked at her and the other Dark Elves. "Since I can't trust any of you not to continue the mission to bring Peirrah back, you're all coming with me. I am going home."

***

Laithrum and his new team stayed with his mother to recover. This was a completely new experience for him, another change in his environment. Yet another shifted air he was forced to breathe but didn't understand; nevertheless, unlike with his first adventure he wasn't alone.

The rest of the group gathered in the mountain city to rest and plan their journey home. Their lives would continue, and their mission was no less difficult. They had to rebuild.

The End